The Way Maker

The Zemyneah Experiment Book 1
The Codes Of Creation Multiverse

Arlie Sheelin

D1741486

THE WAYMAKER

Edited by Dennis Doty

http://www.dennisdotywebsite.com/editing.html

Cover by: Lisa Pederson

Earth Orbiter Font by: Daniel Zadorozny @ Iconian Fonts

FIRST EDITION: July 6, 2021

https://www.arliesheelin.com[1]

To my daughters

You are the beat of my heart, the strength of my bones, the reason for everything

Be who you are

Author's Note

BROOKE'S JOURNEY IS about overcoming, and strength and resilience and hope. Please be aware that her story deals with abduction, slavery, sexual abuse, violence, and sexual situations. If you are sensitive to this kind of subject matter, please be mindful of your mental health. I wish you well in your own journey of overcoming, strength, resilience, and hope.

Dear Reader,

WELCOME TO THE CODES of Creation Multiverse. The Way Maker is the first book in The Zemyneah Series, which takes place in Dimension 2 of this multiverse.

Dimension 5 is the home of the Realm of The Forsaken series. The first book for this series is written and in the editing process and will be released next.

Dimension 3 is the home of the Mystic Haven series.

The first book for this series will be released third.

These three books happen concurrently in this multiverse series. There is no reading order with these first books.

The three series are the beginnings of a vast multiverse of sci-fi/fantasy stories. I hope you enjoy the adventures, and misadventures of my heroes and heroines. Just watch out for the dragons.

Please note that all three books start with the same prologue.

Just one other small thing. I'm Canadian (eh) and The Way Maker takes place in Canada. I use Canadian spelling and grammar. Thank you for your understanding and kindness.

~ Arlie

https://www.arliesheelin.com[1]

---

1.   https://www.arliesheelin.com/

In the beginning...

THEY STOOD SURVEYING their creation, and it was good. A smile crept over Eliana's lips, and she glanced at her brother. Rune had the faintest curve to his mouth. They'd succeeded. Spread out before them was blackness so dark that its shape and form could not be determined, as it expanded in every possible direction at an immeasurable speed. Humans would later try to define this moment as the Planck Epoch, but who could define the moment of creation? Who could define the genesis of something beyond all comprehension? Out of nothing, there was a beginning. There was life. In the next Yottasecond, time began— Ages upon ages not yet realized by any coming lifeform. In the blink of a zeptosecond, lights began to appear in the blackness. Glowing orbs of plasma burned with an unending fire. Colors winked into existence, great clouds shifting, evolving, with such velocity that they began to birth new light. Explosions burst through the blackness as some of the lights lived out their time and died before their ageless eyes.

"What shall we call it Rune?"

Rune looked at his sister. "I thought we could call it a universe, but it is far beyond a single cosmos." He turned to watch their creation. All matter and space spread out before him, expanding without limit for all eternity. His eyes took

3

in time as it flowed out and became one with the blackness and the light. Dimension after dimension burst into being. More matter appeared, forming and reforming into incalculable elements, the elements that would be needed for the formation of life. "It's a multidimensional universe. Do you see, the elements have spread to every level, every depth? It's seeded with the potential for life."

Eliana smiled, this was her brother, so precise, so deeply concerned for every detail. "Shall we call it the Multiverse?"

Rune nodded. "It's a good name."

They turned together, ready to return to the in-between where they existed and paused. Glowing in immeasurable luminosity were the codes they'd formed to create the Multiverse. Rune's codes glowed red, yellow, and blue. Eliana's were the gentler green, orange and violet. Encased in two orbs of light, the codes danced and shimmered, symbols appearing and disappearing, interacting with each other as they sang a sound incomprehensible to any mortal ear. The codes were a concept of astonishing beauty, elegance, and boundless power.

Frowning as a possible future unfolded before him, Rune looked at Eliana. "We've made ourselves vulnerable."

Numerous millennia appeared in Eliana's mind, each one telling its own story. "Our creation is vulnerable."

"Even we are a threat." Rune stilled, his gaze going flat as he rapidly considered and discarded a storm of solutions.

"How is this possible? I don't... understand." Eliana pressed her hands to her chest. "We must protect ourselves and the multiverse!" She stared at her brother. "We cannot allow such an ending."

Rune's eyes met hers grimly and he nodded. "There is one solution. We must destroy the codes."

Eliana lifted her hand to cover her mouth, "Rune." Her eyes turned to the beauty of the code. "If we destroy the codes, what will happen to our Multiverse?"

"It will continue." His voice was hard, unreadable. "Because of their volatility, we have contained the codes separately in two stars. If we crash them into each other they will explode, and the code will disintegrate into fragments of atoms. Dust will spread across every dimension. The code will become part of the very fabric of the Multiverse."

"It's the only way?"

"It's the only way, Eliana."

Closing her eyes, Eliana breathed deeply, then with a nod to her brother, she sent the code star she'd created spinning out into the multiverse. Rune's star followed, picking up velocity as it hurtled through space after hers. Lifting her hand, Eliana brought her star to a halt dead center in the ever-expanding multiverse, and a mere zeptosecond later, Rune's star slammed into hers. A cataclysmic explosion smashed through the Multiverse, as the code stars disintegrated into dust, the shockwaves carrying the fragmented atoms to every corner of every dimension. Stardust mingling with the building blocks of life.

Chapter One

EARTH DATE: JUNE 17 07:30 AM

Secret Communication deeply encrypted in the outgoing messages:

> *Entering the Sol system. Target: Planet Earth. The nightmare continues. Assistance required. Vital that message reach highest level.*
>
> *-Starforge*

Second Secret Communication deeply encrypted in the outgoing messages:

> *Increase guards on DK. Spy aboard Exanthus. Exercise extreme caution.*
> *—DW*

Gardenside, Alberta, Canada
Earth, Dimension Two

BROOKE ST. CLAIRE HATED running, but she loved chocolate, and the battle to keep her size sixteen figure from becoming a size eighteen was all too real. She started her days in the cool, crisp silence of the mornings, running eight kilometers along the worn path that ran the boundaries of her heavily forested land— Land that had been in her family for over two centuries.

This morning she stepped out of her beloved Victorian home into the early morning light, the fading fog still light and wispy on the ground. The sun was shining through the tops of the trees, the promise of another glorious day in the blue of the sky and the early morning bird song. She was in a mood. Right after her run she was going to town and buying chocolate. A lot of chocolate.

Pushing her short auburn hair back, she inserted her ear buds and pressed the play button on her smartphone. *Classic Bon Jovi*, she thought, as "It's My Life" blared out of her earphones. Brooke adjusted the volume, turning the music up a bit, then straightened the bottom of the green tank top that matched her eyes, and began her run.

As a counselor, she knew she needed to let go of this, but honestly, why did the whole world think you needed a man? She'd already had one, thank you very much, and he'd given her two beautiful children and more heartache and pain than she'd needed for a lifetime. Two-timing bastard. The S.O.B. had died of a massive heart attack, in the bed of his secretary.

She never understood why that pretty, young woman had been in bed with her husband. It wasn't like he was any good in bed, never mind the absolute disaster he'd been as a husband. The man could not have found a clitoris if he'd been given a detailed map. She shuddered at that memory. This morning's phone call from her cousin wanting to set her up on a blind date had triggered an avalanche of bad memories.

Forcing her mind off her thoughts, she laughed as the next song in her playlist began. "You Give Love A Bad Name." Yeah, he had, and she wasn't falling for that B.S. a second time. She turned up her music, singing along, loud, and off tune as she pushed herself a little harder. She was going to need to burn a lot of calories before she hit town.

Four kilometers into her run, she contemplated giving up chocolate as the path led her briefly out of the forest and followed the fence line that ran along the south side of her property. A familiar police car drove past, and she lifted her hand in a casual wave at Officer Clay Brendon, knowing he would be waiting at her house when she got there, and he'd probably have another speeding ticket for her. Damn speeding tickets. Her lips curved into a slight smile as she ran. Maybe, this time she would claim her heavy foot was genetic. After all, her son Jaxson and his best friend, Clay, drove race cars in their spare time.

The path turned, taking her back into the cooler depths of the shaded forest. The scent of the damp woodland filled her senses, and she inhaled deeply. Who was she kidding? Chocolate was as close to heaven as she was coming in this life. There was no way she was giving it up. If running was the price she had to pay for that, then she would pay it, even though there was a vast cosmic unfairness to that.

At forty-eight, she should be able to—a bright flash of light erupted out of nowhere almost blinding her, and she threw up her arm to shield her eyes. The next moment she slammed into something... someone... and crashed hard to the forest floor. Her hand scraped the rough ground, and she felt a snap as her wrist gave way under the impact. Pain surged through her a split second before her head hit a rock. She lay on the ground stunned, trying to get past the pain. Fighting the dizzying blackness that was bleeding in from the sides of her vision, she heard movement, and someone crouched down beside her. She found herself looking into the face of a very odd-looking man. Nausea rose with the pain as the man picked her up, and she cried out in agony. Her eyes rolled back in her head, and she went limp as she lost consciousness. Light flashed in the forest, and silence descended once again.

Chapter Two

FOOTSTEPS ECHOED THROUGH the hold. Theiv Draakon looked up with a curse, pocketing the small laser tool he'd been using to override the computer locked doors of the holding cells. Moving silently, he ducked under the wing of the sleek black shuttle craft and edged around to its side door. He punched in the code and the door slid open.

Reactivating the lock, he swiftly entered the cockpit and began to touch screens and controls before he settled into the pilot's chair. The large viewing screen opened before him. He watched as the man in charge of this mission, Drace Aphelion, strode through the holding bay carrying an unconscious Earth woman. Theiv swore viciously. By the Emperor, when was this going to end?

He sabotaged the main components in the flash transporter last night, hoping to prevent this very scenario. The bastard must have a personal flash transporter. He frowned as Drace strode past the holding cells and made for the main doors of the hold. What the hell was he up to?

Theiv quickly exited the small craft and followed Drace from a distance down the main corridor of the ship, and into the science wing. The Exanthus was a fully equipped science vessel on a secret mission, and Theiv had joined its crew a few months ago at the request of the Dragon Warrior's counsel. They arranged for him to take command of the warrior class on board the Exanthus. It was the perfect cover for him, since he was a top-ranking Dragon Warrior, but even a Dragon Warrior could end up dead if he were caught snooping during a mission this secret.

From the moment he boarded the Exanthus, he felt a wrongness. This ship was permeated with a deathly stillness. Something was going on, and if these walls could talk, he might be able to solve this godsdamned nightmare.

He moved silently through the nearly empty corridor, taking care to stay well back. It would not be wise to have his interest noticed. Halfway down the science wing Drace stopped and glanced around, then entered the main lab of the ship. Theiv swore silently. To get into that lab you had to have top level science class, with the highest security clearance.

The sound of hurrying footsteps caused him to duck around the corner. Pressing his back against the wall, he watched carefully as Havyn Aphelion appeared and hurried into the lab, followed a few seconds later by Riak Valkor and T'lain Netron. The Exanthus's highest ranking scientists had just gathered, and he had no way to find out what they were up to. A chill swept over him as he thought about the Earth woman Drace had been carrying. May the gods have mercy on her soul.

Chapter Three

CONSCIOUSNESS RETURNED in bits and pieces, flashes of memory instantly making themselves known. Hands touching her, removing her clothing. Terror. Confusion. Disembodied voices speaking a language she had never heard before. A cold, hard male voice, distinctive in its utter lack of emotion. She swallowed against the panic and nausea rising in her throat. Her head ached, her arm hurt, and she was shivering, filled with a sense of dread.

She forced her eyes open and blinked away the blurriness. She couldn't make sense of what she was seeing. She was in a brightly lit room. Lying on a hospital bed? That wasn't quite right. Was this one of those nightmares where nothing made sense?

A hand touched her uninjured arm and she flinched, startled, horror filling her as she realized her body had not obeyed the reaction. Had she been in an accident? Was she paralyzed? Were these people doctors?

Panic surged inside her as she tried to move her arms. Nothing, not even a finger twitched. Every fight or flight instinct she'd ever possessed surged through her body in an electric wave as her heart rate soared. Her breathing rasped in and out of her chest, a scream built in her throat, and all her muscles tensed as her body made a desperate, futile attempt to catapult her away from the unknown danger. Nothing. A slight buzzing sound began to irritate her ears as a light flashed on, bathing her in its glow.

"The translator has been activated. Subject 459 is conscious. She is in a state of panic. Her adrenaline levels are spiking. Heart rate and respirations are too high. Administering a calming agent."

Brooke felt pressure on her throat, then heard a hiss. Instantly her heart slowed, and she began to feel calmer.

The odd-looking man from her run moved into her line of vision and it became apparent, as he snapped out commands, that he was in charge. She watched him, trying to figure out why he seemed so strange. Another man moved to her right, a woman stepped forward to lean over her, and she found herself staring into large, exotically tilted, golden eyes. The woman was beautiful with fine boned features, high cheekbones, and pale purple eyebrows that matched her hair. Her eyes moved from the woman in front of her to the man beside her, and Brooke's lax mind finally recognized what was odd about them. They were blue.

A wave of bone deep terror swept over her. This was not possible. How could this be possible? Oh god, this wasn't a hospital. They weren't doctors. She wanted desperately to cover herself, to run, to hide, but she couldn't move no matter how fiercely, how urgently she tried.

She was methodically examined, the beings handling her in a coldly clinical way, as if she were an object and not a human being. "Our scans tell us she's given birth more than once. She's overweight. She's past her prime. Perhaps we should find another subject?" the woman said. Brooke closed her eyes, humiliated by their utter disregard.

"No. There will be no other subject. The genome therapy and the serum will take care of those minor issues," That was the man, the one she'd run into, the one with the cold hard voice.

Subject? Genome therapy? Brooke began to shake, not on the outside, that was impossible, but somewhere deep inside.

The group gathered around her in their intimidating foreign uniforms of black with a strange green symbol. The shaking inside her grew worse as they continued their discussion as if she wasn't present. Fear and anger rising, she began to concentrate on moving just one small part of her body. A finger, a toe... if she could just move one part of herself, then she might be able to move more.

Sweat broke out on her skin and her head began to ache, an ache that swiftly turned blinding, but still she tried, forcing herself to concentrate past the pain. Move. Something had to move!

Darkness began to fill the edges of her vision, and she realized that no matter what she did, she couldn't make her body move. A tear slid down her cheek as one of the men turned to her and placed a small blinking black box on her forehead, which, within seconds, eased the pain. *What was this? Star Trek?* She thought hysterically.

"There is no time for another subject. The Emperor has moved my audience to the ninth of Yarl. We must be ready then. I will not lose this opportunity."

"I don't like your plan, Drace. What do you possibly hope to gain from this experiment? So far, we have only seen pain and death. This needs to end." The woman's voice was soft but filled with determination.

"My plan is of great importance to our planet, Havyn." That cruel voice said in a tone dripping with disdain. "I will not allow our way of life to be threatened. You don't like my experiment because you are a wife and usually not subject to the presence of the Zemyneah. You were warned, Havyn, and yet, you insisted on accompanying me on this mission." His voice lowered menacingly. "Be very careful. Your words border on betrayal and treason. I will not tolerate either."

The woman's chaotic golden eyes met Brooke's for a few seconds before she looked away, and it was clear to Brooke that she was furious.

The leader moved closer, giving her a clear view of his hawkish features. His eyes were so dark that they bordered on black, the pupils nearly indistinguishable. His lips were a harsh slash across his angular face, making him appear as cruel as he seemed. There was no warmth to this being, and seeing it up close, leached the last remnants of hope from her heart.

Despite his cold demeanor, he had a striking presence, and that made the look in his eyes even worse. She had no doubt that this alien was the one to be the most afraid of. It was written in the black pits of his eyes.

He smiled, and it was a smile filled with such an eerie coldness that goose bumps broke out on Brooke's flesh. In that instant, she understood that her terror was giving him pleasure. "Hello, little human female. What do they call you?" His voice was completely devoid of emotion, and Brooke knew that she would hear that voice in her nightmares for the rest of her life.

He stroked her cheek and down her throat, waiting for her to answer. Her skin crawled at his touch, at the look in his eyes. Suddenly she could talk. "B-Brooke, my name is Brooke. Why are you doing this? Let me go!"

"Brooke." He nodded. "I am Drace, and this is my crew. We fly the Space Vessel Exanthus. We are a ..." That menacing smile reappeared. "Science vessel."

"Given her age there is a strong possibility of grandchildren, Drace." One of the men spoke up, earning him a frosty glare so potent that he quickly looked away.

"Drace." The woman he'd called Havyn spoke in an urgent voice. "We cannot do this to a wife and life bearer."

Drace threw her a narrow-eyed look of warning. "Do you wish punishment, Havyn?" The hardness of his voice was intimidating, but underlying it was a clear note of twisted anticipation. The alien woman immediately dropped her gaze.

He turned back to Brooke. "You have been brought aboard our ship as the subject for an experiment that is imperative for the lives of all Althaneans."

Her eyes rounded in terror before everything inside of her rejected what he said. "No! I don't want this! Let me go!"

Drace shrugged. "Your agreement is not necessary." He paused as a long silver capsule rolled up beside her. "Ah. The chamber is ready. You needn't be afraid, there is no pain with this particular procedure." But his eyes said that he wished there were. It was like a burning flame in his eyes even as he gently caressed her arm, sending a horrified shiver racing across her skin.

"Our Zepto technology will eradicate every genetic flaw, repair your immune system, and heal every trace of disease. Genome technology will transform your body and reverse the damage caused by aging. These technologies will keep you in peak physical health, and in time, you will adapt to your body's requirements for sexual nourishment."

She felt the blood draining from her face, leaving her skin ghostly white under the unforgiving glare of the overhead lights. Her hands grew icy, her breathing ragged.

His eyes moved over her, and he smiled with cold amusement. "Your new body will require food, water, and scx to survive."

Brooke could barely breathe, nausea rising. "Are you insane?" She struggled frantically to move, to escape this lunatic. Oh, God, why were they doing this?

A cool hand skimmed down her side and over her hip in the lightest of caresses as she stared in mounting horror at the being that had captured her. There was nothing she could do to stop his icy hand as it continued its journey until it came to rest just above her mound. Her skin crawled and her mouth went dry with a soul deep fear that no woman should ever feel. She could feel his exhilaration as he continued his sadistic mental torture, his hand reversing course and sliding up her stomach in a straight line until it rested between her breasts.

"Don't be afraid, little Zemyneah, you will not be required for service until we reach our destination. You will be cared for and kept safe. And best of all," He leaned down to her ear, whispering with vicious delight. "You will love your service to your new master."

"No!" she screamed at him. "No!"

Drace shrugged his shoulders as if suddenly bored of his game and stepped back, signaling his men to lift her and place her into the capsule.

Brooke screamed and began to beg. "Let me go! Let me go! Please don't do this! Please! Please!" Panic swamped her system as tears streamed down her cheeks, her eyes meeting the woman's. "Help me! Please, please help me!"

Drace stepped forward again and stood looking down at her, his eyes glowing coldly with lust. He shut the lid, and suddenly, she could move again. She screamed and kicked, frantically hitting the lid with her fists as hysteria overwhelmed her. A purple gas hissed into the chamber, and then there was only blackness and terror. So much terror.

Chapter Four

EARTH DATE: JUNE 17 08:30 AM
  Gardenside, Alberta, Canada
  Earth, Dimension Two

CLAY BRENDON GLANCED at the time displayed on the dash of his police cruiser and tapped his fingers against the steering wheel. Where the hell was Brooke? She should have been here fifteen minutes ago. This wasn't like her. She was never late, and she wasn't answering her cell. Rubbing his neck, he wondered if she'd twisted an ankle, and was stubbornly hobbling her way home. She had his cell number, and she waved at him as he passed, so he knew damn well that she'd seen him, but that didn't mean she would call. Brooke was too independent for her own good sometimes.

He'd met Jaxson St. Claire on the first day of kindergarten and his mom, Brooke, on the second day. From that point on, Brooke took him under her wing. His biracial uniqueness and his rough home life hadn't made any difference. Brooke showed him the same fierce protective love that she poured out on her own children. He had become one of hers.

He radioed the station and told them his location, grinning over the good-natured ribbing he always got about his cookie breaks, then got out of his car and headed toward the trail Brooke should exit on. She would probably show up any second and tease him for being a worrier.

He called out her name as he walked, carefully scanning the heavily forested area as he tried her cell again, but it rang until it clicked over to her voicemail.

A couple kilometers down the trail, Clay's worry increased. Hell, he was more than worried. He had a really bad feeling. He hoped like hell she hadn't run into a bear or a cougar. Fuck! A few more feet and he came to a stop. Brooke's smartphone lay in the long grass beside the trail. After doing a careful visual scan of the area, he crouched down next to the phone as he took in the scene. The dirt on the trail contained two distinctly different footprints. This was private land. No one else should be on it. There was a flattened area in the grass to the side of the trail, and blood staining a rock buried in the grass.

Grabbing his radio, he called in to the station to make a request for search and rescue. He stood up and looked around for any evidence that would indicate the direction Brooke had been taken. There was nothing. No footprints. Not a fucking blade of grass out of place! He swore as worst-case scenarios began running through his mind. He did another careful scan of the forest, looking for anything out of place, anything that would give him a direction to begin a search. There was nothing. There was fucking nothing!

He pulled out his phone, and with a grim look, called the one other person who knew this land like the back of his hand, his best friend Jaxson, Brooke's son.

Twenty minutes later, a black pickup truck with St. Claire Construction emblazoned on the doors roared into the driveway and slammed to a stop beside the police cruiser. Dust filled the air as the driver's door opened and a blond man stepped out, his emerald-green eyes sweeping the area for Clay, before he walked over to the passenger side of the vehicle where his sister and his mother's best friend were climbing out. He grabbed the backpack that his sister had hastily packed, and they headed out into the forest.

"Jaxson!"

"Have you found anything, Clay?" Jaxson asked, even though he could see from the hard look on his friends face that the answer was no. *Shit.* He'd really hoped to arrive and find his mother and Clay having a coffee and laughing about Clay being a worrywart. He glanced at his sister, Dani, and saw the same worry in her green eyes, before turning back to Clay. "You haven't found Mom?"

Clay shook his head. "No. I've called search and rescue. They should be here any minute." He hugged Danielle tightly. "Where are the kids?"

"I had a friend come over and watch them," Dani replied, holding on to the police officer who she considered one of her big brothers. Heaven knew he was as overprotective as Jaxson. The two of them drove her nuts on a regular basis.

Clay gave Dani a little squeeze before turning and hugging Nissa. "We'll find her, Nissa."

Nissa hugged Clay back and nodded her head. "We will find her," her voice was firm. She had no room for doubt in her mind. They would find Brooke. "I called Chief Wolf, and he said that no bears or cougars have been spotted in this area recently. He's coming with some of his men to help search for her."

Clay nodded. "Thanks, Nissa." He turned and shoved a hand through his brown hair then showed them what he'd found. It wasn't enough. Not even close to enough.

By the time Search and Rescue pulled into the St. Claire property, more police, Chief Wolf and his men, and Brooke's friends and neighbors had shown up to help.

JUNE 18, DAY TWO

They had optimism and hope. It balanced the fear that kept crowding into their minds. The search and rescue dogs hadn't picked up a scent, and with that information, the police became grim, setting up roadblocks and searching vehicles for miles around. The search and rescue team searched Brooke's land and her immediate neighbors' land, sure they would find her or some clue to her whereabouts. But they were wrong. Nissa called the media and organized posters to be distributed province wide, fully aware that the faster they got the information out to the public, the greater their chances of finding Brooke.

JUNE 19, DAY THREE

They were quietly determined, the search area now targeting a fifty-kilometer radius. Nissa, determined and willing to throw a lot of money into solving the mystery of her friend's disappearance, convinced the powers that be to get some helicopters into the search. She interviewed with the local TV and radio stations and put out word that there was a large reward being offered for any information on Brooke St. Claire. She organized a huge force of volunteers to plaster five counties with the missing posters. Clay, along with the rest of the small police detachment, went door to door. The search area was massive, the dire possibilities replaying in everyone's minds, and the situation becoming more urgent with every minute that passed.

JUNE 20, DAY FOUR

They were angry and fighting fear, but resolutely searching a hundred-kilometer radius. They would find Brooke. A national TV crew showed up and interviewed the family. Brooke's disappearance was being reported nationwide. Where was she? No one knew.

It was dark when Clay walked wearily into the yard, the moon high in the sky, and he'd been awake for more than seventy-two hours at this point. He desperately needed coffee and something to eat. Hearing his name, he looked up and saw the haggard face of his friend. Together they walked into the big St. Claire house and straight to the kitchen. Nissa handed them both a coffee, her face marked with the stress and lack of sleep. "Did Dani go into the washroom?"

Jaxson paused mid sip and looked up at Nissa. "I thought she was here with you. I sent her back here this afternoon and told her to try to get a couple hours sleep."

Clay set down his cup. "I haven't seen her, Nissa."

Nissa shook her head. "She came here, called to check on the kids, then drank some coffee and headed back out. She said she was going to catch up with you, Jaxson."

Both men started to stand when Nissa slapped her hand down on the table. "Drink your goddamn coffee!" She snapped, "And you're going to eat something too! What good is it going to do anyone if you collapse on us!" She turned abruptly and started ladling thick stew into large bowls. But they'd seen the tears. Clay looked at Jaxson, then stood up and took the ladle from the slender dark-haired middle-aged woman, turning her in his arms to hug her tightly. "Nissa, we'll find Danielle."

Once she calmed down, Nissa fed the men and fixed them a thermos of coffee before they headed back out. Only this time they were looking for their sister as well.

It was just after midnight when Jaxson stepped out of the forest onto a faint trail that led him up a steep hill overlooking the valley. He glanced around before walking into a clearing that, come morning, would be kissed with the stunning colours of the sunrise. There she was, laying on the soft grass that covered their grandparents' graves. The small family graveyard held seven generations of St. Claire's. Every one of the St. Claires was born and raised on this land. His father wasn't here, but then again, his father had been a Burkman not a St. Claire, and after his terrible betrayal, he had no right to anything St. Claire.

"Danielle." His sister turned her head, and his heart clenched at the absolute hopelessness written across her face. He walked over and sat down beside her, pulling her into his arms. "When we find mom, we are all taking that trip to Hawaii we've been talking about for the last five years." His voice was thick as he fought the moisture prickling at his eyes. "You've been talking to Gramma and Gramps?"

"Jaxson?" Dani clung to the broad shoulders of her brother, tears dripping down her face as she whispered her terrible question. "W-What if she's dead?"

"She's not dead, Dani," Jaxson said firmly. Though deep inside he was beginning to fear the worst. "She can't be dead. We still need her too much. Clay wouldn't survive without her cookies."

"Hey. Quit maligning my good name," Clay spoke as he walked up to them. It looked like he'd had the same hunch as Jaxson. He sat down with his family and pulled out a thermos. This was as good a place as any to talk. As a family they needed to decide their next steps.

JUNE 21, DAY FIVE

The day dawned bright and clear, and the searchers hadn't slept in four days. Where was Brooke St. Claire? There were no answers. It was as if she had disappeared into thin air.

Chapter Five

RUNE AEZORWYN PAUSED as he looked out over the Multiverse and frowned. What in the seven hells was that man doing now? He crossed his arms over his chest, a muscle jumping in his jaw. This being was stubbornly certain of his own righteousness even though his plans were being met with fierce resistance. Rune walked away from the transparent wall that gave him unprecedented views of all that he and Eliana had created. He'd always hated that sect and their twisted beliefs, but this was going too far. The sheer arrogance of thinking that he had the right to cause harm was unconscionable. Inexcusable. Did that man really think there would be no consequences for this? He growled and began to look for the solution to this madness. His mind filtered through the ramifications of every possibility. He unraveled tangled threads of life and death, birth and nonexistence, unforeseen consequences, and of course, the unexpected. Ah. There. Just the person he needed. Rune disappeared.

Chapter Six

EARTH DATE: JUNE 21
  Sol Star System, Starship Exanthus

DAY AFTER DAY PASSED as the ship maintained its orbit around Jupiter's moon, Elara. The newest captive aboard the Exanthus remained deeply sedated as her body was transformed by alien technology. Completely unaware of the desperate search going on seven hundred million kilometers away, her body fought to survive the radical changes taking place inside it.

One by one, the other women captured from earth in the weeks prior, began to die, their bodies unable to adapt to the profound changes demanded by the experiment. The horror of their short existence after the transformation was completed, noted only as scientific data.

When it became apparent that the newest captive would survive, she was transferred to a small cell where she could be observed as needed and her biometrics read by the computer sensors embedded in the sleeping ledge. A warming sheet was drawn over her naked body to keep her temperature stable, and she was left to awaken on her own.

The first thing Brooke felt as she woke up was how her body ached. She felt like she had been run over by a train, and it had backed up. She cautiously eased onto her side and frowned. This was not her bed and she had no pillow. She opened her eyes. Where was she? Looking around, she could see that she was alone in a darkened room. As she studied the unfamiliar design of the walls, her heart began to race as terrifying memories arose. The cold dark eyes of the alien being who'd captured her swam through her mind, and she moaned. Swallowing back the tiny sound, she sat up. Had it been a nightmare? Please, let it have been a dream. More memories surfaced. Not being able to move. Hearing the evil in his voice. His plans. *Oh, god.* His sick twisted plans. Nausea surged, but she fought it off, breathing deeply even as the memory of the lid of a silver capsule closing over her made her tremble. The terror of that moment crashed over her once again and she forced herself to concentrate on her breathing. *Think, Brooke, think.* She took slow deep breaths as she tried to figure out what she needed to do. Escape, of course, but how she could get away from aliens on a spaceship she had no idea.

Carefully, she sat up and set her feet on the floor, soft overhead lights coming on with her movement. She couldn't stop shaking and realized with a shiver that she was still naked. *Damn, Damn, Damn.* What had they done to her? She couldn't let herself think about that right now. She needed to find a way out of here. Later. Later there would be time to panic.

She grabbed the blanket off the bed and dragged it around herself, tucking the ends in as she looked around for a door. There wasn't one. Anywhere. No doors, no windows. Her heart began to race again, her breathing speeding up. *Oh, god. Oh, god.*

She took a deep calming breath, then another. *You can do this, Brooke, you can do this. Just be calm and think about it.* They brought her in here somehow, and if there was a way in, then there was a way out.

She approached the nearest wall and began to run her hands systematically over the smooth surface, looking for any indications of an entrance. Later, hours or minutes, she had no way of knowing, she slid down one of those perfectly smooth walls and sat with her knees drawn up. There was no way out.

She took a deep breath and then another. She would not panic. She absolutely would not panic. She shoved a length of hair back over her shoulder again, irritated that it kept getting in her way, then froze. Her hand trembled as she reached up and felt her hair. It was no longer in the short no-nonsense style that she had kept it in for the last fifteen years. In fact, as she slid her hands down the soft silky length, she realized that it reached her waist. What the heck was going on!

She jolted to her feet and, reaching back, she gathered her hair and drew it forward. It cascaded down her shoulder and over her breast, a deep shimmering wave of purple that would never have naturally occurred. But the colour didn't shock her as much as what she saw next. She looked, really looked at her shaking hands. They didn't look like her hands, she thought as a small whimper escaped. Her hands had been different. Not so slender, the start of age lines just appearing, and the beginnings of arthritis in her knuckles giving them a slightly swollen appearance.

She ran her hands over her face, searching for answers to questions that were too terrifying to even consider. She swallowed against the dryness that suddenly invaded her mouth, unwrapped the sheet and stared down at her body. Firm breasts, slim waist, flat stomach, bare woman parts, and long slim legs... wait! Bare woman parts? She yanked the sheet tightly closed and slumped weakly against the wall. A deep breath and then another. Oh god. What had they done? What had they done to her?

Chapter Seven

EARTH DATE: JUNE 21,
   Sol Star System, Starship Exanthus

THEIV WATCHED THE GOINGS on with interest. So far, two of the top scientists on board the Exanthus had slipped away to the shuttle bay, boarding one of the sleek fast crafts, and now, he was following Drace's wife.

Havyn Aphelion was far more than she appeared to be. Far more than a simple Althanean woman happily bonded to her husband, not that he thought for one microsecond that she was happily bonded to that bastard. She was far more than the obedient honored wife of the greatest scientist in the known universe. He snorted silently. If she had an ounce of obedience in her soul, he would eat his phase pistol.

Dr. Aphelion might have an advanced degree in genetics, but he would lay credits that her true purpose on this ship had nothing to do with helping her husband advance his experiment. He suspected she was playing a deeply deceptive game. The question was, why? Was she a willing participant in this horror story? Was she as much a victim as the women that Drace captured? Or was she something else altogether?

Havyn stepped out of her husband's private chambers, and Theiv glanced at his timekeeper his eyebrow raised. Just enough time for a quick fuck, but when you were a bond wife and your husband was a busy man, you took as much time in his bed as you could get. After all, your survival depended on it.

He also knew that Drace Aphelion was not a man easily pleased. He had listening devices everywhere on this ship, and he'd spoken with the man's Zemyneah Slave, who was carefully tucked away where Havyn would never find out about her. Not that she could have done anything about it, but there were appearances to be considered. Hypocritical protocols still had to be followed.

He glanced at the closed door to the room, contemplating Drace's next action and his reactions to the unpleasant surprise his wife undoubtedly had for him, then casually followed Havyn as she moved through the corridors. He recognized the purpose in her stride and the caution in her movements. She did not want to be found out. He waited until she reached the holding cells before he stepped forward. "Havyn Aphelion."

She whirled around. Her golden eyes widened when she saw the head of the Warrior Class standing a few feet away from her, his rank clearly denoted by the red security symbol on his black uniform and the phase pistol present on his hip. "May I help you?" Her voice was calm and cool, showing only the minor curiosity of a scientist of her caliber being spoken to by a Warrior.

Theiv almost laughed. She was good. He gestured towards the main door leading into the holding cells. "Proceed.

I will accompany you." That made her pause, and he raised a brow at the fleeting look of rebellion that he saw in those golden eyes.

Havyn lifted her chin and stared haughtily at the head of security. "These cells are classified. You are not needed here, Warrior."

He crossed his arms, a huge silent man who was not about to be put off. His purple eyes met her golden ones, and he simply waited. Her options were few. She could call Drace, or she could deal with him. He had a feeling she was not about to call Drace. He was right.

Havyn cursed quietly. Had Drace put this man on her? Was he having her followed? Investigated? She swallowed, her mind running quickly through her actions over the last few weeks. No, she had not betrayed herself. Her messages were so deeply encrypted that there was no way for Drace to know about them. She was confident of that and another important fact snapped to the forefront of her mind. Drace had been furious when his head of the warrior class was transferred to another posting and this man, Theiv Draakon, was sent to replace him. Draakon... a Dragon Warrior. It was an odd placement for a Dragon Warrior.

Havyn would not have gotten this far if she had not been willing to take the risks. She was intelligent, skilled, and driven. In short, an Althanean husband's worst nightmare, if only he knew it. She had been on her way to the biggest risk of her life. What was one more hazard in such dangerous circumstances? What she was about to do would change everything. She didn't expect to survive anyway. Her goal was only to live long enough to complete this final mission. And this mission had nothing to do with creating more Zemyneah slaves. Nothing.

With the slightest of nods, she entered the code and the door to the holding cells swooshed open. She stepped through with Theiv Draakon right behind her. The door closed and she heard the locks engage. She was about to do something incredibly dangerous, and she hoped like hell it paid off. She took a step, her soft boots silent on the polished floors of the hall that ran between the row of holding cells.

She hated coming into this area of the ship. These cells were originally designed to be holding cells for the unlikely event of a crime taking place on the ship. The chances of criminal activity on a science vessel were slight, however, and that was why it was decided that it would be safe for an honored wife to assist her husband on his mission. Not that Drace cared about her safety, his only concern was her skill as a geneticist. Under Drace's influence, the ones who made that decision had no idea of the true nature of Drace's mission, but then, neither had she, at first.

Theiv reached for the woman. It was time for some answers. Only to find himself sailing through the air as she performed a maneuver that no protected, coddled, Althanean wife would ever know. He landed on the floor with a hard thud and instantly flipped and rose to his feet, a dangerous man prepared to engage in battle. He paused when he saw the highly illegal weapon in her hand. "Havyn Aphelion, you surprise me. Star Forge, I assume. You do understand that you have committed acts of treason, and you can be sent to the Zemyneah ranks? "

She shrugged, cool and in control. "I have walked that line for many years. You are simply the first to find out, to discover my messages. Why are you here? Did Drace send you?" She was fully prepared to kill this man. Her mission would succeed. Even if it were the last one, she would finish.

"The Dragon's would never align themselves with a man such as Drace." Theiv replied, watching her carefully. He could see a cold determination in her eyes that did not bode well. "I've been sent to find out what is going on in this ship. What it's true mission is. We are obviously not studying the effects of Zepto Technology on the dying star of Marginus. The Bergice system is in the opposite direction than we have traveled. We are also obviously not studying the genetic origins of the Althanean people, as your paper points to a remote system in the Paxeon Expanse. We are nowhere close to the Expanse, nor could we get to the Expanse traveling in this direction.

We are, in fact, hiding behind a moon named Elara, which is in a prograde orbit around a planet called Jupiter in the Star System Sol. This system has one populated planet named Earth and has been designated Non-contact 100. So, as a Dragon Warrior, I must ask. What in the Seven hells are we doing here, Havyn Aphelion?"

She stared silently at the man. Kill or trust. To kill a Dragon Warrior was to incite the whole Dragon Clan. One did not anger a dragon lightly. In fact, one did everything they could to avoid even a slight misunderstanding with the Dragons. They were the elite, the best, the most powerful of the warrior class. Men of honor and courage, they protected the mighty Dragons who they fought with. Finally, deciding that perhaps the legendary Dragons might be the only ones who could help to stop the madness, she spoke. "Drace is conducting experiments to create the ultimate Zemyneah. He has been charged with gaining control of the Emperor, to protect Althanean interests."

Theiv listened and watched the woman, his mind turning over the possibilities. "You are speaking very freely. Are you not afraid that Drace will hear you?"

The woman tapped the small green science insignia on her black uniform. "This contains a dampening field that will prevent any electronic listening or viewing devices from functioning within a 200-meter circumference around me. I tapped it before I entered."

"That is a handy piece of Sarisian Technology, lady." She nodded once and he paused again. Games. This lady was playing a dark and dangerous game. "The Emperor is not interested in appropriating Zemyneah slaves. He has a wife, and from all appearances, he is committed to her. Your husband is on a fool's mission."

"Be that as it may, Drace is no fool. He created a Zemyneah, who is irresistible. It's taken many experiments, and cost many lives, but he succeeded, Theiv Draakon. The Emperor will not be able to resist her."

"So, the Emperor gets to have his own personal sex slave, why is that even a concern? She probably won't live long anyway. The Empress is not known for willingness to share her man."

Havyn arched a slender brow. "This woman carries the unique ability to bond with two men. She will be bonded to a handler before she ever reaches the Emperor. Once he takes her, he will long for her, he will crave her. She will be his addiction. The enhanced Zepto health protocol that Drace smuggled to a double agent on the Emperor's medical team will see to that. It contains very specialized zepto technology that will recognize hers. If she is killed, he will die too."

Theiv froze. "You've created a bonding circuit? That is impossible."

Havyn laughed. "Of course, it's possible! Just because an Althanean is a male doesn't make him impervious to a bonding protocol. That is a myth created by the males of our society as part of their justification in enslaving the females of our world. Think about it. We are both Althanean. For centuries, females have been kept away from any information pertaining to the Zemyneah Industry." When he started to interrupt, she ignored him and continued. "Women are not weaker than the men of our world. We are not more easily led astray, nor are we less intelligent. It has taken centuries, but finally, we have women in a position to unravel the secrets of the Zemyneah health protocols." She lifted her chin, her eyes meeting his. "I am the worst nightmare for the males of our society. In allowing me to work on this project, Drace has revealed the Zemyneah Secrets. The bonding secrets. I have sent that information to those who can stop this enslavement. It will take time, but we will unravel this and put a stop to it."

Theiv crossed his arms. She was talking about the Rebel faction that had been making its presence known more and more over the last twenty years. He had a lot of questions, but he dismissed them all except the most important. "What will happen if the Emperor is bonded to this Zemyneah?"

Havyn gave him a grim smile. "Perhaps a form of justice. He will be able to be controlled. If it were any other man, I would simply allow it, and continue to gather the information we need. But the Emperor has been seeking to change the laws around the making of Zemyneah slaves. He has been trying to get laws regarding the equality of women to be passed throughout the whole known Universe. He has publicly condemned the Zemyneah practice of Althanea. And that is what has made him a target.

"The Althanean government hoped an Althanean on the throne would lead to prosperity for our world. It has not happened." Havyn gave Theiv a tight smile. "The Emperor might be Althanean, but he was not raised on our world. He has shown no respect for 'the Althanean way', and our leaders refuse to allow this to continue. So, they have commissioned Drace.

"In the last few months, Drace has had certain successes. And now his latest, and he hopes, his final success awaits in the holding cell. The ultimate Zemyneah slave. Irresistible, exotic, utterly dependant on sex for her survival, and totally innocent of any of this.

"She is an Earth woman, a woman who was stolen from her life and family, to fulfill a perverse and evil mission. We experimented on many women, Theiv. But it was here on this unprotected planet that we finally found what Drace had been looking for. We found a woman who could survive his experiments. She could be altered and changed into what he was after. A woman who will not only enslave the Emperor but will deal a death blow to the fight for freedom for the Althanean women. She will enslave us all, for all eternity."

"Then she must die." Theiv said quietly, determination in his voice. "I will do it if you can't."

Havyn looked at him steadily. "If you go into that room, you will not be able to resist her. From her eyes to her scent, she is the most erotic creature I have ever seen. And Drace has sped up the process. He wants her ready as soon as possible. He has an audience with the Emperor in a few weeks.

The woman is releasing pheromones designed by her Zeptos to draw a sexual partner. It is not quite what we expected, of course, but it is very effective.

She is innocent in this, Theiv, and too many women have already died. My plan is to return her to Earth."

"You what?" Theiv was furious. "You can't just return her. She is not a pet. She is an intelligent being who has been given advanced technology. Do you know what that could do to Earth's natural path of learning? They are not ready for this. That is why they are slated Non-contact 100. It will be at least a hundred years before they are ready for outside contact."

"They are about to get a steep learning curve then, because if we don't give them the means to protect themselves, they will be extinct long before a hundred years." Havyn began furiously. "I refuse to kill another woman. I refuse to allow her to be killed. She is innocent in all of this, and what Drace has done to her is unconscionable. I have a plan, and I am returning her."

Theiv moved so fast that Havyn didn't have a chance to stop him. He disarmed and cuffed her before she even understood what was going on. Then he moved to the single cell that held a prisoner. The door opened with a swoosh,

and he entered prepared to kill a woman who had done no
wrong.

Chapter Eight

EARTH DATE: JUNE 21,
  Sol Star System, Starship Exanthus

BROOKE WHIRLED AROUND, nearly tripping over the trailing ends of the sheet. A huge dark haired alien male she hadn't seen before stepped inside. There was a hardness to his purple eyes and a grim set to his jaw. Her head tilted up as she looked at him and her eyes widened. *Wow.* She swallowed, suddenly conscious of how much bigger than her, he was. *Warrior! Danger!* Her brain shouted and she took an unconscious step back. And yet despite the danger signals, or maybe because of them, Brooke felt a very feminine awareness of him.

He never said a word, simply watched her, and she tightened her grip on the sheet wrapped around her, wondering what he was thinking. He carried himself like a military man, his stark black uniform with its red insignia lending to that impression. Their eyes met and held, and in those purple eyes, she could see an internal battle taking place. Unnerved by the connection she felt to this man, she tore her gaze from his, her arms crossing over her chest. What did he want? Why was he here? She wondered as she chanced another glance at him. His left hand was closed over the butt of the weapon holstered to his hip, and her breath caught in her throat as she realized the hard unnamed emotion that she had seen lurking in his eyes was death.

She took another step back, terror filling her, and her eyes jumped back to his. She bumped into the wall behind her and stopped. There was nothing she could do, nowhere for her to run, nowhere to escape to. She lifted her chin, determined if he killed her, he would do so with the full knowledge that he was killing a person who had done nothing to deserve death. As they stared at one another, she saw the moment he decided to let her live.

She was beautiful, extraordinary, and he fucking wanted her. His cock had hardened the moment he had walked into the cell and caught her scent. Her eyes, an exotic green color, sucker punched him right in the gut. It took all his strength to push aside the totally inappropriate fantasies of tearing that sheet from her hands and taking her right there against the wall. He was supposed to kill her, not fuck her.

Her pale ivory skin almost glistened under the lights in the room, and her lips were a beautiful shade of rose that he'd once seen on a flowering plant his sister cultivated on the planet of Giastea. It was the thought of his sister, who looked so much like his mother, that made him realize that he could not kill this woman. She was not guilty of any crime except being in the wrong place at the wrong time and capturing the attention of an evil man. He swore mentally. He had a duty to protect the Emperor. How the hell was he going to prevent this woman from being used to destroy so many? One thing he knew, he was going to have to stay close until he knew she was no longer a threat.

His eyes drifted over her again. Gods, she was all lush feminine sexuality. He inhaled the exotic scent that was uniquely hers, and he could almost taste her. His cock throbbed, and he took an unthinking step closer. A craving to taste her hit him hard. He paused as a thought struck him. If he could forge a telepathic link with this woman, he would be able to find her anywhere. He took another step closer, his tongue sliding over his sharper eye teeth as he felt them pulse again. Having a telepathic link to this woman, would help him to protect the Emperor, and that was his priority.

Brooke stared into the man's eyes as he moved closer to her. Her heart was beating hard in her chest, and she licked her dry lips. What was he doing?

Theiv braced a hand on the wall by the woman's head, caging her in. This close her scent seemed to flow all around him. Even his skin seemed to absorb the wonderful fragrance. He leaned in closer, fought the urge to tear the sheet from her tightly fisted grasp. "What's your name?"

"Brooke." Her voice was shaky, and she put a hand on his chest to hold him at bay. This close she could smell the wild clean scent of him, and it was doing crazy things to her. "Are you going to kill me?"

"No."

She felt his breath against her neck, and shivered. She could feel the heat of his body under her hand, could feel the rapid beating of his heart. She wondered what he would look like without his uniform and bit her lip as an image of rock-hard abs flitted through her mind. Oh god, what was happening to her? Her nipples peaked, and she could feel the heat building between her legs. His big body pressed against hers and she inhaled, her eyes fluttering closed. She should be screaming. Why wasn't she screaming? She inhaled his scent again and everything in her sighed. He smelled so good, so right.

His mouth moved over her neck and she tilted her head giving him better access, as her other hand found its way under his shirt, the heat of his skin enticing her to slide her hand up his skin.

Theiv felt the sheet as it slipped to the floor, and he looked down at the body of a goddess. His breath rushed out of his chest and he groaned, a harsh sound that jerked his attention back to the task at hand. He needed to establish a telepathic link to the woman, not fuck her. But gods, he wanted to. Badly. Gritting his teeth, he forced himself to not look at that beautiful body again. The glide of her soft hands over his skin, as she pushed up his tunic, was killing him. He swore his dick had never been this hard. *Focus Theiv,* he told himself as he hesitated. *One hard bite will do it.*

He swallowed and a second groan tore from him as he felt the brush of hard nipples against his chest. The scent of her arousal filled his senses, and he couldn't help breathing deeply as if he could fill himself with her essence— A sensory memory he would never forget. Somehow forcing his mind back on the task, he crowded her against the wall, his body preventing her escape. Not that she seemed to want to escape he thought as he felt her leg wrap around his and her hands stroke his chest. He had to do this now, or he was going to end up fucking her. With a harsh growl, he dipped his head and bit down on the smooth muscle where her neck joined her shoulder. The copper taste of blood flooded his mouth as she stiffened, then to his shock, she bit him back. He growled and his arms closed around her as he felt her slender body shudder and convulse. Had she just come?

Releasing his hold on her neck, he licked the small puncture marks his teeth had made and fought the need to take her hard and fast against the wall, as he felt her lick the bite on his chest. Information poured into his mind from her, and he knew the link had been established. He had to get out of there. He had to get out of there right now, or he was going to fuck her, and consequences be damned.

He eased back from her, his eyes traveling over her naked body once more before he turned and strode across the room. It was all he could do not to turn right around and take her. No. He gave his head a shake. He was a Dragon Warrior. He would behave with honor. Pausing for a moment at the doors, he adjusted himself and straightened his tunic, then he activated the door and stepped through it. The door slid silently closed behind him and he took a deep breath of the clean sterile air outside that room.

Theiv walked over to Havyn and released her hands. She whirled on him and slapped him. He stepped back, his eyes watchful, but he did nothing, said nothing about what had transpired in the holding cell he just exited. Havyn was a wife and not used to being treated with harshness. Finally, he spoke. "Havyn, what is your plan? I did not kill her, but I need to know about this plan. I cannot allow her to be used to harm the Emperor."

Havyn narrowed her eyes and stared at Theiv. The son of a bitch had handcuffed her, but she knew that, if he helped, her plan had a much better chance of working. "It's simple. We take her to Earth. To a military installation near her home, then we tell them what has happened. They will provide her two males to bond with, and she will no longer be of any use to Drace. The biggest problem we have is that this might be a one-way trip for us. We cannot come back to the Exanthus, and we have no means of communication with the Emperor."

Theiv nodded. "Get the woman to the ship. Yes, I saw Riak Valkor and T'lain Netron skulking around. You science class are not made for clandestine escapes." He shook his head and started to turn towards the door to the main corridor. "I will take care of finding a way for us to communicate with the Emperor. I will meet you in the shuttle bay."

Havyn watched the man leave and sighed in relief before she stepped over to a small nook and opened it, taking out a simple science tunic and pants, she walked into the cell holding the prisoner.

Another swoosh and the wall opened again. Brooke looked up from tucking the ends of the sheet in so it would not fall. She was mortified. The first orgasm she'd ever had that hadn't been from her own hand, and it was with an alien stranger who hadn't even touched the correct parts. What was he thinking? What had she been thinking? She'd never behaved like that in her life! She rubbed her neck where the man had bitten her, puzzled why there was no pain. The woman from earlier walked into the room, a curious look in her eyes as she examined Brooke. Swallowing the fear that wanted to overwhelm her, Brooke summoned all her anger and stood to her full height, glaring defiantly at the alien female. "Let me go."

"This is what I am here to do." Havyn answered calmly.

Brooke paused, startled. "Oh..." She sagged against the wall, tears burning her eyes. *Thank God.*

The woman stepped closer and held out a bundle of clothing. "Take this."

Brooke hesitantly took the bundle, her fingers trembling as she understood how close to death she had come. It was a uniform, just like the one that the aliens wore. Black with a green symbol on the tunic. "Why..."

"Put it on. Hurry, there is not much time."

Deciding to trust the woman, Brooke dropped the sheet and dressed quickly. "Why are we hurrying? You said you were letting me go."

"I am letting you go. My husband, Drace, is not." She glanced at a small tablet in her hand, keeping her gaze off the woman as much as she could. The medical results on the screen confirming what she could already feel about this new breed of Zemyneah. They were designed to be irresistible, their bodies completely bent to the will and preferences of their masters. The potency of the enhanced pheromones was undeniable. And the full scale of the evilness of Drace's plan struck her. He would not only enslave women, but he sought to find a way to control those in power. Havyn swallowed. If he succeeded... they would all suffer.

Havyn tapped the screen, this Zemyneah was not what Drace had expected. Her initial levels were much higher than any other test subjects, and where the other Zemyneah affected only men, she could feel herself responding to the peripheral views of Brooke's body and the pheromones that perfumed the air. The possibilities with this Zemyneah were too great, too horrific to even consider. It was why she'd decided to risk everything and free her. If Drace realized...

She snapped herself out of her thoughts, beginning the sequence to delete all the files on Brooke off the system's hard drive. "We need to get to the shuttle craft before he awakens and discovers what I have done." Looking up and seeing that Brooke was dressed, Havyn took the woman's arm and ushered her out of the room. "Do not look at the crew, keep your eyes down." She whispered sharply as they entered the lift, and seconds later they disembarked on another floor.

Brooke hurried to keep up, fear pounding an unwelcome rhythm throughout her body. Her stomach churned, her hands grew clammy, and her pulse rocketed through her veins. Damn it. Of course, they weren't just letting her go. That would have been too easy.

"Pay attention." Havyn spoke in a low tone as they headed down another corridor. "We will enter the launch bay and then enter the craft. You must do as I tell you. There is no room for error," she said emphatically. "You will keep your eyes down at all times. You will not speak to anyone but me. If you don't want what Drace has planned for you, you must do exactly as I say. This is your only chance of escape."

Brooke glanced at the woman and met her golden gaze, nodding her understanding as she saw the stark truth painted in those unusual eyes. Havyn was deadly serious. As they walked down the halls at a brisk pace, she started to ask Havyn why she had been taken, but Havyn shook her head and brought them to a direct stop in front of a door. Putting a finger to her lips to signal for silence, she touched a dark metallic plate on the wall.

A section of the wall slid away with a silent swoosh and they slipped inside to a large, cavernous space with several sleek black shuttle crafts. The front one had the hatch open, and Havyn drew Brooke over to it.

Freedom was so close, but part of Brooke was terrified at the thought of stepping into a metal box that was going to hurtle through space. The hesitancy she felt didn't stop Havyn from pulling her up the ramp, nor did it stop the blue-skinned alien from pushing her into a seat.

The door sealed with another of those silent swooshes and Havyn moved to the front of the craft to speak to the man at the controls. "Are you sure you can fly this?"

The man turned and looked at Havyn, his expression sardonic. "I've been flying ships since I was a young teenager. There are few ships I can't handle."

Brooke caught her breath. It was the man who had come into the room she'd been held in. The two male scientists from the lab where she had woken up the first time, came from the back and took seats in the cockpit beside the big man.

The men started to touch symbols on the console in front of them. "You can take your seat, Havyn. We have all been trained to fly the shuttle crafts in the event of an emergency. You have no need for concern. Whether we will be able to evade Drace is the real issue. We are not warrior pilots. We are scientists."

The big man beside them shook his head. "Speak for yourselves." He touched a few more symbols and sent an encrypted message to the Captain of the Exanthus, warning him of their departure. If not for that man, the Dragon Warriors would not have known about the experiments being performed on the Exanthus.

Havyn looked annoyed, "Theiv, just go to the coordinates that I have given you. Drace should not awake for several hours. Make sure that you have disabled the tracking programs," she ordered, picking up the tablet from where she had temporarily discarded it. A percentage reader wound around and around as data was deleted, her fate and Brooke's sealed with one press of her finger.

Havyn returned to Brooke's side. "Do not look at them." She snapped quietly.

Brooke looked away from the two aliens and met Havyn's eyes. "Why?"

Golden eyes shifted away, breath becoming shallower as she focused on the answers the other woman would need. "In our language Zemyneah means essence. Zemyneah women are the essence of sexuality. From your eyes to the pheromones you produce, you are designed to be irresistible. We cannot trust their ability to resist you." She took a seat across the aisle and buckled herself in, tablet on her lap. "They are not warriors like Theiv."

Theiv, the man about to pilot this spacecraft. Brooke took a deep breath trying to calm herself. Somehow, she had more faith in his ability to fly this machine than the two scientists. She snuck another quick look at him. He was built much differently than the two scientists Havyn mentioned, the control in every movement of his body reminding her of the soldiers she had seen throughout her life. The struggle she'd seen in his eyes suddenly made terrible sense. Zemyneah. A tendril of dread worked its way down her spine, and she remembered Drace calling her that, his eyes filled with an animalistic lust.

There was a slight shudder as the shuttle lifted off, and she jerked her head up in time to see the wall of the ship simply disappear and then they were hurtling into dark space. Looking out the small, rectangular windows, she frowned in confusion as they flew farther away and, as bright colours came into view, she suddenly realized they were flying over a massive planet. She looked down at the planet, her eyes as round as saucers as she saw swirls and dots of blue, gold, and orange. It was magnificent and so utterly alien.

The tiny craft they flew in was traveling unbelievably fast, and as they gained more distance from the planet, she saw a huge red spot along the planet's curve and realization dawned. Jupiter. They were flying past Jupiter.

The shuttle seemed to hesitate and then space disappeared into a swirling vortex. She gasped and grabbed at her harness, her stomach trying its best to leap up into her throat.

"It is safe." Havyn said calmly as she looked across the aisle. "You are safe. We are taking you home. Now, you must obey me." She said in a tone that brooked no argument. "Look down."

Brooke met the woman's eyes, finding compassion and pity in that golden gaze. She swallowed and obediently looked at her feet. What had they done to her? She licked her dry lips, afraid to ask the questions that she needed to ask. Afraid to know the answers.

"We don't have much time. We will be entering earth's atmosphere in just a few minutes." Havyn's voice with its exotic accent was quietly determined. "We cannot return you to the exact place where you were taken from. That will be the first area that Drace will search-"

"Then where am I supposed to go?" Brooke demanded.

"I have determined the safest location is a military installation." Havyn looked at Brooke, tapped a finger over the map on her tablet. "We have pinpointed one with a bunker hidden in a mountain. It should be a sufficient location to hide the presence of our craft."

There was a slight shudder as the craft rapidly began to lose speed, then a flash of light created as the craft slowed. The black endlessness of space surrounded the craft, and she raised her head to look out the window, gasping as she saw a blue planet floating in the darkness. Tears stung her eyes as she stared, her hands clutching the armrests. Earth.

Home. She was almost home.

The craft shook as they entered the atmosphere and Brooke tightened her grip on the armrests, terrified that the spacecraft was going to break apart.

"Havyn. We have armed aircraft approaching." Theiv announced as if it were the weather he was discussing.

"From our studies of this planet they have a multinational, civilian bandwidth for emergency communications." Riak said.

"It is an archaic system, but our computers should easily be able to find it." T'lain added.

Theiv opened a channel, and they heard some static before he spoke. "We come in peace with an urgent message for your leaders."

If Brooke wasn't clutching the armrests, her heart racing and staring at the armed fighter jets flying alongside them, she might have laughed. *We come in peace,* she thought with a touch of hysteria. Instead, her stomach tightened, lurched as she watched the jets. In this day and age, they were more likely to shoot first and ask questions later.

A crackle of static sounded, then she heard Theiv speak again. "Earth aerial craft, we are on a mission of peace."

A long static filled pause, then a Canadian voice spoke. "Unknown vessel, identify yourself."

Theiv glanced back at Brooke for a long moment then finally answered, "This is the craft Sun Seeker, from the United Universe Accord. We are on an urgent mission. We carry critical information, and we have on board an Earth woman we have rescued. May we land?"

This was followed by another long silence, the static filled seconds ticking by and Brooke felt her chest getting tight. *Please, please,* she thought. So close to home. Just as a small whimper was crawling up her throat, the Canadian voice came back and cut it off. "Sun Seeker. You have permission to land. Follow my aircraft down. Do not deviate from the flight path or you will be fired upon."

They followed the jet in and as the first aircraft landed, the Sun Seeker hovered then gracefully lowered to the ground. Brooke watched as two more jets taxied in, on adjacent runways. The differences in the sleek black alien craft and the most advanced fighter jets that earth had were unbelievable. Earth had a long way to go before they were anywhere close to developing the technology these aliens had.

The door to the craft opened with a hiss, and the safety harnesses released. Brooke stood on shaky legs and looked towards the open doorway. She took a step and then another, terrified that the aliens were not really going to let her go. Havyn touched her arm and Brooke looked at her, seeing the compassion in her golden eyes. "You are home, Brooke."

"Wait." Theiv commanded and they all turned to look at him. "I am Brooke's protection. I will be right behind her. The rest of you go first. Keep your hands in plain sight and do what they say." He waited while Riak and T'lain moved ahead of Havyn. He knew the risks, but he needed a moment with Brooke. He put his hand on Brooke's shoulder and leaned down to speak in her ear. "Brooke, it's going to be hard over the next few days. I can help. If you have need of me, just let me know. I will come." She started to twist to look at him, but he spoke again. "They will separate us. We'll all be examined by their medical staff, and they will perform tests. Cooperate with them. Perhaps they will be able to find a cure." He hesitated, then used the newly formed bond between them to speak to her telepathically. *"You can always talk to me like this, the telepathic bond will work both ways. Try it."*

Brooke froze. He was speaking in her head. Numbly, she accepted that real life was stranger than fiction. *"How are you doing this?"* She thought at him.

"There is no time to explain right now, but just know you can contact me if you need me."

Chapter Nine

EARTH DATE: June 21,
   Sol Star System, Starship Exanthus

Secret Communication deeply encrypted in the Exanthus' outgoing messages:

Will attempt sabotage. High risk of capture. Go to full alert status. Repeat. Go to full alert status. Require response from the highest level. Urgent response requested:

-Starforge

Second secret Communication deeply encrypted in the outgoing messages:

Going dark.

-Starforge

Third secret communication deeply encrypted in the outgoing messages:

Suspicious behavior on the Exanthus. Danger exists for the Emperor. Send reinforcements.

-Dragon Warrior

EARTH DATE: JUNE 21
   Sarisia, Galadin Star System

THORNE FERAL WAS A big brute of a man, standing well over six feet tall. There was not a spare ounce of fat on his massively muscled body, and he was not pretty. He looked like what he was, a hardened warrior, savage and wild. But that had never stopped the women from flocking to him. He was a natural leader, a rebel, and a law unto himself. He would never be called good, and he just didn't care.

He touched some symbols on the console before him, and then turned to look at the man who'd invited himself along for this journey. Fuck that. That was no mortal man, and he'd more or less, commandeered Thorne's ship. Fucking Rune Aezorwyn. Anyone else Thorne would have shot and thrown out the airlock. It was a little harder to do that with a Creator. He crossed his arms over his chest and glared at the being leaning against the wall. "So, let me get this straight. You want me to go to Earth, a non-contact 100 world that I could get thrown into prison for even approaching, and pick up some Terrans? Which, again, is a prison sentence or worse."

Rune shrugged easily, his long white hair slipping over his shoulder. "It's a matter of some urgency, Thorne Feral."

"No kidding." Yeah, that was sarcasm, but Thorne was irritated. "I figure the universe must be in imminent danger if one of the Creators is getting personally involved."

"Multiverse." Rune frowned. "Why are all of you mortals so small minded?"

Thorne growled, and yanked the leather cord off his wrist to tie back his long blue hair, helping to hide his pointed ears. "Small minded? Why are all of you Creator's assholes?"

Rune burst out laughing. "Don't let Eliana hear you say that. She might decide to give you a lesson in manners."

Thorne merely stared at the man. "I take it the 'Multiverse' is at immediate risk of total annihilation?"

Rune eyed the scarred warrior before him. "Not presently, but I am curious why you think I would call on you if it was."

"I have the fastest ship in the known universe. Oh. Excuse me. I mean in the 'Multiverse'. I'm a damn good pilot, and you came to me."

"Hmm." Rune eyed the man. "The mission is to save a Zemyneah slave, and to prevent the extinction of the Terran people."

"A Zemyneah slave? Way out there? How the fuck did she get anywhere near the Sol star system?"

"Did you not receive the communication?" Rune straightened and walked over to the ship's communication center. "Your technology is just so slow. I do not know how you mortals exist like this." He tapped some symbols. "Ah, here it is now. Starforge is attempting to sabotage something, expecting to be captured, and requesting full alert status." Rune looked at Thorne. "That means the situation is bad."

"No shit." Thorne strode over to the com center and read the message for himself. "I'll alert the resistance. Anything from Starforge goes directly to them."

"What is going dark?"

Thorne jerked around. "What the hell are you talking about?"

"It's in the second message."

Swearing Thorne scanned that message, and then he swore some more as his fingers flew over the communication console. "I've alerted the resistance. Whoever Starforge is, he's in trouble. Now what does this have to do with the Sol star system and a lost Zemyneah slave?"

"That's in the message coming in. The Zemyneah slave is not lost. She is a Terran."

A soft beep announced an incoming message and Thorne scowled, then read the encrypted message. "You didn't tell me this involved Theiv Draakon, and how the fuck did a Terran become a Zemyneah slave?" His fingers flew across the controls as he opened a channel to his contact. "Kahea, we have intercepted a message that warns of a threat to the Emperor. Stay on your toes. No, no details. It's from Dragon Warrior. He's requested assistance. I'm on it. Feral out." Turning and leaning against the console, Thorne stared at Rune.

"What are you waiting for?" Rune asked, irritated that Thorne was just watching him.

"Why don't you just snap your fingers or whatever you do, and we'll be there instantly."

Rune looked at Thorne as if he were crazy. "I can't interfere with the normal course of events. That would be a massive breach of the Creator's code."

"Then what the hell do you call this?" Thorne waved his hand between him and Rune.

"Guidance." And Rune disappeared.

Swearing Thorne took his seat. "Computer, set course for the Sol star system, planet Earth. Engage hyper warp drive."

Chapter Ten

EARTH DATE: JUNE 21
   Sol Star System, Starship Exanthus

DRACE STORMED OUT OF the holding cells, shouting for warriors. She would not get away with this! But when he spoke into the communication system mounted on the wall outside the cell, his voice was eerily cold. "Ship status alert. All decks, lockdown. Subject escape, possible pathogenic contagion, Theiv Draakon report to the main lab."

Instantly, he began to hear the sounds of force fields engaging and heavy blast proof steel doors sliding into place, as the whole ship went to alert status. Knowing that the warrior class would be searching every square particle of the ship he walked back into the holding cells, his eyes seeking out his next subject.

He needed to get started on replicating that experiment as soon as possible, his time was fast disappearing. He stopped before each cell and looked at his data pad considering the data on each subject before moving on to the next. By the time he was to the last cell he knew that none of these subjects would do. He needed his experiment back.

Turning abruptly, he walked out of the holding cells and went to his quarters. His Zemyneah slave was still sleeping in his bed, and he frowned as he strode past. He had been a bit excessive last night after taking the last readings on the earth subject. A man was allowed to celebrate his achievements. He continued into the private holding cells that were only accessed through his quarters.

These were for his special projects and only he knew of their existence. Subject 396 was unconscious but had strong vital signs. Subject 397 was unconscious and her vital signs were weak and fading. He shrugged. She'd served her purpose. He'd gotten the DNA and other samples he wanted, and he'd run a Zepto experiment. It failed, of course. Her species just wasn't compatible with the Zepto technology without a lot of tinkering with the Zeptos, and he had no time for that. He turned her over to the men in the warrior class that he knew were loyal to him.

The fact that she was still alive at this point spoke to the hardiness of her race and was one reason he took the risk of acquiring her. But she was a liability now. If she were discovered on this ship, he would have to explain, and risk having his experiments under the scrutiny of the scientific community. His experiments were too important for that kind of delay, and frankly, he was far more interested in the male they had captured with her—her mate, or almost her mate. He smiled, a cold evil twist of his lips. Fortunately, they had been captured at the most opportune time, during their mating rituals. A few more minutes and he would not have been able to use the male at all.

He touched the communication device and contacted the man in the warrior class that he knew would follow his instructions to the letter. Privately. "Jaixe, I need you to fly a disposal run." He listened as the man asked where and when. "I think Sarisia would be a good place to dispose of this matter and right now." It would take Jaixe off the ship for a few days, but he knew that the Sarisian wilderness was an exceptionally dangerous place with many predators and scavengers, the perfect place to dispose of a body, or a soon to be body, and on the off chance that any evidence was ever found, it would simply result in a war between the Sarisian's and Subject 397's race. Nothing of consequence.

He walked away from the communications panel and went back through the doors, locking them behind him. His Zemyneah had obviously awakened and returned to her quarters. *Good.* He looked around and decided to run his data one more time before he met up with Theiv Draakon and then returned to earth to capture another subject.

A frown appeared on his face, and then a scowl as he discovered his files had been tampered with. Sitting down at his computer alcove, he began tapping the keys and fury began to burn deep inside as he discovered file after file had been erased. He brought up the backup files and they were gone too. His heart thumping hard he ordered the computer to restore all deleted files and gave his security code. The computer began to work, and he turned around in his chair and stared out the port window at the stars. He was going to have to find a suitable punishment for his wife. Death was too easy. Moments later the computer spoke. "Restoration failed. All Data lost."

Drace's face tightened, and he turned slowly in his chair to face the computer waiting for its next command. "Locate my wife."

"Havyn Aphelion is not on board the Exanthus"

Drace's eyes narrowed. "Computer, locate T'lain Netron and Riak Valkor and have them meet me at the main lab right away." He stood up, a plan forming in his mind. T'lain and Riak could create a zepto tracking device that would be able to locate the zeptos in his wife's body. Then he would solve the problem of Havyn Aphelion––permanently.

The computer spoke as he reached the door. "T'lain Netron and Riak Valkor are not on board the Exanthus."

Drace paused then continued from his quarters to the main lab. Theiv Draakon was said to be an elite Dragon Warrior. He would have the resources to locate Havyn, the two missing scientists, and his experiment.

He arrived at the main lab moments later and was not pleased to find that Theiv Draakon was not waiting there for him. That man was too arrogant by half. He would need to be taught a lesson. The computer scanned him, and the doors to the lab slid open. He stepped inside and strode to his computer console. "Computer, tell Theiv Draakon that he is late and to go to the main lab immediately!"

"Theiv Draakon is not on board the Exanthus."

Drace turned slowly and stared at the computer, his hands opening and clenching into fists. Ice cold cascaded through his body and he forced himself to take a breath, to allow no reaction. So, he had enemies. He would deal with them when the time was right. His mind was already turning over the possibilities.

Chapter Eleven

EARTH DATE: JUNE 22
Canadian military base, Rocky Mountains.

THEIV GLANCED AROUND, then quickly used his scanner to break the code for the primitive locking system and entered the room. He reengaged the lock, ignoring the gasp he heard when he slipped inside. Turning, he looked at the only occupant of the room. "Hello, Brooke."

"What do you want?"

"I want to make sure you're alright. Your Earth doctor isn't being very forthcoming."

Brooke frowned, and crossed her arms. "Earth doctors are never forthcoming. It's against the law for them to divulge private information to a complete stranger."

"I'm not a stranger, Brooke." He frowned and looked at the little Earth woman. Her cheek bones were more pronounced. His eyes traveled over her body. There was an air of fragility about her that concerned him. "I can smell the pheromones you're releasing. You're hungry."

Brooke felt her cheeks heating up, and abruptly turned away, walking over to look out the window, knowing that he was referring to the state of her arousal. It was humiliating how easily he read something she was trying desperately to ignore. "That is none of your business."

Theiv stared after Brooke. He didn't understand her. *Dragon's breath!* He cursed silently, no one understood the Terran people yet. He tried again. "You need nourishment. Have you been with anyone since we arrived?"

Brooke's mouth dropped open, and she turned. "No! Of course not!"

Theiv watched her, ignoring his body's responses. "I can—"

"No!" Brook shook her head. "I'm not discussing this with you."

"Have you discussed it with your Doctor Reed, or Havyn?"

"Look," She began, "You brought me back to Earth. Your job is done."

"My..." He frowned as his translator gave him information on her words. "You're not my job. We're connected. I don't wish to see you harmed. There are options if you don't wish to meet your needs with me. Havyn could—–"

"Havyn?" Brooke's eyes widened.

"It's not the ideal solution, but as a temporary stopgap it might work. She is also in difficulty as she's unable to be with her husband at this time."

Brooke stared. "Theiv, I'm not gay."

"I don't think you are happy, Brooke. I know this has been a diff—"

"No." Brooke cut him off again. "I'm sexually oriented to a male/female relationship not female/female."

Theiv watched her as his translator updated the information. "Zemyneah are capable of any sexual orientation their owner wishes. You don't have an owner so the zepto technology inside you should be able to adapt until you find someone to bond too."

Brooke shook her head. "I don't wish to bond with anyone. I don't wish to be with anyone."

"You will die."

"There are some things worse than death, Theiv."

"But you're not a woman who gives up easily, Brooke. You've had the courage and strength to fight what Drace did to you. You survived what no one has survived before you. Do not give up now. If you change your mind, and wish me to come to you, call me. I will come." Theiv turned and let himself out of Brooke's room. He would speak to Dr. Reed and Havyn, insist they send someone to Brooke. It was the only solution. And he ignored the internal resistance he felt to that thought.

Chapter Twelve

EARTH DATE: JUNE 23
Canadian military base, Rocky Mountains.

"HOLD IT, WARRIOR."

Theiv paused in the hallway and thought about ignoring Havyn's order. He didn't have time for this, and then he wondered if Brooke had finally sent for him. Clenching his jaw, he turned, waiting as Havyn and Dr. Reed, the head of the human medical and science team, and two human soldiers, joined him in the hall. "Where have you been? We need blood tests, and I want a scan done. Your secret little bonding session with Brooke, before we brought her home, concerns me."

"I don't have time for this. We're stranded here until we can contact the Emperor." Theiv gritted out, a muscle ticking in his jaw. "I'm working with human techs trying to create a reliable communication system, and there are a million problems."

"I'm concerned as well, Theiv." Dr. Reed spoke up. "We don't know enough about the alteration to Brooke at this point to understand how this will affect either of you. It was a dangerous thing for you to do."

Theiv glared at Havyn and Dr. Reed, shoving a hand roughly through his hair, regretting that he told them about his ability to track Brooke.

Havyn stared at him, her eyes widening. "Theiv, you're shaking."

Theiv clenched his jaw and stared back at Havyn. That's when he noticed the two soldiers watching him. What were their names? The one with the dark hair was Storm Kenyon and the other one was Sev Conder. He had no doubt that they were dangerous. He could see the truth of what they were in their eyes. Tough, hard, deadly. Warriors much like him. He considered his options, knowing the two men were there to ensure that he got the tests done. Scowling, he gave an abrupt nod. "Fine. Do the tests, but this needs to be quick. I have work to do." Turning he stalked down the hall, towards the medical center, restraining his urge to pull out his phase pistol and shoot the two men. This was a waste of time.

Dr. Reed and Havyn hurried along behind them, and it suddenly struck him that these two soldiers might be more than just soldiers, they might be potential candidates to bond with Brooke. The thought made his vision wash red with fury, and he started to turn. His mind automatically seeking the telepathic bond, he shared with Brooke. Just as it had every few hours since they'd brought her back to earth. *Keeping track of her, he was just keeping track of her, as he should. So, why did the thought of her having sex with either of these males disturb him so much? Why was he even giving it a second thought? In full blown holovid detail.*

"Don't even think about it, man." Sev shoved him roughly into the wall and shook his head.

Theiv narrowed his eyes, his voice rough. "Get your hands off me."

"You need to cool it. Let Havyn run her tests." Storm stepped up, watching Theiv intently.

"Theiv!" Havyn snapped. "Stop it! We need these tests, and you know it."

Theiv shoved away from Sev with an oath. Turning, he pressed his hands against the wall, letting his head hang, breathing, and trying to find a scrap of the legendary Dragon Warrior control he was supposed to have mastered. *What in the seven hells was going on?* And suddenly he was struck by an appalling thought. "Havyn!" he rasped, jerking around, and staring at the slender woman. "Were Brooke's Zepto's coded to the Emperor's DNA!"

Havyn frowned at Theiv. "Yes. Drace wasn't leaving anything to chance. In fact, he put an unbreakable bonding process into the Zepto's that would activate with the smallest DNA exchange with the Emperor. What does that have to do with anything? It doesn't matter that the Zepto's were coded for a specific person, they will never encounter the DNA they were coded for."

"What if there was an anomaly?"

Haven was shaking her head, "What anomaly could there be? The Emperor was the only child of an Altanean couple who lived on Sarisia!"

Theiv swore violently, slamming his fist into the wall.

Sev crossed his arms, his expression grim and exchanged a look with Storm.

Havyn frowned. "What's going on Theiv?"

Theiv ignored her question as he forced himself to breathe and think logically about this. There is no way that tracking bond he'd created with Brooke could have become anything more. It just wasn't possible. But... He looked at Sev, and swore again, knowing that it had to be checked. He handed the soldier his laser gun. "We need those tests. It's imperative. I've set my weapon to stun. If I lose it again, shoot me." Sev raised an eyebrow, and then nodded grimly.

As soon as they reached the medical center, Dr. Reed and Havyn started snapping out orders and running scans. Theiv sat on a gurney, sweat beading on his face as he struggled to control the building need to get to Brooke. What was happening to him? Sev leaned against the wall, his arms folded over his chest, holding the gun in a deceptively relaxed grip.

"I don't understand these readings. How can this be?" Havyn muttered as she tapped the screen of her scanner. "This is not possible."

She turned to Dr. Reed. "Can you clear the room?" Dr. Reed nodded and immediately ordered everyone out.

Theiv stared at Havyn, his jaw clenched. "What exactly do the tests show?"

Havyn shook her head and threw her hands in the air. "The tests show the impossible! My best guess, and this is only a guess, is that when you bit Brooke, to create the telepathic bond, and she bit you back, you exchanged a tiny amount of DNA and Zeptos. A tiny amount, but enough that the Zeptos activated the bonding protocol in both of you. Your telepathic bond is far more than you were expecting, Theiv.

Far more." She looked at him, her eyes betraying the depth of her concern. "Theiv, this bond could mean your death. You are irrevocably tied to Brooke. If something were to happen to her," She hesitated, then forced herself to say the words. "You would not survive."

Theiv stared at Havyn, his face expressionless, his eyes cold. "Your team programmed the Zeptos to kill the Emperor if he did not fall in with your plans?"

Havyn stiffened, "Team? This was not a choice we made, Dragon Warrior. Drace refused any reasonable alternatives. His success was all that mattered, regardless of the consequences."

Forcing himself to contain his fury, Theiv considered the questions he needed answered. "The Zepto technology malfunctioned. I'm not the Emperor."

Havyn gave a single nod. "Your DNA is slightly different because you are the Emperor's brother." She gave Theiv a look that spoke volumes. He stared back silently, his arms crossed over his chest.

"And yet," Havyn continued, "the Zeptos perceive it as the correct DNA. As you said, it's an anomaly." She paused, her eyes traveling over him. "Brooke's deteriorating condition is understandable, but the fact that the Zeptos are affecting you before you have even engaged in coitus with her is deeply concerning." Havyn pulled her scanning device out of her pocket with a frown and began to scan Theiv again. She punched some data into the screen of her scanner and almost growled. "The Zeptos are an interdependent system. They were designed with the ability to adapt to different situations. But this... we never expected this. I don't even know how to explain what this is." She shoved the scanner impatiently into a pocket. "The tests are detecting trace amounts of DNA from all of the species that were integrated into the Zemyneah formula Drace used on Brooke. The males of each of those species are naturally dominant, with exceptional strength and highly developed instincts. I'm seeing changes that suggest that your natural physical strength is being increased, your instincts and reflexes as well.

In 24-48 hours the Zeptos, in both of you, will enter stealth mode. Which means that they will be undetectable to any test we have." Havyn rubbed her temples in frustration. This experiment is proceeding exactly as Drace predicted it would. Your bond with Brooke will render the experiment invisible. From my understanding of the process, as the first man to bond with Brooke, you are now her handler.

Theiv gave an abrupt nod, swearing in his head. "This stealth mode was how Drace would've got Brooke past the Emperor's security. No scan would have detected his bond to her. She would appear to be an unbonded Zemyneah slave. Cunning bastard."

Dr. Reed watched the alien male. They didn't need further complications with this situation. Now, there were two people's lives on the line. She clenched her fists. She'd been doing everything she could to convince those in command that they needed to save Brooke, now they had to save one of the Aliens too. Unless they wanted to risk a war with a far more powerful race of beings. "Can we do something to alter this bond that Theiv has with Brooke?"

Havyn shook her head. "The Zeptos perceive Theiv as the one they were programmed to create an unbreakable bond with. And frankly, I have no idea if that makes him the handler or the target. What I do know is that the Zepto technology has radically multiplied since entering his blood stream." Havyn looked at Dr. Reed. "As the data we've collected shows, both of their lives are now endangered. Theiv needs to go to Brooke."

Chapter Thirteen

EARTH DATE: JUNE 23
Canadian Military Base, Rocky Mountains

THE DOOR OPENED AND closed but went unnoticed. Brooke crouched, her arms locked around her knees, in a corner of the room. Skin glistening with perspiration, her hair was a wild tumble of damp curls covering her bare breasts as she rocked back and forth. Her eyes were tightly closed as an internal war waged deep inside against the raging sexual needs that were bordering on insanity. Nothing she tried helped. Cold shower, hot shower, cold bath, hot bath, multiple attempts at a little self love. Nothing worked! She was desperate. Should she contact Theiv?

The scent of wild clean air and hard masculine power washed over her, and Brooke's eyes shot open. She knew that scent. Her eyes traveled up, and she found herself staring at the alien who had given her a stunning orgasm with a single bite. He was as tall, and powerfully built as she remembered, well over six feet, with extraordinary purple eyes, messy dark hair, and pale blue skin. He might have been in his mid thirties, but she couldn't seem to care about that as she took in the way his black uniform stretched over his chest. His tight black pants rode low on his lean hips, the material cupping what appeared to be something impressive.

Theiv. Had she inadvertently called him to her? Her eyes traveled over him again. There was a wild dark intensity about him that instantly brought her darkest forbidden dreams to her mind. She drew in his scent in a long breath. Lust slammed through her body, and she squeezed her eyes shut, rocking back and forth.

A wave of warm exotically scented air flowed around Theiv, his nostrils flaring as he recognized the scent that swamped his mind and sent sensations straight to his groin.

She was even more beautiful than he remembered. Long thick purple hair trailed over her shoulders and back, her deep green eyes vibrant and alive with need. Lush pink lips that begged to be kissed, parted as she stared at him, and he felt another wave of desire rush him. He took a step forward, his eyes darkening before his brain kicked in. She was like some erotic Pixie from his darkest fantasies—and he wanted her.

Theiv crossed the room and crouched down in front of Brooke, reaching out to lift her chin until her eyes met his. "Hello, Brooke."

Brooke found herself staring into the deep purple eyes of the man who was crouched down in front of her. This close together, his scent rushed over her, surrounded her in a cloud of unrelenting need. She tried to speak past vocal cords that seemed paralyzed. Finally, she managed to rasp out a soft plea. "Help me. Please, help me. I don't know how to make this stop."

Theiv lifted a hand, gently pushing a damp strand of hair back from her face that had her cheek turning in toward the heat of his palm. "I will, I promise. I won't leave you like this. I can make this stop." His voice was a powerfully low sound that sent shivers racing across her skin. He slid his hands down her arms before he stood, lifting her to stand in front of him. Brooke shuddered and swayed, her breasts sliding briefly against his cloth covered chest.

She was a goddess.

Purple strands of hair brushed the tips of large, firm breasts, the straining peaks engorged and flushed. Every soft, panting breath she took stroked them against his chest, sending a rush of sensations straight to his groin and the flesh that was hardening more and more by the second as his lust rose to meet hers.

Grimly, he reminded himself, she was under the control of the Zepto technology and the genetic changes that were happening inside her. That thought helped him to regain some control.

He could see that there would be no talking this through with her. She was held in the brutal grip of a relentless hunger that was slowly stealing her humanity. If he was going to save Brooke St. Claire, then this was the time for action.

Reaching out, he slid a hand into her hair, the silky softness sliding along his skin creating a burst of sensations that sent his nerve endings firing. His other hand gripped her slender waist and he pulled her up against him as he lowered his head and took her mouth. His lips moved over hers, their breaths mingling as the spice scented pheromones she was releasing flooded his taste buds.

Gods, she was nirvana; and as the rational side of his brain was taken over by the need to fuck, he didn't know if he was ever going to get enough of her.

His tongue stroked over her bottom lip to coax her to open for him, his teeth capturing the soft flesh and gliding over it to entice her further. A soft moan escaped her as she parted her lips and he surged inside, plundering the sweet depths of her mouth.

He drew back slowly, his eyes meeting hers as they fought to catch their breath. The hand on her waist tightened briefly, his thumb stroking her skin.

She bit her swollen bottom lip as she stared into his turbulent eyes. She didn't know if it was the consuming needs her body was demanding or if it was the sensual magnetism she felt radiating off this man, but if he asked her what her name was, she wasn't sure she'd be able to tell him.

She licked her lips and raised a trembling hand to his cheek as a deeply hidden side to her personality rushed to the forefront. Her hands slid up the muscled slopes of his arms as she rose on her toes.

Theiv recognized the look in her eyes. Hell, any male, no matter the species, would recognize that look. His head lowered as the hand that was tangled in her hair bunched the silken strands in his fist, and as their lips met for the second time, she eagerly met him half-way.

His tongue swept into her mouth with bold certainty, stroked and circled hers before retreating. When her tongue chased after his, his cock jerked again, his hand tightened on her hip, and the brief thought he'd had about going slow was lost in the fire of lust that was surging through him. The hand on her hip moved urgently over her skin, skimming down over her ass to knead the firm cheek as he devoured her mouth.

He tasted so infinitely masculine that her knees went weak, and Brooke was suddenly thankful for the support of the arm he had around her. She felt out of control, untamed and wild, as her hands began to tear desperately at his shirt. She needed to feel the heat of his bare skin against hers. Gone was all logical thought, all her natural inhibitions cast aside as the burning blast of ravenous desire swept through her again, fiercer, hotter than any that had come before. She was starving for this man. Starving. She didn't want to stop. God help her, she was going to hell, because she wouldn't have stopped even if she could.

Theiv momentarily broke the frantic kiss to strip his shirt off and release the fastening on his pants, his heart racing a mad beat.

Brooke made a desperate sound as her fingers dove into his hair, fisting in the course silkiness before she fiercely pulled his head back down. She needed his mouth on hers. Needed it with a fervor that shocked her. His rough laugh against her mouth only fueled the fire that held her in its burning grip. She nipped at his neck.

"Hold on, Dragoness." His voice was husky and low, promising all manner of erotic sins and teasing her hypersensitive nerves. The command in his voice brought her head up, her fingers once again tightening in his hair.

Theiv nipped her bottom lip in reprimand, and licked away the sting, then took charge of the kiss. Lifting his hand to cup her breast, he brushed his thumb across her erect nipple as their mouths moved together.

A gasp and she broke the kiss as his fingers closed around her nipple, the tug sending pleasure shooting through her body to her core. Her fingers released the dark strands as she tried to jerk away from the intense sensations.

He caught her face in his hand, firmly keeping her from moving away. "Easy." He murmured against her lips before deepening the kiss again. He reached for her other breast, rolled her aching nipple between his thumb and forefinger. Her gasp against his ravaging mouth told its own story of need. He moved away from her damp lips and kissed her jaw, bit down lightly on the silken skin, then moved down to capture a hard nipple between his lips. He sucked the sweet nub into his mouth, his tongue lashing the sensitive tip, before he grazed it with his teeth. She jerked in his grasp. Ah, she liked that. He did it again to her other nipple then sucked hard.

Brooke's hands stroked hot male skin as she writhed under his onslaught. Lifting her leg, she hooked it around his thigh trying frantically to climb closer to him. Just as she was about to settle against him, he shifted away from her, briefly shocking her with the violence of the protest that formed inside her. He lifted his head from her damp nipple and savagely took her mouth before she could form a verbal protest, his tongue roughly thrusting in and out. His arm banded around her slender waist and he backed her up against the wall, his knee parting her thighs. The hand on her hip traveled across silken skin, over the soft pad of her mound and down, stroking over her silken flesh. Hell, she was so wet. He stroked through swollen feminine lips to glide over that little bundle of nerves and got the reaction he wanted, as she gasped and arched into his touch. He nipped her bottom lip and lifted his mouth from hers, murmuring. "Mmm that's it, just like that, Dragoness." He circled her clit with his thumb as he eased a thick finger into her, then a second one. She groaned and panted and tilted her hips to take his fingers deeper. His breath ghosted over her lips as he curled his fingers to stroke her, and she cried out as a deep shudder shook her slender body. So, he did it again. Crowding her back, he leaned in, his teeth grazing that sensitive spot where her neck joined her shoulder, his fingers fucking into the heated depths of her pussy, as his free hand plucked at her nipple. She groaned and went stiff, and he thrust harder, stroking his fingertips over that exquisitely sensitive spot high up inside of her. She cried out and convulsed, her hands clenching on his arms as she flew apart for him. He eased off continuing to lightly stroke her clit, as she clung to him trying to catch her breath, a lazy male smile curling his lips because he knew exactly what he had done to her. "Again," he said and leaned down to suck her nipple into his mouth. He felt her shock, and the slight jump as he grazed sensitive flesh between her legs. He thrust his fingers building a steady rhythm but not going as deep. He lifted his head and his eyes met hers. Her eyes were still filled with the lust that had been riding her hard, so he continued to play her body, taking her up into a second blazing orgasm, then a third that finally had her clinging weakly to him as she struggled to catch her breath.

He kissed her again. Long, hard, and deep. "We are going to need to talk more later, when this need isn't driving you so hard. I can help you to meet these needs, but if you don't want this then just say the words Dragoness and I'll go. if you want what I'm offering, then all you need to do is say yes." His goal had been to get her past the desperate sexual frenzy and give her a chance to decide what she wanted. "I know it's never going to be as simple as that, but I want you to have a choice. I want you to make the decision."

She realized that this man was giving her a choice. The first choice she'd had in days. What she wanted more than anything was to have a clear brain again and from the stimulating lesson he'd just given her, she understood what she needed to do to get her mind back. So, she did what any smart woman, abducted by aliens or not, would do. She said yes. Yes, because of this insatiable lust that held her prisoner and yes, because this alien was the hottest man she'd ever met.

He instantly took her mouth in a hot searing kiss as he tore off the rest of his clothes.

"Hurry!" She gasped, her hands stroking over his chest. The feel of a hot hard shaft against her stomach made Brooke suck in a sharp breath, and she reached for it.

Theiv caught her hands before they came in contact with his aching cock and pulled them behind her back. Fuck, he would not last if she touched his dick and he had to last. "No." His voice was firm, refusing any argument.

Brooke froze for a split second, her eyes meeting his in shock, then anger. Unreasonable and hot, it shot through her as she surged up on her tiptoes and bit his lip hard.

Theiv jerked his head back with a harsh curse, then caught her chin and tilted her face up. "Look at me, Brooke."

Brooke opened her eyes, her breathing laboured, her body on fire. Why was he stopping? Didn't he know how desperate she was?

Her eyes rose to meet his, as her heart began to race, and butterflies rioted in her stomach. She felt his hand glide down her skin to her mound, lower. She moaned as he cupped her, a thick finger sliding between her swollen folds. She sucked in a soft gasp, her eyes fluttering shut as he circled her clit.

"No, Brooke, look at me." His voice, low and dark.

It was a command. Unyielding, with a dangerous edge that sent heat spiraling through her body. Brooke forced her eyes open. She could see the flush of desire colouring his high cheekbones, his eyes glittering with arousal. His hard masculine length pressed firmly against her stomach leaving a damp trail with every harsh breath they took.

Theiv inhaled the intoxicating scent of Brooke's arousal, his mouth flooding with the need to taste her. He wanted nothing more than to sink his tongue between the plump lips of her pussy and feast on her to see if she tasted as good as she smelled.

First, he thought, his breath rasping, he needed to get inside this beautiful Earth woman. He groaned at her whimper as he slid his fingers through her heat, then back to circle her swollen clitoris. His cock pulsed against her soft warm stomach as her hips arched, and he couldn't resist the urge to grind forward once, twice.

She moaned and arched for him while he circled the small swollen bundle of nerves again. "Please." She was begging, and she didn't even care, "Please, Theiv!"

"Keep your eyes on me," he demanded, his voice harsh with the effort it was taking to control his hunger for this wild sexy woman. His finger slid inside her, testing her readiness.

As he stared into her dazed green eyes, listening to the sexy little sounds she was making, he lifted her with one arm, and drew her legs around his hips as he pressed her back against the wall. His shaft glided through her wetness and lodged at her entrance. His jaw clenched when she gasped and moved against him, then his hips rocked forward to ease the tip of his cock inside her. When she instinctively pushed down to take more of him, his hands gripped her hips to stop her. He stared at her beautiful face, flushed with wild abandon, and felt himself harden impossibly more. Holy hell, he was not going to survive this. "Look at me."

Wide green eyes filled with carnal promise met his. With her firmly pressed against the wall, he braced himself and took her hands to raise them over her head. The fingers of one hand wrapped around each of her wrists, shackled them there as his hips surged forward. She moaned as his length filled her, stretched her and, in that moment, the potency of the need that had been building with each passing second hit them both full force. Like fire, they burned hotter and hotter, their bodies moving against each other.

His hard cock rubbed over hidden pleasure spots deep inside of her, places that she had never known existed. She arched helplessly, low feminine moans and harsh masculine groans filled the air as the inferno soared higher, her body a ragged jumble of ultra-sensitive nerves.

Theiv drew a shocked ragged breath as her snug sheath pulsed over his hard cock and he could feel himself growing thicker. He couldn't slow down. His hips pistoning back and forth. His shaft burying itself over and over again in the lush heat that, with each thrust, was driving him closer and closer to the edge of insanity.

Euphoria, madness, pleasures never felt before, never even conceived of, rushed over them, sending them racing towards the promise of an even greater pleasure. Brooke's whole body tensed, fire erupting and sweeping her over the edge as she shuddered and cried out her release, her green eyes locked to the turbulent purple of his as something changed inside her, expanded, and reached for something inside him. She heard his harsh groan and, as the hot spurt of his seed filled her, something deep inside her settled.

She felt his hands move down to hold her before he shifted them around. He slid down the wall until he was sitting on the floor with her in his lap, their bodies still intimately connected. He was breathing heavily, panting, and he looked as shocked as she felt. He reached up and rubbed her cheek then gently drew her head to his shoulder.

Chapter Fourteen

EARTH DATE: June 23
  Canadian Military Base, Rocky Mountains

BROOKE RELEASED A BREATH, her body slowly relaxing into a trembling mass. What was that? What had happened? Then reality settled back in with a wicked punch to her gut. Oh, God. She'd just had sex with an alien! With one of the ones who'd done this to her! She froze for a breath, and then she was scrambling away from him, almost falling in her haste.

He reached out and caught her arm to steady her, surprise on his face, and she jerked away from him. "Don't! Just...give me a minute."

He let her go and rose to his feet, watching her carefully. He hadn't expected this reaction, but he couldn't say he was all that surprised. She had been through a hell of a lot. He glanced around the room and saw the blanket laying across the foot of the bed. He reached for it thinking that she probably was feeling vulnerable right now.

Brooke turned her back on the wildly beautiful man, tears burned her eyes and she fought to calm the panic racing through her body. "Oh, God." She whispered. What had she done? Her hands started to shake, and she wrapped her arms around herself, trying to find a calm she was nowhere near feeling.

Frowning with a growing concern, Theiv settled the soft blanket over her shoulders. "Brooke. Brooke, listen to me. I'm—" He broke off. *What the hell? What did you say to a total stranger that you'd just taken complete sexual control of?* He cleared his throat and shoved a hand through his hair.

An impotent fury swept through Brooke, and she raised livid green eyes to the man's face. "Get out."

But with her rage came blazing hot lust, rushing through her body at the speed of light. With an appalled moan, she stumbled back against the wall, the confusion and terror shivering through her doing nothing to lessen the stunning arousal burning in her. The alluring scent of spices filled the air, and she watched his nostrils flare, his eyes narrowing dangerously. He took a step toward her, his shaft hard and rising to rest against his belly.

"No." She whispered.

Theiv stopped. He shook his head and took a step back, then another. "Fuck." He closed his eyes, clenched his jaw, and swallowed hard, fighting the powerful desire that had gripped him at the mere scent of the pheromones she produced. *Control, man, control. Get a godsdamned grip here.* With his training he had better control than this. His cock jerked as another wave of pheromone scented air drifted by. He'd never had a hard-on as intense as the one he now sported. The need gripping him was brutal. "Fuck!"

Abruptly he turned, grabbed his pants, tugged them on and struggled to get the fastener over his raging erection. He didn't bother with the last one. What the hell was going on here! Shit! He dragged a hand through his hair trying to gain control of his rapidly escalating lust. Finally, with a frustrated growl, he turned back to her.

My God. She was the sexiest thing he'd ever seen. Her purple hair was tousled from their frantic fucking. Her green eyes glowed with the aftermath of her orgasm. Her skin seemed to almost shimmer, and he wanted nothing more on the face of this earth than to taste her pussy, to lap up the taste of those enticing spices that he knew he would forever associate with this woman. And he would, but not now. Not now, damn it!

He forced his gaze back to her face. Her green eyes were wide under her arching purple eyebrows. Her nose was small and straight, her chin stubborn yet somehow fitting the delicate features of her face. What Drace had done to her was simply amazing. She was every man's walking wet dream, and she was his, bonded to him. Owned by him. His cock flexed as the already engorged organ filled with a fresh rush of blood.

Shit! He gritted his teeth together, furious with his thoughts. He did *not* own her. What the fuck was going on in his brain? He refused to allow that line of thought to continue. He was her protector and her lover. End of story.

Brooke pushed farther back against the wall as the man stared at her with such heat that she wanted to hide from his fierce perusal. She could feel the arousal roaring through him and, as she let her eyes wander away from the harsh lines of his face, she noticed a strain in his body that had nothing to do with sexual need. It was then she knew with sudden clarity that he was holding on by a thread. Terribly aware of the vulnerability of her nakedness, her hands clenched on the blanket covering her.

"Brooke." He spoke quietly, his voice deliberately low and soothing as if he were talking to a wild creature. "You understand what's happening, right?"

Brooke shook her head, shuddering as she breathed in his wild clean masculine scent. Her nipples hardened. Liquid heat slicked her folds. She fought the arousal, forcing her mind to work. "The other alien. Drace." She spat his name, ice filling her chest at the oily feel of his name on her tongue.

She took another ice filled breath as she fought the nausea suddenly churning in her stomach. "He succeeded." Her voice was flat, bleak.

"The woman. Havyn? She kept saying I was a.... Zemyneah." Brooke looked at Theiv in confusion as she clung to the blanket covering her. "She said men are not able to resist a Zemyneah." Her fingers were trembling, and she clutched the blanket tighter. "I'm human. I know they made me young again, but I'm human."

"Drace changed you." Theiv rasped hoarsely. "But you're still human. They cannot take your humanity from you. We won't let them do that, Brooke." He clenched his jaw, a sick feeling beginning low in his gut.

Brooke swallowed, tears welling in her eyes. She nodded jerkily as the terrifying memories of being closed into that strange capsule flooded her mind.

"What else do you remember?" Theiv prompted her gently. "Do you remember what the doctors here told you?"

Brooke stared at the man, struggling to contain the arousal that all the intense emotions were forcing on her. Had she seen doctors here? She struggled to remember, but the unrelenting needs surging through her body were making it hard to think. Finally, she shook her head. "I don't remember seeing any doctors."

"Fuck!" He shouted.

Brooke flinched.

Theiv stalked toward the door, fury rocketing through his body. He was going to fucking kill them all! He stopped, his fists clenching and unclenching. He wanted to hunt down every fucking person involved in this fucking situation. He ground his teeth together, fighting the urge to throw the door open, storm down the hallway, find those bastards, and have them realize exactly why he was a Dragon Warrior. Fuck. He was aware of Brooke watching him anxiously. How could she not be when his fucking cock was hard as titanium, and every fucking breath of those wild pheromones was a harsh lesson in endurance and self control.

He grabbed the door handle with one hand, then growled, knowing he couldn't go out there and find those fuckers. He slammed his fist against the wall and heard her gasp. Ah, hell. He leaned his head against the door. Shit. Calm the fuck down. He took a deep breath and slowly released the door handle. Fuck. He couldn't leave.

He turned slowly and faced the woman he was bonded too. She was staring at him with huge green eyes, pressed against the wall, clutching the blanket around herself with a white knuckled grip.

He shook his head contemplating what kind of man this made him. She had consented, but was it a true consent if she were in a state of such desperate arousal that she would agree to anything for relief?

He shook his head and straightened away from the door, feeling totally off his game. "Brooke, we need to talk." Some part of him cringed. Didn't he normally exit as fast as possible if a woman said those very words to him? Well, welcome to his fucked-up life. Maybe this was destiny? He gave himself a mental shake and tried again. "We need to talk about Drace and what was done to you."

Brooke narrowed her eyes. If she'd learned anything in life, it was that men did not like to talk. Have sex, yes. Talk, no. He had the sex part down pat, she had to admit, but she was not going to have sex with this alien again. No way. She had a growing concern that he could be addicting. Even now, she was struggling against the totally insane urge to drop her blanket and throw herself into his arms for another round of Theiv Draakon. In all her life, she'd never wanted a man as much as she wanted this stranger—deep, deep inside of her.

Her eyes got large as she realized what she was thinking. "Uh, talk?" She cleared her throat. "Talk is good. We can talk." Oh heavens, she was babbling. She needed her brain to start working. Now.

Theiv took a deep breath. How the hell did you explain to an alien woman that you were bonded together? "So just bear with me while I try to explain what's going on," he said as he glanced around looking for a place for them to sit and talk. His eyes landed on the bed and he just knew that would not go over well at all. So, he sat on the floor, his back against the wall, adjusting his rock-hard dick. "This is going to sound unbelievable." He looked at her as she slowly sat down beside him, tightly holding on to her blanket. "Though, I guess that you have survived many unbelievable things these last few days."

She nodded and watched him warily.

That was good, he thought, good that she was wary. "Drace and his scientists were doing some fucked up experiments on human women." He saw a shadow cross over her face. "You survived, Brooke. That is the most important part of this. You survived, and you are going to continue to survive. My job is to protect you, to not let Drace take you again."

The look on her face would have made him chuckle if this situation hadn't been so damned serious.

"That was protecting?" She crossed her arms as she arched a delicate purple eyebrow, and he could see her anger, her fury.

He shrugged uneasily. "This situation is... complex. When I came into this room..." He hesitated, gauging her response, and decided to take the risk, because if nothing else, she deserved to know that she would always get the truth from him. "I don't think you were interested in talking."

Brooke glared at him. "Can I just go home? I really am not interested in talking or anything else you might want to do. I want to leave."

Theiv shoved a hand through his hair. "I wish it were that simple. Do you remember what happened when you were on board the Exanthus?"

Oh, for heaven's sake. "I remember everything. Can I go now?"

He raised an eyebrow. She remembered everything. The scent of her arousal was lessening, and he began to wonder if that was why she hadn't been able to remember the doctors examining her earlier. If the need for survival was critical, her brain would have pushed aside things like memories it didn't need at the moment. Would she have been able to remember everything that happened while consumed by the starvation of her body? He knew that, under extreme stress, the brain did that very thing as a coping mechanism.

"No, ma'am." He said in a deceptively mild voice. "We need to talk. I'm not about to let you walk out of here and fuck the first man you see."

She gaped at the man beside her. "I... wouldn't!" She choked out, totally aghast.

"I hate to burst your bubble, but you did." He looked her in the eye and then looked down at himself and back at her. The evidence was irrefutable. "I intend to be the only one you fuck from now on."

There was a first time for everything, Brooke realized. Like right now for instance. This was the first time she had ever wanted to kill a man. "Exactly how is this your concern? And if you ma'am me again, I won't be held responsible for my actions."

Theiv laughed. He couldn't help it. She was fierce. "It is my concern because we have bonded. A bond that should have been impossible but is now an unbreakable reality for us both." He broke off and wondered if she was going to try to kill him or believe him. It was a far-fetched tale, and yet, it was the absolute truth. "As Havyn explained to you in the shuttlecraft, your whole sexuality has become a necessary part of your survival."

Brooke stared silently at the beautiful man who had lost his mind. Well, this was just the icing on the cake. She'd had sex with a crazy alien! "How did you get into my room? I mean, did someone let you in, or did you escape your padded room and find your own way here?"

Theiv stared at her in surprise. "What?" And then it sunk in. He narrowed his eyes. "You know I am not averse to handing out a damn good spanking when needed."

He folded his arms over his chest and returned his fierce dragoness's glare. "You need to pay attention. I am telling you the truth about what that bastard did to you. For your own survival, you need to pay attention."

The man was serious. She frowned and nodded stiffly for him to continue. But in the back of her mind, she was making plans. When the next round of technicians showed up looking for more blood, she was making sure he left with them. Maybe all aliens were insane.

Theiv glared at the ceiling for a long moment then turned his gaze back on the woman as he stood up. "Brooke, what you are feeling is not normal for any human." *Or Althanean for that matter.* "We are total strangers, not even from the same planet and we just had unbelievably amazing sex. You came apart in my arms, several times." He ignored her glare. "And yet, now, you are ready for me again." He held up his hand when she opened her mouth, no doubt ready to verbally blast him. "I know because I can smell the pheromones you release when you are aroused.

"Drace changed you. He performed a genetic experiment on you and injected you with microscopic computer bots. Here on earth, you would call it nanotechnology. This particular type of Zepto technology is cutting edge even for our world. We can't fix it, and we can't shut it off. And I sure as fuck am not willing for you to be used as a pawn by Drace and those he works for. Do you understand?" His voice was a hard furious demand.

Brooke trembled and searched his eyes. He was telling the truth. She swallowed and struggled against the lump rising in her throat and the terrible knowledge pounding away at her brain. Images of her moments on the spaceship filtered through her mind, haunting her with the absolute horror she had felt. Finally, she nodded, unable to speak.

He watched her face. He had been brutally honest, but if she did not start to believe him then they were fighting a losing battle. Finally, she whispered. "I understand."

"Brooke, this need to have sex several times a day, isn't going to go away. Ever. The Zepto's and the genetic manipulation have seen to that. Sex, with me, is now essential to your survival." He looked at her and oh, fuck. As impossible as it was for a human's eyes to glow, hers were glowing, and he would take bets it was not pleasure driving that glow. "I understand that you don't want to hear this, but by whatever God you pray to, you will listen to me. There is more to this than you can imagine. There is a potential galactic war! There is the very real danger that your whole species could be destroyed if they get their hands on you again. They are searching for you. Your only hope is me. Gods, you do not want what they had planned for you. Do you hear me? Do you fucking hear me?"

"I don't need *any* man to meet my needs. I am perfectly capable of handling my own needs and looking after myself!" Her hands were shaking as the red-hot feeling of rage poured through her, and yet she was all too aware of the scent of those pheromones and the silky dampness seeping through her folds. She strode up to the big blue alien and poked him in the chest. "Did you hear me? I don't need a man! I don't want one!" And yet, now that the idea was there, her mind was filling with images. Images of her naked body beneath this hard bodied alien, his hands touching her, coasting up her flesh, taut male skin under her fingers as she explored his body, hungry lips and teeth on her nipples, pressing kisses over her flushed skin. She felt herself growing wetter, and without realizing what she was doing, she flattened her hand onto his chest and stroked. The heat seemed to scorch her flesh and she moved a step closer to the warmth that seemed to radiate off this man. He had the most beautiful eyes she'd ever seen. They fascinated her.

Theiv stared at her, trying to ignore the way her fingers felt as they moved over his chest.

She reached up and put her hands on his shoulders to pull him down so she could see his eyes better. He came willingly, his breath ghosting over her lips. She breathed him in as they stared at one another. He was such a beautiful man. Temptation flowed through her. His scent was like a drug, and she couldn't get enough of it. She leaned up and brushed her lips over his. His hands settled on her hips and she shivered. Then he hauled her up against his heat, and she pressed her lips to his mouth hungrily.

Theiv took her mouth, just as hungry for another taste of her. Her eager hands found his zipper and soon she had his cock in her hot little hands. He groaned and when she dropped to her knees in front of him, the control he'd regained as they talked almost vanished completely. *Holy fuck.*

He took a deep breath, that unique spice scented aroma flooding his senses, and the only thing on his brain was tasting her. He took a ragged breath, pushed his pants down, and dropped to his knees in front of her. "Touch yourself," Theiv watched as she slid a hand up her body to stoke her nipples, her small frame shivering with pleasure. His jaw clenched as he watched her, his hand grasping his cock in a tight fist as he was visually assaulted by the sensuality of her pleasuring herself.

She gasped and then her other hand found her core, her fingers slipping through her wetness before finding and caressing her clit. There was something so erotic about staring into his eyes as they both pleasured themselves, something she had never experienced before, and she let out a moan of approval as the slick, pre-cum coated tip of his cock touched her belly. The air felt cool on the damp section of skin as his length moved away from her, eliciting a shiver from her as her fingers rolled and stroked around her clit. How was it possible that she was so close to coming already?

He was so fucking hard again. Hearing her desperate moans, he knew she was close, so fucking close, and he wanted her hovering right on the edge. "Stop." He growled. She stopped, heavy shudders running through her body. "I want you to slide two of your fingers inside that hot pussy of yours. I want to taste and see if it's as sweet as it smells."

Her hand slid down her stomach, over her mound, then two fingers dipped between her folds and into her entrance. She moaned, green eyes glowing with the unsatiated lust raging through her as she pressed deep, withdrew, and pressed deep again. Just a few more thrusts of her fingers and she would be right where she wanted to be.

"No coming." He said, his voice as commanding as ever, and he effectively ruined her plans in two words.

A soft panting moan escaped as she bit her plump bottom lip, her fingers frozen in place inside of her in quiet obedience. Reluctantly, she forced herself to withdraw fingers glistening with her juices, the scent of sex and exotic spices flowing through the air.

Finally, fucking finally, he was going to get to taste her. Her wild sensual scent had driven him half mad with lust and as he leaned forward, all he could think was: *Fucking finally*!

He caught her slender wrist in his hand and brought her fingers to his mouth, watching her as his tongue slowly slid up her fingers. Hints of cinnamon, cloves, ginger, and something else he had no way to identify burst to life in his mouth. Something foreign. Alien. Powerful. He sucked and licked until the smoky sensual flavour was gone then slowly released her fingers, his eyes locked on hers.

"I want you inside me."

Her voice was a low, husky plea that somehow drove his excitement higher, but he hadn't had enough of that spicy flavor. "Not yet." He picked her up and laid her on the bed before kneeling beside her, then slid a hand up one quivering thigh and slowly spread her legs.

Moving between her slender thighs, he feasted his eyes on her. Her pussy was swollen with arousal, glistening with the evidence of her desire. He grasped her ankles and pushed her legs up until her heels touched her ass. Her legs spread automatically, and he watched her outer lips flower open. She was wet, her clit swollen and begging for his attention. He could do that. He could give that sweet bit of heaven all the attention she could handle.

He looked up and met her eyes as a whimper escaped from her throat, then he dipped his head and licked slowly. His tongue slid between her folds and across swollen, pink flesh to stroke over that tiny bundle of nerves. When she arched up with a broken cry, then he got serious, because she tasted as intoxicating as ambrosia. Like an addict, he couldn't get enough. Gripping her hips, he took her clit into his mouth, and at the same time, pushed a thick finger deep inside her.

She drew a sharp breath and fisted a hand in his hair. That was —She'd never felt anything like—"Ooh!" She was panting, her fist clenching on his hair, and she didn't know if she wanted to push him away or pull him closer. She writhed and felt his hand tighten on her hip. Her head tossed against the pillow as he bit down gently on her clit and added a second finger, stretching her. She arched, then cried out, a silent plea of *don't ever stop!* Floating through her brain.

Her cries of pleasure spurred him on, and he fucked his fingers into her faster and harder, curling them to stroke across her g spot, as he alternated lapping that sweet little clit and sucking hard on it. He felt the tiny convulsions start deep inside her pussy, her body stiffened, and he bit down.

Brooke arched, a tiny scream leaving her throat, as he bit down on her clit, and she came apart, as a powerful orgasm rolled over her, leaving her limp and gasping for breath.

Theiv lifted his head. His eyes were wild with lust, as he rose on his knees between her thighs. Grasping her hips, he pulled her closer and thrust deep, her pussy a hot wet clasp of pleasure as he felt the aftershocks of her orgasm rushing through her. He reached for her nipples and tugged on them, pulled them up and twisted. She cried out and her hips rocked, a grimace of lust and pleasure crossed his face, and he began to thrust.

She was on fire with pleasure, a trail of fiery pleasure pain winding around her, through her. Her fingers, hands, arms, the fire burned higher and hotter, touched every erogenous zone she had and places she had never considered erotic before. The areola around her nipples heated and her nipples stiffened further, became ultra sensitive, as he tugged and twisted them. She arched and moaned, her head thrashing on the pillow as she was flooded with sensations. Everywhere he touched a trail of fire followed. Her hip lit up as his fingers skimmed across her skin, her stomach, her mound, and then slipped between the swollen folds of her sex. She writhed and gasped as she burned for him. This was like nothing she had ever felt before. What was happening? She groaned as he circled her clit, the fire trailing right around that nerve laden area. She panted and arched helplessly as that fiery pleasure/pain branded her. "Theiv, what's happening?"

What was happening was that they were burning the fuck up. Holy fuck, he'd never had sex that felt like this. "I got you, Brooke," he said as he fucked into her hot wet pussy, holding onto his control by a thin thread. "Just like that, baby, just fucking like that." He growled, his control almost slipping as he felt her moving against him. Control. He had to stay in control. He felt her sheath grip him tightly, and ease to a caress of fiery sensation, then tighten again. Ah, fuck it. He had no control. He moved over her, going deeper. "Fuck!"

The air filled with the sounds of abandoned wanton sex, the slap of damp skin against damp skin, harsh gasps, and rough groans, soft pleas, and hoarse swearing, and underlying it all was the wild, alien scent that filled their senses and drove them on. Her hands were all over him, touching, stroking, and driving him insane. He sucked a hard nipple into his mouth and slid his hand down between them to work her clit.

She felt his deep shudders and groans of pleasure as her whole body lit up with that fiery pleasure/pain, she stiffened and cried out as a powerful orgasm blazed through her whole body, sweeping her into its fiery embrace.

Theiv swore as she clamped down on him, and fire swept up his spine as his balls drew tight, "Fuck! Fuck! Fuck!" He came hard, his semen leaving his body in hard jets as he shuddered in her embrace, a harsh groan rasping out of his corded throat.

Chapter Fifteen

EARTH DATE: JUNE 24
Canadian Military Base, Rocky Mountains

THE NEXT MORNING, THEY were awoken by a loud knock on the door. Theiv got up, pulled on his pants before going to the door and pulling it open a few inches. After a short discussion, he shut the door and turned back to Brooke, who was looking sleepily bemused and sexy as hell as she stared down at her arm.

"Theiv?" Her voice held an uncertain quality that caught his attention. "Look."

She held out her arm as he walked back over to the bed and sat down beside her. Taking her arm into his hand, he studied the faint, barely perceptible white line that was wound around her arm. He paused, his eyebrow raising. That hadn't been there last night. He looked closer and began to see tiny leaves and flowers. It looked like a pale white tattoo of a flowering vine. He looked up into Brooke's worried eyes.

"I think I know what this is." Theiv said, pulling away the blankets she had pulled up to her chest and seeing the vine marking was covering her whole body.

It wound in a delicate trail over her breasts, down her stomach, around her hips, legs, and even over the tender flesh of her pussy. It was one of the sexiest things he had ever seen. And it marked her as his. Why the hell did that give him a deep sense of satisfaction? The bond was tightening. He should be making a fast exit. Except there was nowhere for him to exit to. He was stranded on this planet until he got that communication system going. "I don't want to say much until Havyn has a look at this. I don't believe it will cause you any harm." He stood up. "Let's shower and then go find Havyn and Dr. Reed." Theiv looked up into Brooke's eyes and saw her conflicting emotions, tempered with a brief flash of anger before she looked away and nodded. She headed into the bathroom first, and as she walked away, his gaze hardened. He was going to get answers. A Zemyneah bond was one thing. An Amberisian mating was quite another.

"BROOKE." DOCTOR REED stepped around Theiv and smiled at her.

"Doctor." Her mouth was dry, and her hands were trembling as she glanced around the office, looking for another way out.

"You're looking much better. Being with Theiv helped? I'd like you to listen to what Havyn was just telling me, and then I need to examine you again."

All Brooke wanted was to leave. Right now. Her heart was pounding, and she felt like she couldn't breathe. Memories of waking up on the ship and seeing the aliens flooded her mind. She tried to push the thoughts away, tried to remember that Havyn had saved her, but fear was a living breathing thing inside of her. "I don't want to be examined again."

Havyn stepped forward, a small black device in her hand. "Did you complete the bonding?"

"No." Brooke shook her head, flinching as Havyn lifted the device. Brooke glared at Theiv, focused her anxiety on him, allowing her anger to rise, her words firmly dismissive. "I am not your... your... Zemyneah!" She spat the word as if it were foul tasting dirt.

Theiv crossed his arms and regarded Brooke. He had no interest in owning a Zemyneah slave, but it was becoming crystal clear that neither his nor Brooke's interests were going to play a part in this situation. "We fucked like Dragons in heat." He stared icily down at Havyn and the human Dr. Reed. "It's done. And now we deal with the consequences." He reached over and lifted Brooke's arm, pushing her sleeve back.

Brooke tried to snatch her arm back, frowning fiercely at Theiv.

"Be still." Theiv commanded, giving Brooke a look that clearly showed he expected to be obeyed.

Brooke narrowed her eyes. "No. Let go."

Theiv moved faster than Brook could have ever expected, got right into her space. "Don't push your luck with me right now, Brooke! You're not the only one having a hard time with this. The sooner you accept this, the sooner this situation will re—"

Brooke narrowed her eyes and jumped into the middle of his furious speech. "Or? Let's be clear here. I am a person!

Not some object or sex toy, to be used and manipulated until you are ready to discard me. I will not be dictated to by you or by your Alien society. I am a human being with all the same rights as you have. I. Make. My. Decisions. Not. You." She jabbed him in the chest hard with every furious word.

Theiv stared at her, his jaw clenched so hard a muscle ticked. Purple eyes locked with green in a silent war, then with a curse, he turned towards the door. She was right. She was right, and he knew it. He took two strides then stopped and turned, shaking his head, and came back to her. "Brooke." He reached out and tipped her chin up so he could see her eyes. "We'll work this all out. You're safe. I won't let anyone hurt you or ignore your wishes." He didn't like the fear in her eyes or the anger. Not after what he'd experienced with her.

Brooke stared into his eyes, searching for some understanding of this man. She'd been married, and yet somehow, she knew that she'd never known a man like this one. And she was not entirely sure that was a good thing.

Brooke shifted and glanced at the Doctor, then at Havyn. Shrugging uncomfortably and not wanting to show them because it seemed very intimate. She pressed her damp hands against her pants then lifted her arm. "Do you see it? It's white and kinda hard to see. It was just there when I woke up. I noticed it because it was still dark in our room and the mark was kind of glowing..." She trailed off as she became aware of the intense interest of the doctor and Havyn.

Dr Reed looked at Brooke's arm and leaned in. "This is extraordinary. Do you have it anywhere else?"

Brooke nodded. "It's everywhere."

"Everywhere?" Havyn was looking at Brooke's arm, a puzzled expression on her face. "Does it hurt? What were you doing when it appeared?"

Brooke shook her head. "It doesn't hurt. I don't know when..." She hesitated as a memory surfaced. Last night when she and Theiv had been—. Her eyes got big as she remembered the fiery pleasure/pain that had seemed to trail from his fingers.

Havyn tilted her head as she watched Brooke's face. "During sex." It wasn't a question. "We need to take some blood. I believe I know what has happened, but it is a very unexpected side effect."

Theiv took that moment to excuse himself and stepped out into the hall, closing the door quietly behind him.

Dr. Reed nodded at Havyn. "I agree, but before we do that, we need to discuss this situation with you, Brooke. Please, sit down." Brooke sat down. Havyn took the seat beside her, and the doctor took the seat behind her desk. "What exactly did Theiv tell you?"

"The same thing that you all have told me," Brooke stated her voice sharp, clasping her hands together so they wouldn't see her trembling. Doctor Reed frowned and Brooke had a tiny flicker of hope that this was all some crazy bad misunderstanding until Havyn spoke up.

"Brooke." She began in her exotically accented voice. "You have been with Theiv. You must have seen the truth of our words. You felt better after you had sex, yes? That is the proof that the Zemyneah protocol has taken hold"

Brooke shook her head. "I'm not a Zemyneah. I can't be a Zemyneah. Just give me the cure so I can go back to my life before any of this happened."

Doctor Reed rubbed her brow. "Brooke, please. This cannot be undone. If it could, we would have already done it."

Brooke stared at the Doctor numbly, her words echoing in her mind.

Havyn took her small scanner from her pocket and began to scan Brooke. "Dr. Reed, Theiv is correct in saying that their bond is complete. She is not releasing nearly as many pheromones as she was."

"That is one piece of good news. Brooke, Havyn needs to explain a few things about her culture to you. It's important that you listen to her. It will help you to understand what's happening to your body."

Havyn reached out and gently touched Brooke's shoulder, the shimmer of tears in her eyes even as she fought the urge to scream her rage, to rip aside the facade that carefully hid the fury that was burning her alive and expose it to the whole universe. "Ah, Brooke, I am sorry. We have done a terrible thing to you. My heart and soul apologize for this atrocity." She paused, fierce bitter outrage sparking bright in her golden eyes. "In my world, there are two kinds of women. No. No, that is not right. I will not cater to that way of thinking. I will not lessen the horror of the Althanean women with pretty words. Women in my world are forced into one of two roles by our men's fears and sexual greed. We are wives, or we are Zemyneah slaves." She stood up and began to pace the small room.

"Whether Zemyneah or wife, we are bonded to men through a process that our ancestors created hundreds of years past when our women began to demand equality."

Brooke listened carefully, focusing on Havyn's words, trying to understand.

"You have no idea what we are trying to save you from, Brooke. How could you? How could you know what it is to rejoice at the birth of your son, and weep at the birth of your daughter. As a wife—no, as a woman, I could not condemn you to such a life.

My choice was to kill you or find a way to save you. Too many women have died, Brooke, many of them Earth women. We must stop Drace's experiments. We have to prevent him from succeeding." Havyn stared at Brooke for a moment, then whispered "I could not kill you." She lifted trembling hands. "I am guilty of so many deaths already. I could not face killing another woman," A silvery tear tracked down her cheek, "may the gods forgive me. So, I brought you home."

"But just coming back to Earth isn't enough to save me." Brooke said quietly.

Doctor Reed's eyes filled with regret. "The bond you formed with Theiv will help you, but we must prevent Drace from taking you again."

Havyn touched Brooke's arm. "This mark you showed us, it's not something we would have expected. It's the Amberisian mating mark." She shook her head and stroked the vine-like mark. "You are amazing Brooke. A miracle, in a universe that desperately needs a miracle."

Havyn took a deep breath and told the Earth woman a zealously protected secret. "A Rebellion has begun. There are whispers that our freedom approaches, that this evil will finally be destroyed. We need you, Brooke. You have no idea how important you are to this fight for freedom. How your survival gives us all hope. Be brave, Brooke. Be very brave. Stand against this evil, and if it is somehow possible, forgive us, and find a way to reach out to a people who are not your own, a people who have caused you great harm."

Brooke stared down at her hands. Forgiveness? Her mind filled with a red-hot anger, a bitter taste filling her mouth as she tried to sort through the violent hate filled words that wanted to spew out of her. In the end, she chose to avoid Havyn's plea, allowing only the words that marked her soul. "You think he's still after me."

Havyn's eyes met hers, searching for something that Brooke could not give her in this moment. Finally, regret filled her eyes, and she spoke. "You are extraordinary Brooke. I do not know of any man who could resist the pheromones you release. Even women are tempted by you. My husband succeeded beyond his wildest dreams. You are the very essence of Zemyneah. Yes, Drace is coming for you. You are all that he sought to create, the perfect pawn in his game."

Brooke's hands trembled, rage churning inside of her, a violent storm that began to reshape her very soul. "I will not submit to that monster. I will never submit to him or his vile plans!"

"He is a cruel man, Brooke." Havyn's eyes met hers, and Brooke saw the horror she had survived. "By the time he was ready to present you to the Emperor, you would do anything he wanted. Anything, to escape his perversities."

"Theiv won't let that happen." Brooke was shocked by the words that came out of her mouth. And yet, on a soul deep level, she knew they were true, but she shook her head. "I won't let that happen!"

Havyn stared at her, her eyes grave. "I have no doubt that Drace would love to get his hands on Theiv. To have a Dragon Warrior in his power would be an unbelievable victory. To incorporate the DNA of a Dragon Warrior into his experiments would be a feat he would never have dared dream of. But in the end, Brooke, Drace would kill Theiv to prevent any potential problems with your bonding to the Emperor. I can assure you that Theiv's death would not be an easy one."

Brooke swallowed as nausea rose in her throat.

"It is critical that you understand the danger you face," Havyn continued. "If you are recaptured, Drace will force you into a state where your pheromones are at their most potent. At that point, the Emperor's fate is sealed, and so is yours. Drace will command you to find out all kinds of information and bring it to him. You cannot discount how powerful your influence will be over the Emperor, nor Drace's power over you. With Drace as your handler, the potential for harm is far too great to allow."

Doctor Reed looked at Brooke, deeply concerned. "Brooke, perhaps none of us can fully understand the depth of the violation that you've experienced. Your life and your body have been changed without your consent. You've been forced into a nightmare. It will take time for you to heal from this trauma. But you will heal. You will adjust. Theiv will help if you give him the chance. And he is, perhaps, your only chance of safety."

"And what about my life? Have any of you even considered that?" Brooke burst out, her voice anguished, a fury she'd never known before flared through her blood, her vision painted vivid scarlet. Heat raged with the savagery of a firestorm, burning through her fear, and the numbness that had been turning her slowly to ice. She shot to her feet, her hand lashing out to strike everything off Dr. Reed's desk! Turning, she snatched the scanner from Havyn's hand, and threw it as hard as she could against the wall. The alien technology shattered, the pieces falling to the floor. "What about me?" She screamed. "My life is not going to simply stop because of your plans. You're not taking my life from me! I refuse to allow it. You're going to need to adjust your plans and schemes. I don't owe you my life, and I sure as hell, don't owe you my loyalty or my body. I did not consent to what was done to me by that evil bastard, and I sure as hell am not going to consent to giving up my life because of what he did." She turned her gaze on the military doctor assigned to her. "This is no better than the human trafficking that goes on every day on this planet! Do you even have a conscience?" She stared at the two shocked women, her hands clenched tightly into fists, her eyes radiating her fury.

Chapter Sixteen

EARTH DATE: JUNE 24
Canadian Military Base, Rocky Mountains

THEIV HAD BEEN HESITANT to leave Brooke with Havyn and the human, Doctor Reed, but it was critical that he spoke with Riak and T'lain. He needed more information on this new type of Zepto technology that Drace used to genetically alter Brooke, and he wanted answers about that Amberisian mating mark. He had a feeling that Drace's experiment was about to spin out of control. It was imperative that he knew exactly what they would be dealing with.

He found the two scientists in a temporary lab set up for their use. The few pieces of Althanean technology they possessed were set up on the table in front of them, and they were examining the Earth tech they had been given. He could hear T'lain cursing softly. Both men looked up when he walked into the room. "Theiv, these tools are primitive, and we need to collect important data on Subject 459."

Theiv crossed his arms and looked at both scientists for a long moment. "Her name is Brooke. She is a human from Earth, with a family and people who love her. Not a subject.

Not an experiment. You do not get to distance yourself from what you have done."

The two men stared at him, the blue of their skin darkening over their cheeks. Riak finally gave a stiff nod. "You are correct. We did protest Drace's choice, but we should have done more."

"We cannot change what has happened, but we are seeking ways to help Brooke." T'lain's voice was quiet as he held Theiv's gaze. "The biggest problem we face, that Brooke faces, is that the formula was still being adjusted by Drace. He didn't inform us of the components he used to make those adjustments. What we do know is that all the previous females it was used on died. Brooke's survival to this point is an anomaly. We don't know what this formula will do to her. It is urgent that we get the data."

Riak nodded. "The Humans have provided us with their nanotechnology, but it's so far behind our Zepto technology that we are basically starting over. There is no possibility of reversal, Theiv."

Theiv exhaled, his gut clenching. "The bond happened last night. Brooke is with Havyn and Doctor Reed now, so data should be coming soon. I will return to the Exanthus and retrieve some equipment for you. I need a list. Before I go, there is something I need to speak to you about—another anomaly." Both scientists stopped what they were doing and focused on Theiv intently. "Brooke has developed an Amberisian mating mark. Can you explain this to me?"

The scientists exchanged a look. "An Amberisian mating mark? Are you certain?"

Theiv gave a curt nod. "I saw it clearly. It is iridescent and nearly invisible unless light is shining directly on it. I have no doubt, in the moonlight, it will glow."

"It has to be the genetic modifications." Riak cursed and T'lain looked grim. "Drace was using genetic material gathered from captives. We don't know how much he gathered or where from. What he was doing was unethical. Unprecedented.

Chapter Seventeen

EARTH DATE: JUNE 24
Canadian Military Base, Rocky Mountains

THEIV WALKED INTO THE medical ward and frowned as he heard Brooke's angry words. His eyes met Doctor Reed's, and he raised a brow. He was glad to hear Brooke's anger. It was justified. She'd been violated in ways no person should ever experience. He was relieved to see that she'd found her courage, and she wasn't going to quietly accept what happened to her. "What's going on here?" Brooke jerked around, wide green eyes meeting his. "Fierce warrior woman." He gave her a look of approval as he settled his arm around her shoulders, ignoring Dr. Reed and Havyn. "I've arranged for you to meet the men your government has assigned as our protection unit."

Brooke felt some of the tension ease in her shoulders at this man's support. She was still angry, but somehow, knowing that this big tough man had her back, gave her the boost her confidence needed. No matter what they'd done to her, she was still Brooke St. Claire. They could never take that from her. She would not simply submit to their agenda.

It didn't take them long to reach their destination. She paused outside the door, glancing at Theiv. It still boggled her mind that she'd had wild crazy sex with this man. "Is this protection detail really necessary?"

Theiv reached up and tucked a long strand of deep purple hair behind her delicate ear. "Yes. Drace is not going to stop until he gets you back. I refuse to let that happen. He can't have you. You wear my mark. You belong with me."

Brooke narrowed her eyes, and the man had the audacity to grin. "Fire. Like the fiercest Dragoness in my world. I like that fire, Brooke. Keep it burning." Reaching out, he opened the door, and with his hand on her lower back, ushered her through.

"Brooke!" Clay was on his feet in an instant, yanking her into his arms for a hard hug. "Damnit, Brooke. You scared the shit out of me."

Brooke froze as Clay's arms closed around her. Tears welled in her eyes. "Language," she said, her voice shaking.

She heard him let out a strained laugh, but the strength he was hugging her with told its own story. When he at last let her go, she stared up into his red-rimmed eyes. His hair was in total disarray as if he'd run his hands through it multiple times. Several days' growth of beard covered his jaw, and his clothes were a wrinkled mess. She reached out and straightened his collar, fussing a bit because that's what mothers did. "Are Jaxson and Danielle here? Are they ok?"

Clay shook his head. "I'm sorry Brooke. I was the only one allowed to come. They contacted us this morning. Just landed a military helicopter right on your lawn. They gave the search and rescue teams a short briefing that basically said you were alive and safe, and told me to get on the helicopter. The rest of the family was told that you would contact them today. It was on the flight here that they informed me that this is a highly classified UFO incident. I didn't buy it." He shoved a hand through his hair. "Not even after I read the full report, until I was introduced to two alien scientists. They are trying to keep this all hush-hush. I don't know how the fuck they plan to do that." He took a deep breath. "Jaxson and Danielle have been frantic with worry. You need to call them. And Nissa has taken over your kitchen to feed the searchers."

"Searchers?"

"Of course, there were searchers, Brooke." Clay frowned, then reached out and touched her purple hair. "What did they do to you?"

"I'm surprised you recognized me." Brooke bit her lip and touched her hair, her eyes searching his.

Clay snorted. "You look just like Danielle when she was fifteen and used Kool-Aid to dye her hair."

Brooke choked out a broken laugh. "I don't feel fifteen." She looked away before lifting her eyes to him again and gave him a wavering smile. "Don't get abducted by aliens, Clay. They don't know anything about Star Trek or the Prime Directive."

Theiv hated to intrude, but he needed to introduce the others. He stepped forward and put his hand on her back, directing her attention to the other men in the room. "Brooke, this is Storm Kenyon and Sev Conder."

Brooke watched as Storm stood up. He was a tall powerfully built man, with long dark hair and serious grey eyes.

"Ma'am." He offered his hand to her. She looked at Theiv, and at his slight nod, she hesitantly shook the man's hand, terrified of triggering the insane uncontrollable arousal that had consumed her for days. After a few seconds of contact, she realized the stability she had gained from being with Theiv was holding.

Sev held out his hand next, his dark hair was a wild tangled mess with platinum tips, his brown eyes more pronounced due to the guyliner he wore. When she shook his hand, she could see tattoo's peeking out from under his sleeve. She let out the breath she hadn't known she was holding, relieved to be able to shake these men's hands without wanting to throw them down on the floor and have her way with them. Immediately horrified by the thought, she turned away.

They all sat down around a table and Clay gave her a cup of Chai tea. She blinked away the tears and closed her eyes as she inhaled the aroma. She took a sip and smiled at Clay. "Thank you."

He nodded, his eyes sharp, not missing the way her hands trembled and the fear in her eyes. Never in his life had he felt the desire to kill outside the line of duty, but he'd become deeply familiar with that feeling over the last days. "We're going to keep you safe, Brooke. I promised Jaxson and Danelle that I would bring you home, and I fully intend to do that."

"When it's safe." Theiv interjected. "Right now, we don't want to lead Drace to your family unit."

Brooke's eyes widened. "You know about my family?" Her voice was sharp.

He inclined his head. "Drace is very thorough. Havyn spoke to me of the details." Theiv watched her for a moment. "Brooke," He hesitated, his hand coming up to gently squeeze her shoulder. "Clay, Storm, and Sev have been informed about the details of your abduction. It was necessary for your protection."

She swallowed. "A-about everything? What they did to me? What I am?" Her voice broke off and she stared down at her hands, her shoulders hunching"

Theiv reached over and tilted up her chin. "You are a courageous woman who survived what many have not."

Clay watched them, his eyes reflecting none of his inner turmoil. The alien part of this fucked up situation was real. There was no longer any doubt in his mind about that. He'd met them all, saw their ship and tech. Hell, he'd even demanded to see the medical reports on them. They were real. They were fucking scary real. He'd questioned why an alien soldier could walk around a Canadian military base armed and was taken to meet with the fucking Prime Minister and the President of the USA who'd been on a fucking tour of the base when that damned space craft had landed. It was explained to him that the only reason he was brought into this so early, was his background as a member of the JTF2 team. The two heads of government for the neighboring countries had met with Theiv and Havyn. In that meeting, they'd come to understand that if the fucker who'd captured Brooke, found her, there would be nothing they could do that would stop him from taking her again. Technologically, Earth was far behind these Aliens. Theiv was charged with Brooke's protection. The curve ball was that he, Sev, and Storm were charged with keeping Theiv in line.

Being a cop didn't make him exactly comfortable with all this. His mind was filled with questions. Was this really, Brooke? She was too young, her hair was too long, and it was purple and what was that fucking mark he could barely see on the back of her hands, neck, and face? Fuck the medical reports, he had his own test. "SoSwI' SoH'a'?" *Are you my mother?* He waited and watched. Even if these aliens had some kind of star trek translator technology that knew Klingon, the answer was not yes or no. Would she give the correct response?

Brooke turned and looked at Clay, then reached over and gently set her hand on his cheek, as she'd always done when asked this question. "tIqwIj puqloD SoH". *You are the son of my heart.* He closed his eyes and released the breath he hadn't realized he was holding, and looked at her with troubled eyes, eyes that saw too clearly. "Brooke, I don't care about any of that. You're my family, and that's never going to change."

"Ma'am," Storm spoke up, "We needed to be fully briefed so we could protect you. None of us think less of you because of what those alien bastards did."

Theiv raised his eyebrow but remained silent.

Brooke nodded, fighting to blink away the tears that filled her eyes, but inside, she wondered how they would treat her when they knew she was an alien's lover. Havyn talked about her world and the way the women were treated, but here on earth, women were not always treated any better.

She listened to the men talking for about an hour, adding in her thoughts and opinions when asked, sitting back, and listening as they all argued about why she couldn't immediately go home. But with each passing minute, she could feel herself growing more and more tired. Clay noticed and suggested she lay down in the bedroom attached to this suite. With a nod she gratefully found the bedroom and curled up on the bed, instantly falling into a deep sleep.

Clay shut the door behind Brooke and fought the urge to slam his fist into the wall. He'd never seen Brooke so emotionally fragile in his life, not even after he'd had to tell her about the circumstances around her husband's death. He walked over to the small bar set up along one side of the suite and helped himself to a glass of whiskey. He tossed it back in one shot and poured himself a second, before walking over to rejoin the three men who were helping to protect the woman, who was practically his mother.

A knock on the door interrupted the planning session. Storm opened the door to Dr. Reed and several military personnel. A few bags were brought in containing clothing and personal hygiene items. Then Clay, Sev, and Storm were escorted to their new quarters and Theiv was informed that this was his and Brooke's new rooms. It was certainly better than his last room he thought as he began to put things away. He needed to talk to Havyn, but before he left, he checked on Brooke. She was sound asleep, so he set a bottle of water on the nightstand and determined to return as quickly as possible.

SHE WAS COLD. A SHIVER worked its way through her body, and she curled up, trying to find some warmth. Where was she? She opened her eyes and blinked against the sudden brightness. There was almost a clinical feeling to the room she found herself in. "Doctor Reed?" She called out softly, searching for the military doctor.

"There are no humans here."

She shot up, her heart racing as the voice, that cruel icy voice, that haunted her, echoed through the room. She scrambled to get off the bed, almost falling to the floor in her haste. No. no. no. She frantically looked around the room. He couldn't be here!

She pressed herself up against a wall, looking for the door. She had to get out. She had to get away! She caught her reflection in a mirror hanging on the wall and she moaned. She was naked. Oh god, she was naked.

Amused male laughter, and the sound of a chair being pushed back. Seeing the paper sheet from the exam table laying on the floor, she snatched it up and wrapped it around herself.

She was dreaming. She had to be dreaming.

"Hello, Zemyneah."

That voice pierced her like razor-sharp shards of ice, leaving her shaking, and terrified. She turned slowly and came face to face with the alien who abducted her. "This is a dream. It's only a dream."

Drace laughed again and walked around her. "It may be a dream for you, but for me this is simply a continuation of my experiment." He held a slender electronic tablet in his hands. "The DNA from Subject 498 has integrated well." He input some data into his tablet and continued to walk around her. "What is this?" Reaching out he touched her arm.

She jerked away, and glanced down at her arm, her skin crawling. The tattoo-like mark that appeared after she and Theiv—she pushed the thought away. Her eyes lifted to meet his and she shuddered at the look of cold clinical curiosity.

A slow menacing smile curved his lips. "How curious, an Amberisian mating mark." He input more data into the electronic organizer and looked at her. "You were uniquely designed to mate with two men, the mark I saw indicates you have been assigned a mate. I hope they at least chose a male who could give you some training. If you are like the wives on my planet, you will be grievously unprepared for your duties." Staring at his tablet he tapped it a few times as he thought. "You are not putting off near the number of pheromones that you were. It is of no consequence to my plans. I can deal with that inconvenience when I retrieve you."

"No."

"You didn't really think that I wouldn't come for you, did you Brooke?" Drace looked at her curiously. "Earth is woefully behind on their technology. Your planet is ripe for the picking, and I intend to harvest your women. Just think of it as a higher calling to serve the great cause of Althanea. I'll come for you soon, Zemyneah—and for my errant wife."

Brook shot straight up in bed, choking off a scream. A sob broke from deep in her chest. It was a nightmare. Not real. She sobbed again and reached for the bottle of water by her bed. The water sloshed in the bottle as she brought it to her lips and took a drink. She pushed the memories away and took a second drink before setting it back down. It was normal to have nightmares after what she'd survived, she told herself. Except nothing felt normal about this dream. It was too real, too vivid, too much.

Shaking, Brooke got up and stumbled into the bathroom. Putting her hands on the counter, she stared at the image in the mirror. Was this really her? She wasn't the kind of woman to have mind blowing sex with a total stranger, let alone an alien. What was happening to her? There were no answers in the mirror, and she turned away, and started the shower. Shedding her clothes, she stepped into the warm flow of water, and where no one would hear her, she let the tears fall.

When she was finally able to get control of herself, she began to wash her body, determined to rid her skin of the feeling of that evil bastard's touch. Even though it had only been a nightmare, there was a sick feeling in the pit of her stomach, her skin crawling at the mere thought.

She lathered her skin with the rich bubbles from the soap, and as she washed, she became aware of a difference to her body. She glanced down and frowned, hastily rinsing the bubbles from her skin. "Oh, no!" she whispered, staring at her smooth flat belly. She ran her hands down her stomach. "No, no." She shook her head in denial, shocked horror running over her. The white caesarean scar that had once marked the birth of her children was gone. As if it had never been. Her hands shook and she blinked as her eyes filled with tears, blurring her vision. She'd always hated that damn scar. She should be happy it was gone, not filled with this aching sense of loss. A hard sob caught her by surprise, and turned into a stream of tears, slowly sliding down to the floor of the shower, she drew her knees up. The hard beat of the water pouring down on her, she wrapped her arms around legs, and rocked back and forth, each breath an agonized gasp.

The water had turned icily cold before she regained control. Standing up slowly, feeling like she had aged a thousand years, she reached for the shampoo with shaking hands, grieving the loss of yet another piece of herself.

By the time she rinsed the conditioner from her hair with shaking fingers, she'd regained a fragile control over her emotions. She pulled a towel from the rack and stepped from the shower.

A spark of anger began to burn inside of her. Fucking aliens! She hated them! If she had half a chance, she would––she would––she didn't know what she would do. She clenched her hands. She didn't hate them all, even though some part of her wanted to. Havyn, Theiv, T'lain and Riak risked their lives to save her.

She closed her eyes, breathing deep. She would not lose the person she was. She would not let hate color her view of every person she met.

She took a deep shuddering breath and opened her eyes to stare at herself in the mirror. They had no right to do the things they'd done to her. How dare they force this on her! How dare they think they had any right to force her into some sick, twisted, relationship with their damn Emperor! How dare they change her body!

She glared in the mirror, picked up a brush and began to furiously yank it through the long purple curls that reached to her waist. She paused, cocked her head to the side. Hold it. What was she doing? How many times had she counselled others to not allow a victim mentality to control them? There might be some things in this mess that she couldn't change, but did that mean she had to accept everything?

She began pulling open the drawers on the vanity, rifling ruthlessly through the contents. Razor, nope, it went sailing over her shoulder, suntan lotion, nope, condoms, she snorted and tossed the box. There. Finally. Scissors! She grinned triumphantly. Then she picked up a lock of hair and chopped it off an inch away from her head.

She was nobody's damn victim! Another lock fell to the floor. She wasn't just going to sit back and let them dictate who she was! Snip, Snip, Snip. The scissors felt good in her hand. She wielded them furiously until she had hacked off all the long purple hair that she hadn't chosen.

Theiv opened the door. He paused, his eyebrow lifting as he followed the path of stuff littering the floor until he came to the first long lock of curling purple hair lying beside dainty bare feet. He looked up. Brooke was glaring defiantly at him. All that defiance was glorious, and her hair was a short choppy mess.

Theiv carefully closed the door and locked it, then he reached back and fumbled the robe off the back of the bathroom door, unable to stop himself from letting his eyes travel one more time over that lush, beautiful body, before he held the robe out to her.

Brooke's eyes widened, and she snatched the robe away from Theiv and quickly jerked it on, her cheeks warm.

Ignoring his hard cock, he stepped up to Brooke and caught her chin firmly in his hand, turning her head one way then the other. The cut was sexy, reminding him of some of the warrior women of Sarisia. He tilted her face up until she looked him in the eye. "You have the spirit of a warrior. Resist what has been done to you. Fight it with everything you are. You will not be defeated." He brushed a stray strand of hair from her cheek, and because he couldn't resist, he leaned down and gave her a gentle kiss, "I must return to the Exanthus. There are things that Havyn, Riak, and T'lain urgently need. And I must get a message out requesting assistance." He shook his head when she started to speak. "I am the only one who can do this." Then he picked up the scissors. "You missed a couple of spots, Dragoness."

Chapter Eighteen

EARTH DATE: JUNE 24
Sol Star System, The Starship Exanthus

THEIV FLASHED INTO cargo bay nine and stood absolutely still in the dark room, waiting to see if any alarms would sound, or if there were any unpleasant surprises waiting for him. After a full minute of silence, he moved to the left, skirting a huge pile of containers, then continued down the narrow pathway left between the massive shipping crates until he came to a juncture. He turned left again and stopped at the 14th container on the right, taking out a tiny scanner he tapped a code into it, and waited as it scanned the huge cargo bay. No lifeforms flashed across the small screen. He tapped in another code and seconds later a small section of the container slid to the side. He stepped into it and the door slid closed, locking automatically. The design so precise that there was no way to tell the door even existed.

Inside was a small room, lined with Ryolyzia, an extremely rare mineral that was invisible to all technical scans. Theiv double checked to ensure that all the locks had been engaged. When he was satisfied that the room was secure, he sat down at the small computer console and ran a security scan of the interior. No one had been in the room since his last visit. He began to type out a coded message that would mingle with the daily messages sent out from the ship to the Dark Star communication array. He had no doubt that the intended recipient would find it.

Mission compromised. Exanthus must be stopped. DN extremely dangerous. Approach with caution. Capture is imperative. Risk of Galactic War. DK must be protected at all costs. H.N. Dark. T.N. Dark. R.V. Dark. T.D. Dark.

He ensured the message was heavily encrypted, then hit send. Grabbing a pack, he began to fill it with things he knew they might need in the coming weeks, as they waited for the ship that he knew would be sent.

After a last look around and a careful check that the message had indeed gone out, he activated the auto self destruct on the room and exited. As he made his way out of the cargo bay, he could smell the smoke and the arid scent of the high heat accelerant that had deployed as soon as the self destruct sequence had completed. There would be no trace of the electronics left in that secret room, in fact, the whole shipping container would be reduced to ash. The cargo bay was about to be the scene of a major fire, and a later check into the roster would reveal a small amount of an unstable chemical. The authorities would assume it had not been stored properly.

Theiv made his way through the ship as the alarms screamed, heavy steel fire doors were sliding into place to contain the fire to cargo bay nine, and personnel were rushing to the scene.

It was the fire alarms that alerted Drace to the fact that Theiv had returned to the Exanthus. A fire in the cargo hold was just too coincidental to be an accident. He'd been waiting, knowing full well that the Dragon Warrior would not simply disappear. They would need weapons, and possibly medical technology to protect the Zemyneah. They would fail. He would take his property back, and Theiv would make an interesting addition to his experiment. He'd wanted to get his hands on a sample of DNA from the Dragon Warriors for a long time. *You know,* he mused, *things always have a way of working themselves out.* He activated his com device. "The target has arrived. Apprehend him and bring him to me. Alive."

Theiv had just put a small med scanner into a pouch he wore crosswise across his chest when the door to the med bay slid open. He whirled around, his phase gun lifting as three men came through the door, their guns drawn. He fired and dived behind a medical station cursing. Vhalett, Zholaka, and T'Vass, Drace's men. Zholaka was swearing and Theiv figured he'd hit him with that shot but, not enough to take him out of the action. He moved to the edge of the med station and peered around the corner. The men were working their way towards him. He fired repeatedly, and the men dove for cover.

Chapter Nineteen

EARTH DATE: JUNE 24
Canadian Military Base, Rocky Mountains

PACING IN HER ROOM, she'd had time to think, and she was furious. She couldn't just sit here and wait for everyone to protect her, couldn't allow them to risk their lives for her. She wished that Theiv had returned, but he hadn't. She was worried, and all too aware that the longer she remained here, the more vulnerable she was, no matter what anyone told her. Drace had found her and got to her even if it was only in a dream. She knew he wouldn't stop until he got her in his clutches, and that was not something she was willing to accept. She would not be his experiment again. The problem with Drace was that he was arrogant and full of his own importance. But he'd made a mistake, and she was going to take full advantage of that error. While he'd been in her head, in her dream, she had also been in his. And she picked up a very important bit of information—information that terrified her, but that information would get her out of here. She had to act now, before that damn arousal overtook her. With any luck she would be far away before it struck again, far enough away that no one would ever find her.

Opening the door to her room a bare inch, she asked the two soldiers if they would get Havyn. She wasn't feeling well. They'd agreed, then while they radioed Havyn and Dr. Reed. She walked over to the closet, stepped into it, and shut the door. Stripping off her socks and runners, she stuffed her socks into the shoes and tied the laces together. Her bare toes curled into the carpet as she draped the runners around her neck. Taking a deep breath, she looked up at the ceiling. Another deep breath, while she shook hands and flexed her fingers as she thought about what she had seen in that monster's mind, it was something he called the Giastean Factor, something he'd added to his evil concoction. But what she had seen in his mind... She looked up at the ceiling and then she jumped, straight up. Claws bit into the ceiling. *Holy Mackerel!* She was hanging from the ceiling and her fingers and toes had sprouted claws. She took deep calming breaths and clung to the roof. *Just a few minutes. Just a few minutes*, she told herself over and over again. She heard the door to the room open, and voices, then the sounds of a frantic search. They opened the closet and saw the obvious, it was empty, they never looked up. Eventually they took the search elsewhere and she overheard Havyn's voice saying that Drace must have found a way to get to her.

She waited several long minutes after the room became silent before dropping down to the floor. Shaking, she rubbed her arms and pushed from her mind what she had done, she had to move if she was going to get away. Using every skill she ever possessed for playing hide and seek she made her way out of the building and across the grounds to a remote stretch of fence and then she jumped again and cleared the fence. Oh heavens! This was terrifying. She stumbled on her landing but regained her balance and ran.

Chapter Twenty

SHE SAT ON A BENCH along the edge of a small park in this city that she'd never been to and knew she didn't have a lot of time. The base that she'd run from couldn't be more then a mile or two from where she currently was. She had to get out of this area as quickly as possible. But how? She had no money, not even a credit card, and hitchhiking was not an option she could risk—not with her out of control hormones. She sighed and stared blankly at the gas station/convenience store across the road. What she wouldn't give for a chocolate bar right now. She saw a young man pull up to the pumps in an older SUV and she smiled, her son Jaxon had an SUV like that for his first vehicle. The young man got out and went to the pumps. He used a card to pay at the pumps, lifted the nozzle and set it to self pump. He shrugged out of his jacket, walked around to the driver's door and tossed it inside, then pulled out a backpack and searched through it. Pocketing whatever he'd taken from the backpack he tossed it back into the vehicle and closed the door.

Brooke's head tilted and her brow furrowed. He hadn't locked the door. She knew because a vehicle of that age had manual locks. She stood up slowly, her mind racing. The young man finished pumping his gas then turned and walked into the station's convenience store. She swallowed, thinking about how many times she'd warned Jaxon to never do that. Never leave your vehicle unlocked. She rubbed her hands on her pants and, after looking both ways, crossed the street. What she was about to do— Clay wouldn't just give her a speeding ticket; he would arrest her! She swallowed, and after a quick look around to make sure no one was watching, she opened the driver's door and got into the SUV. She locked the door. Then she quickly checked all the obvious places for a spare key. She found it in the ashtray.

The vehicle started with a throaty purr and she pulled out onto the street. A glance in the rear-view mirror showed that no one had noticed her descent into a life of crime. She turned the corner and then another. Glancing at the gas tank, she saw it was full. She drove several miles before she pulled over into a rest stop along the side of the road. Opening the glove box, she pulled out the map she found. She studied it for a moment, then pulled back on the highway and drove to the intersection of a secondary highway that wound its way through a mountainous national park. Her goal was simply to get back home where Nissa waited. From there, she would make more permanent plans.

Two hours into the drive, high up in the mountain pass, the first snowflake fell. This high up a snowstorm was not that uncommon, even in summer. Her hands tightened on the steering wheel, and she glanced up at the sky. Please, let this just be a few flakes.

Within minutes, snow was falling steadily, and the temperature dropped several degrees. Brooke turned on the heater in the vehicle to keep the windows clear, then tried to find a radio station with a weather report, but in the mountains, there was hardly any reception, and she couldn't find anything more than static. The wind was picking up. She shrugged her shoulders trying to ease the tense muscles and peered through the windshield into the driven snowflakes.

Her fingers began to ache, and she eased her one hand away from the wheel for a few seconds to flex her fingers. The roads were snow covered, and she could hear the undercarriage hitting the drifts that were building up. She took a deep breath, debating if she should pull over, but she had no idea where the shoulder of the road was or if she was even in her own lane.

She stared harder through the driving snow, trying to catch glimpses of anything that would tell her where the lines on the lane were. She seemed to be the only one on the highway. While she was relieved not to be meeting anyone, it was almost eerie. The silence of the falling snow seemed to muffle all noise, except for the odd blast of wind that shook the vehicle and the slap of her windshield wipers. This oddly silent world was a place of danger though and she gripped the wheel even harder. Where was the nearest town?

She drove around a curve in the road, touching her brakes to slow down. The backend of the vehicle slid to the side. She gasped, her heart thumping hard in her chest as she tried to steer out of it. The world swung in a crazy arc. Gripping the steering wheel, her knuckles white, she fought for control as each slide took her closer and closer to the sheer cliff that ran alongside the road. She almost had it. Almost, and then the vehicle was hurtling over the edge of the road. Down, down the steep walls of the ravine. The SUV tumbled over and over, slamming into trees and rocks. Glass shattered, metal screamed, shrieked as it bent and buckled with each impact. The airbags detonated with a bang, and Brooke was flung forward into the protective sack, earth and sky flashing by her in a dizzying spiral. *Stop! Stop!* She thought as something struck her hard and her vision began to dim. The world spun by her again before the battered vehicle came to rest partly on its wheels and partly on its side. Silence filled the air. Snow fell softly, bringing a hush to the wilderness as it silently covered all indications of human encroachment.

Long minutes passed, then a soft groan broke the stillness as Brooke moved, her body slowly responding to her return to consciousness. She groaned again and clumsily pushed the airbag away. Everything hurt.

She blinked against the icy particles that were raining against her face, trying to understand what had happened. Snow. It was snowing. She took a deep breath as a hard shiver wracked her body, crying out when even that slight movement seemed to trigger a growing cascade of pain. She carefully took another breath, then another and slowly her mind filled with the knowledge that if she were to survive, she would have to move.

Carefully, she began to move her limbs. Her legs seemed to be fine as was her left arm and hand. She gasped in agony as pain radiated up her right arm. Oh, heavens, that hurt!

She tilted her head back against the headrest and tried to breathe through the pain. A trickle of warm liquid slid down her face, and she swiped at it with the back of her left hand––blood. She needed help, but with no phone, she was on her own.

A gust of wind filled the broken interior of the ruined vehicle with a shower of snow and Brooke shivered. Looking around, she realized that all the windows were broken, snow was swirling in and piling up on the seats and the dash. She shivered again, her breath a white cloud in front of her. She had to get out of here.

Looking around she saw the young man's jacket and backpack lying on the passenger side floor. She dragged them over, clenching her teeth against a short, throttled scream when she jarred her arm. Closing her eyes, she breathed through the pain. Carefully, she eased her left arm into the jacket, then struggled to get it around her, almost giving up before she finally found a way to get the zipper started. She zipped it up, slowly easing over her damaged right arm that she'd cradled against her chest. By the time it was done up, she realized the snow was falling harder and several more inches had accumulated on the ground.

Sobbing softly, she swiped at the tears on her cheeks and realized she was still bleeding from the head wound. She found a napkin and pressed it against the cut, her breath hissing out at the pain. Knowing she had to get moving, she tried to open the drivers side door, only to discover there was no way it would even move. Crying and swearing, she managed to half crawl, half drag herself over the console and push open the passenger side door.

She could see a faint trail leading into the woods, and even though she knew that leaving the vehicle wasn't the best idea, it offered no protection against the brutally cold wind and snow. Maybe the trail would lead to shelter.

The slight trail was slippery, full of snow. The going was hard and slow. Her feet were soaked and cold within minutes, but she continued until she slipped and stumbled against a tree, jarring her arm again. She fell to her knees in agony, silent sobs shaking her body. For several seconds she leaned helplessly against the tree, then took a deep shuddering breath and stood up.

The day darkened with the storm. The snow fell harder and harder, with the wild wind driving it across the harsh landscape. Brooke could no longer see the trail she hiked on. She kept going. She was hot and then she was cold, and in her mind danced images of Theiv—shockingly, graphic sexual images. The experiment continues, she thought bitterly. Those tiny invading monsters first job was to ensure her survival. They must need more energy. She began to shake uncontrollably, and as her reality again burst into her mind, she wanted nothing more than to run.

When she came across a huge boulder, she huddled down beside it out of the wind, feeling weak and dizzy. After a while, she realized that the weakness wasn't leaving so she rose and continued, her legs shaky.

She was cold, so cold. She longed for nothing more than to be safe in the warmth of her bed, a mound of blankets piled on her and the warmth of Theiv's arms surrounding her. She was struck by how weird it was to even think that way about an alien, who was still virtually a stranger to her, and she laughed weakly. The wind howled through the trees, driving a stinging gust of snow into her eyes. She staggered on, until she ran into a massive tree that had been toppled by the storm.

The path was completely blocked, she couldn't climb over the immense tangle of branches and roots, going around would take her off the faint trail she was following, so she tried to crawl under it. She fought her way through the twisted, broken branches and found herself in a small space that was sheltered from the worst of the storm.

She huddled there, relieved to be out of the relentless wind even as she shivered. Realizing she needed to move, she collected the broken branches that were scattered on the ground and piled them together, then sat on them, hoping there would be enough to help insulate her from the cold ground. Finally, she lay down and tucked her uninjured hand under her armpit. *Stay awake, Brooke.* She stared into the darkness, listened to the storm blowing, and wondered how long it would take them to find her body. At least that alien monster would not win. Her eyes closed, then snapped open. *Don't fall asleep, Brooke!* Her mind filled up with nightmarish images of Drace and his experiments, and she pushed the thoughts away. She was safe from him, and if she died here, she would be dying in her world. She could accept that.

Chapter Twenty-One

EARTH DATE: JUNE 24
Sol Star System, The Starship Exanthus

"YOU MIGHT AS WELL COME out, Draakon, you are not going to get past us," T'Vass said.

"Don't make me kill all of you." Theiv replied, pissed that his plan had fallen apart.

"Drace doesn't want you killed, Draakon." T'Vass returned. "He didn't say we couldn't injure you, though. Do you think he might want to make a Zemyneah, out of you?" The three men laughed. "Ass fucked, Dragon Warrior. Do you think you will like it as much as a Zemyneah?"

Theiv ignored their words. He was a Dragon Warrior, and he'd long ago learned to control his emotions and his actions. He coolly laid down fire as he sprinted towards another station closer to the door. Return fire lit up the room, as Drace's men tried to take him down.

From his new position, he looked up and paused. A mirror was mounted on the wall opposite him, and he could see the exact position of every person in the room. From that moment on, this fight was his. Coldly, systematically, Theiv Draakon, Dragon Warrior, worked his way around the room, killing each of the men who Drace had sent to apprehend him. There would be no experiments on a Dragon Warrior this day.

Chapter Twenty-Two

EARTH DATE: JUNE 24
  Sol Star System, The Starship Exanthus

DRACE LOOKED AT THE four men in his suite. They were hardened warriors, but ones with few scruples, the kind he needed for his missions. They thoroughly discussed the plan, and he was satisfied that they covered every contingency. He turned to grab his phase gun and saw his Zemyneah, Laila, tied naked on his bed, her legs spread, her cunt on display for all the men in the room. Her breasts, and body still held the marks of the last hours spent in service. He walked over to her and released her bonds. She rose gracefully to her knees, never meeting his eyes, her head bowed submissively. "When we return, I'll expect you to entertain my men again. You may return to your rooms. You'll be notified when you are required."

"Yes, sir." Laila replied with a soft voice.

Drace handed her a black silk wrap. She put it on and stood up, walking gracefully towards the exit, pausing as he spoke. "And Laila, I will expect your total compliance this time." His voice was gentle. "I am sure you learned your lesson."

Laila swallowed, and pressed her trembling hands against her stomach. "Yes, sir." Her voice a husky sound in the silent room.

"Off you go then, get some rest, you will need your energy when we return."

"Thank you, sir." She said, and stepped in front of the exit, feeling the lust of the men in the room. The door slid open with a slight hiss, and she walked out.

Drace turned to his men, his eyes traveling over them. Knowing the situation, they would encounter with his missing experiment, he'd made sure that these men glutted themselves on Laila. "It's time to collect my missing Zemyneah slave. Please remember that it is entirely possible she will be putting off an extraordinary quantity of pheromones. Laila will fill all your needs when we return. You will maintain control until you are with Laila." He looked at the leader. "You have the readings?"

The big warrior looked at his device and nodded. "The coordinates are stable."

"Let's go then." Drace said.

The room lit up with a brilliant flash and they disappeared.

Chapter Twenty-Three

EARTH DATE: JUNE 24
Sol Star System, The Starship Exanthus

THEIV STOPPED OUTSIDE a door in the crew quarters, glanced around carefully, then touched the pad that would let the occupant know of his presence. Moments later the door slid open, and he stepped inside.

Laila was waiting just inside the entryway. She was a tiny woman, with large grey eyes and black hair that curled down to her waist. She'd been a Zemyneah slave her whole life but owned by Drace Aphelion for only three years. "Theiv! Drace was looking for you!"

"Laila. I don't have a lot of time." Theiv paused and looked at her face. Something seemed off. "Are you ok, Laila?"

"Theiv, he flashed to the planet with his men. They're going to try to recapture his experiment!" Her voice was urgent, her hands clenched.

Theiv swore. "Do you have what we discussed?"

Laila hurried over to her computer station and opened a hidden compartment. She took out a black pouch and handed it to Theiv. "That is all I could get. If Havyn is careful, it should last her a few days."

Theiv took the pouch and tucked it into his pocket. "Do you want me to get you off here? I won't be back."

Laila shook her head sharply. "I need to stay here. Drace and his men will need to be... distracted. I am good at that."

Theiv nodded once, gravely, knowing the risk she was taking. "Be careful Laila, Drace is dangerous."

Laila gave a short off-key laugh, her arms crossing her chest. "I can handle Drace."

Theiv's eyes searched hers. There was nothing more he could say, they both had their missions, and they both understood the risks involved. Laila had the courage of a Dragon. "I'm going to flash, turn away so your eyes are not damaged. May the Creators keep you safe." He waited for her to turn around and then activated the military flash technology. A bright light filled the room, and he was gone.

Chapter Twenty-Four

EARTH DATE: JUNE 25 12:17 AM
Canadian Military Base, Rocky Mountains

THEIV FLASHED INTO chaos. Absolute chaos. Armed men were rushing around. He could hear orders being issued from commanding officers, and then he heard his name called. He turned, caught a brief glimpse of Havyn, Riak, and T'lain just before a dark-haired man barrelled into him. He went down amid a flurry of punches and curse words. He didn't know what the hell was going on, but he was a trained Dragon Warrior. He tossed the man and sprang to his feet. The fight was brutal. Hard punches exchanged. Blood flowed. They went down a second time, and hard hands tore them apart. Sev and Storm. Staggering to his feet, he wiped away a thin trickle of blood and glared at the man who'd started it. "What in the seven hells, Clay? Why did you attack me?"

"Where is she, you bastard"

Theiv raised his eyebrow, wincing at the pain and ignored the blood trickling down his face. First, he was attacked on the Exanthus, now here. Crossing his arms, he ignored the question and looked at Sev who was holding

Clay back. "Explain what is going on." He looked around the room and saw armed guards holding Havyn, Riak, and T'lain. His stare could have frozen boiling water. Storm was the one who answered. "Brooke is missing. We've turned this base upside down. She is not here. Where have you been?"

Theiv growled. "You lost my woman?"

Clay began to struggle against Sev, cursing violently. "She isn't yours, you bastard. You fuckers kidnapped her and experimented on her. Did you give her back to that bastard that took her in the first place? Or is he just a part of some fucking elaborate story you made up to con us into believing you were the fucking hero." Theiv's eyes narrowed.

"Release Havyn, she's in no condition to be manhandled, and held as a hostage for things she didn't do. If it weren't for Havyn, Brooke wouldn't have survived." His words were icy. "While you are detaining me and my people, Drace could be on his way out of this galaxy with Brooke. Have you considered that?" His hand itched to shove into his pocket and activate the flash technology, he could be out of here in a microsecond. The tracker he'd put on her would tell him instantly where to look, but what would happen to Havyn and the two scientists if he did? "Let me go, I will find Brooke."

"You'd like that, wouldn't you?" Clay sneered, fury in every line of his body.

"Clay." Havyn's voice, filled with urgency, carried across the area, "For Theiv to harm Brooke, would be for him to harm himself. You don't seem to understand that he is bound to her, just as she is to him. He is our *only* chance of finding her. Let him go. He is a Dragon Warrior, a man of honor. You must trust him."

Clay shoved Sev hard away from him and turned to face Havyn, his face set in harsh lines. "I don't have to trust him or any of you. You are all guilty. You fucking experimented on her."

Havyn gave the men who guarded her a furious look, then pushed past them to stride over to Clay. "I'm guilty. Riak and T'lain are guilty." She stopped right in front of Clay and glared. "Theiv is not. He isn't a scientist, nor is he controlled by Drace. He's a Dragon Warrior, an elite class of warriors whose motto is honor, integrity, and justice. He's not guilty of anything but saving a woman that he did not know. Of attempting to save your race."

"Enough." Theiv shouldered a black pack sitting among the containers he'd transported in with, and walked over to Havyn and Clay, ignoring Storm and Sev as they moved into places where they could stop any further violence. "Clay, you have every right to your anger. The Zemyneah Protocol is wrong. What Drace attempted to do through Brooke is evil. I will bring your mother home." Then he touched his flash device and disappeared in a bright burst of light.

Chapter Twenty-Five

EARTH DATE: JUNE 25 12:45 AM
Canadian National Park, Rocky Mountains

THEIV REAPPEARED IN a flash of light that lit up the driving snow in a spectacular burst, reminding him of how the stars appeared when you entered hyper-warp drive in a starflyer. He looked around glad to see that he was not on the Exanthus. He'd engaged the homing mode when he'd activated the flash device. A simple failsafe he'd put into the transport tool to enable him to flash directly to Brooke, if Drace took her. The wind blew a hard gust and frozen bits of snow stung his face. Ignoring the sting, he turned, initiating the light built into the sleeve of his uniform. Scanning the area, he paused, his light sliding over a twisted broken traveling machine. His gut clenched, but he forced himself to walk over to the wreck. Crouching down to look inside, relief surged through him. She wasn't there.

He shrugged off the pack he'd brought back from the Exanthus and took out a small scanner. Sweeping it back and forth, he frowned at the series of beeps, indicating the presence of blood, then looked at the screen. Brooke had been in this mangled steel trap. The scanner showed an exact match. Swearing at the amount of blood indicated on the small screen, he stood up and turned the scanner to sweep across the area. It began to beep again, and he contemplated the snowdrift covered landscape. She had, of course, gone in the direction that was most covered in snow, totally obliterating any tracks. The temperature was a cold minus eighteen degrees Celsius and falling fast. His climate-controlled uniform at least made this a doable rescue. He checked the scanner again for direction to make sure the signal remained strong. When it showed a clear signal, he took out his flash device and looked at it regretfully. The signature a flash jump left behind was highly distinguishable to scanners. He'd used it with the hope of landing exactly where Brooke was. It hadn't worked that way. The technology had taken him to a five-kilometer radius of where she could be. The storm created issues with its targeting protocols. He could not risk another jump. The chance of Drace homing in on the signal was too high. With regret, he tossed the small device onto the ground and brought the hard heel of his boot down on it, smashing it to tiny pieces. There would be nothing to trace now. Shouldering the pack, he set off through the blowing snow, on an alien world, knowing he was the only chance Brooke had.

Chapter Twenty-Six

EARTH DATE: JUNE 25 4:00 AM
Canadian National Park, Rocky Mountains

BY THE DRAGON'S BREATH it's cold on this planet. Theiv rubbed his hands over his face, then rubbed them brisky together in a vain attempt to warm them. His scanner showed the temperature was at -27° Celsius. With a low growl he tapped the sleeve of his uniform, extending the invisible climate control energy field to cover his whole body. Flexing his hands as they began to warm, he read the information filling the screen of the scanner with blue light. In the distance, he could hear the howls of an unknown creature, and he wondered what animal would be out in a storm like this or what had disturbed it.

The data on the scanner indicated that he was close to his target. The tracker had not moved for a long time. He prayed to the Creators that she had found shelter. The snap of an energy weapon discharging filled the air a split second before the distinctive sound of laser energy filled the air. The energy burst hit the tree he was shelter behind, a mere millimeter from his head. Bark sprayed out in a cloud of dust and debris. Cursing, he dove for cover. Peering, carefully around the bush he pocketed the scanner, and palmed his laser pistol. Drawing deeply on his connection to his Dragon, his eyes began to glow with purple light. His dragon enhanced night vision clearer than it had ever been. A quick scan of the forest around him revealed members of Drace's private security team moving silently through the trees. Fuck!

His eyes swept over the night dark landscape, and he growled low in frustration. The snow clearly showed every footprint. His and Drace's team.

An icy gust of wind swept through the forest, swaying the trees, and sending snow devils swirling. Taking advantage of reduced visibility, he jumped up, and caught the thick branch above his head swinging himself to land under the next tree. He repeated the action and managed to land behind a large shrub that grew at the base of a large evergreen tree. He hadn't gone far, but he hoped it would give him a slight advantage. His eyes fell to the footprints of the enemy soldiers and he began to plan his next move. The hunters were about to become the hunted.

Dragon scales rippled over his body, and he felt his dragon connect to him over the vast reaches of space. *F'tal.* He touched the mind of his partner and friend. Knowledge of the Dragons of Althanea was murky at best for those who were not of the elite Dragon Warrior class. Some thought the dragons to merely be an animal controlled by the Dragon Warriors. Others believed the lies the powerful Protectors of the Sacred Way Sect spread in their hatred for the Dragon Warriors, proclaiming that the Dragon Warriors were possessed by the evil dragons they rode and fought alongside. The truth of the dragons was something the sect would never accept. For the Dragons of Althanea where an ancient race, some of them capable of shifting to humanoid form. They were beings of power with a great intelligence that surpassed even the wisest of the Sect's rulers. A Dragon Warrior was connected through blood and mind with the Dragon he rode and fought beside. They were partners, and most formed deep friendships. When the dragon chose the warrior he would fight beside, he bit him, an agonizing moment that carried the risk of death with it. That instant started a chain reaction in the Warrior, changing him forever. A silent communication path developed. The warrior gained the protection of the dragon's scales and the mark of the dragon appeared on his body, in the form of a dragon's image.

Do you have need of me?" F'tal's voice in his head was remarkably clear.

I'm too far away, old friend. I'll be fine. The dragon snorted in his mind and he grinned.

I sense a change in you, Theiv. F'tal's voice conveyed his concern.

Yes. There is a change, F'tal. We have much to discuss when I return.

I knew I should have come on this mission with you.

Dragons don't exactly fit on spaceships, even one the size of the Exanthus.

I would have come as a man.

Next time I will listen to you. And with those words, Theiv closed the communication path and selected his first target. Pulling a wicked knife from his boot, he silently moved through the forest of this alien world. Keeping to the shadows, he took advantage of the wind gusts and swirling snow to cover his movements, moving only with each snow filled gust. The first man died easily, silently. The struggle brief. The second man turned at the last moment, and managed to get a shout out, before Theiv's dagger ended his life. From then on, it was a battle. Two men rushed him, laser pistols firing. Theiv threw his knife, burying it deep in the first man's throat. The man dropped lifelessly to the ground, and Theiv ducked and rolled beneath the laser shots of the remaining target. He snatched up his knife and swung a wild punch to the jaw of the man with the laser pistol. The man staggered back dropping his weapon, then regained his footing and tackled Theiv. They went to the ground in a flurry of punches and disappeared from the view of the oncoming soldiers as a snow devil swirled around and over them. When the snow cleared, the man was dead on the ground with a broken neck, and the Dragon Warrior was nowhere to be seen.

Cursing and swearing, Drace stood with the last two of his warriors. The forest was silent except for the howl of the wind and the eerie call of an alien creature stalking the night. "Flash." Drace snapped, and a brilliant white light filled the forest at the exact same time as the snap of a laser pistol firing sounded.

Chapter Twenty-Seven

EARTH DATE: JUNE 25 5:00 AM
Canadian National Park, Rocky Mountains

BROOKE'S EYES SNAPPED open as a hard masculine hand pressed firmly over her mouth. Her muffled scream vibrated against warm skin as her arm was bumped. Dazedly, her heart racing with adrenaline, she recognized Theiv.

He gave her a little shake when she tried to jerk away from him, but she was so cold she could hardly move. "H-how—"

"Shh!" He hissed out as he slowly released her. "You have enemies here, Dragoness." His whisper was furious as he carefully looked around.

"Enemies?" Brooke huddled against the thick trunk of the tree, shaking from the cold, and carefully holding her arm.

Theiv frowned and touched her face. "You are too cold." He shrugged out of his jacket and draped it over her shoulders, deeply concerned with her injuries and the level of exposure she'd been subjected to. "We have to get you warmed up." He began to break branches to make more room in this most unlikely of shelters.

When he'd cleared a big enough area, he shrugged off the backpack, and pulled out a thin black material, thanking the gods he'd thought to bring his emergency go-bag from the ship. He worked efficiently, moving quickly to fit the high-tech waterproof cloth all around the roof and sides of their tree cave. The material clung securely to every surface he pressed it to, and in short order, they had a tent, of sorts. "This will help keep out the wind, light won't shine through, and it muffles sound."

He pulled a small square box out of the pack and set it on the ground. It began to glow a soft orange and Brooke felt a gentle heat. She scooted closer and held out her hand to the warmth.

Theiv took out a thick roll of material and spread it out on the floor, then he scooped Brooke up in his arms and settled her on the mat. Tugging a soft fleece-like blanket from his pack, he tucked it around her as best he could without covering her injuries. Brooke moaned softly when he jostled her arm.

"My apologies, Brooke." He murmured, as he assessed her injuries. He'd seen the blood around the vehicle's crash site, knew she'd been hurt, but the sight of her injuries made his gut twist. "Why, in the seven hells, don't your traveling machines have safety protocols?"

The wind outside blew against the walls of the shelter, but Brooke's violent shivering slowed as the little shelter warmed. She watched Theiv gather medical supplies, some of which looked foreign. "How—"

"How did you end up here?" He interrupted as he un-zipped her jacket, pausing when her posture stiffened. "Easy. I must check your injuries."

She nodded, steeling herself against the pain she was certain would come.

Theiv tried to be gentle, taking care not to cause more discomfort than necessary as he checked her over. His frown deepened as the extent of her injuries became clear to him.

"I was going home. Hit some black ice. Rolled down the cliff face."

"I found the wrecked travel machine." He flashed a small light in her eyes, his jaw turning to granite at her answer. *So, she'd run away.*

Pulling a small, blue packet from his pack, Theiv ripped it open and took out a damp cloth. On his planet, the medicated wipe was used to prevent infections. He had no idea if it would be as effective on this planet, but it was what he had, and it would have to do.

He gently wiped her face with it, wincing when he saw the long, jagged tear that sliced across her forehead and down her temple. He carefully cleaned it. "This cloth contains antibiotics to prevent most infections."

He carefully taped the wound closed, then helped her to take off her jacket. Her arm was swollen, badly bruised, and the angle of her forearm was wrong.

Brooke closed her eyes breathing away the nausea that rose in her throat.

"I need you to lie down, Brooke, your arm is broken, and I must immobilize it. If you faint. . . then you will not aggravate your injuries."

Brooke nodded and let him assist her. He knelt over her and searched through his bag some more. He brought out what looked like a netted material, assuring her it would turn into a hard splint when he applied it.

He gave her a shot of something for pain, and then he quickly and efficiently splinted the arm and wrapped it. Even with the pain shot, it was agonizing. Brooke clenched her teeth and fought to contain her groans of pain, fighting the darkness that was threatening to encroach. A cold sweat broke out over her body and she shivered.

"I'm sorry for the pain I caused, Dragoness. I did not have time to put together a full medical kit." He gently lifted her and tipped a container to her lips. She drank thirstily. When she finished, he eased her back down and tucked the fleece blanket securely around her, before sitting back against the tree trunk. "So, Brooke, we are finally alone."

Brooke burst out laughing. "There are easier ways to be alone with me."

"You're not afraid of me?" Theiv gave her a dark look.

"I probably should be, you look angry enough to scare the bravest, but you've never hurt me."

Theiv reached out and gently tugged a short spiky piece of hair. "I am angry. And there will be consequences for this foolish course you have chosen, but not here while you are hurting." He ignored the anger that flashed in her eyes. "We must leave as soon as the storm abates. I believe that Drace has a team in the area. I saw a flash in the forest to the west, about 5 km away from your crashed machine."

"He found me again? So soon?" Brooke closed her eyes and took a deep breath, and then another as she struggled to contain her urge to jump up and run. Was there nowhere she could escape him?

Theiv watched her intently. "I have the same questions. Especially when we consider that I neutralized all the tracking devices he implanted." He paused and tilted his head as if he were listening, holding up his hand for quiet. "I think the wind has stopped." Edging out of their shelter he looked up into a clear night sky before crawling back inside. "The storm is over."

He began to dismantle the little tent he'd created and put everything away into his pack, then he shrugged into his uniform jacket, and took a second identical coat from the pack. "This will keep you warmer than the one you were wearing." He helped her to put it on, and as he drew up the fastener, their eyes met. He could smell her pheromones and his dick hardened, but he understood the cold hard facts that surrounded the sexual tension they were both feeling. Her body was attempting to heal her, and it could do that more efficiently if it had access to more energy. Zepto technology was an unfeeling bitch. He broke eye contact and assisted her out of their shelter. As they stood, he brought out the scanner once more, determined to retain his control. "According to the GPS there is a small town approximately seven kilometers to the east." He turned his gaze to the woman at his side. "Are you able to journey that far?"

Brooke nodded. "I run that distance every day. What are your plans after we get to that town?"

"Finding a safe place to rest and getting something to eat is the priority." He looked out over the forest assessing the easiest way through the towering green trees. "Then, Brooke, we will talk."

Never in her life had Brooke been so tempted to close down communication with a "whatever," as she was at that moment. There was an FFT for everything, she thought, "Effing first time." Not that she would say the full acronym out loud. Though, come to think of it, it was possible there would be an FFT for that too, especially if her future continued to spin wildly out of control. She cast a mutinous look at the tall alien beside her. "Communication is good," she said, as they started to walk. "As long as you understand this is my life we are talking about, and I will be the one who makes the decisions for my life."

Theiv held on to his temper, a muscle in his jaw jumping as he clenched his teeth. "This is my life, too, Brooke. The decisions will be made together."

She wanted to scream, but she simply kept walking. *His life? Really?* He was not the one they experimented on. He was not the one whose body was out of control. She hated what those aliens had done to her. Hated it! *How dare those blue skinned*—she cut off her thoughts, horrified. *Blue skinned?* What on earth was she thinking? Never in her life had she judged a race based on their skin colour. Was she going to allow what that evil man had done to influence the bedrock of her values? Was she going to let what had been done to her change even the most important parts of her? To be angry with the man who committed such a great evil was justified, to hate his entire species because of his actions, was not. She took a deep breath, her mind and heart heavy.

Chapter Twenty-Eight

EARTH DATE: JUNE 25 4:00 PM
Canadian National Park, Rocky Mountains, Unknown Town

SHE WOULD HAVE LIKED the procurement of a "safe place to rest and eat" to have been a simple matter, but her new normal seemed to include her life spinning wildly out of control. Apparently, simple was not in the plans of the universe. She stood, shivering, in the alley between the bank and a diner, as she waited for Theiv to use his device to convince the ATM to give him some cash. Heavens, she was a criminal now too! And she wasn't even going to think about the vehicle that she stole and wrecked. Clay was going to arrest her! She put her hand over her face and breathed deeply. She knew that Theiv was right, if they contacted the base, they would be taken back there and right now she needed time to think and adjust to her new normal. Even if that time was likely to only be a day. If they could get a motel room, she would be able to contact her family and Nissa.

Theiv appeared at the entrance to the alley. He glanced around, then hurried over to her. "You did not tell me cameras were recording everyone at the ATM. It's a good thing that my scanner detected it before I entered the building. I was able to disable it for the time I was in there." Theiv handed the thick stack of cash to Brooke and paused when he saw her eyes widen. "I did not know how much would be needed." He shrugged. "I took what was in the machine."

Oh heavens! She nodded and swallowed, *Clay was going to freak out*, then pointed to a sign attached to the side of the building she faced. "We could try this bed and breakfast. It will be more private than a motel." Stuffing the money into her jacket pocket, she waited to see if Theiv could bring up the place on his weird GPS thingy.

A few minutes later, they stood on the outskirts of town, looking at a beautiful yellow Victorian house. Brooke thought wistfully of her own home before looking at Theiv. "I'll tell the owner that I had an accident in the storm and need a room for the night. I look the part." She said with a sigh, "And this jacket you gave me almost looks like a police issue jacket. With luck, they will think I was dropped off here by the police. Wait out of sight." He gave her a silent nod and walked around the corner of the building. Taking a deep breath, she opened the door, and stepped into the warmth. She was back outside minutes later, clutching keys and looking for Theiv. He stepped out of some trees that lined the edge of the property, and she led him to the second-floor entrance of their room.

The door closed behind them and they both just stared at each other and the room. It was beautiful— a king sized bed, fireplace with a sitting area, and a huge bathroom.

Walking over to the bathroom, she peeked in. *Oh. My. Gosh. The bathroom of my fantasies!* A huge deep tub, and a massive shower took center stage. She sighed longingly, then turned and looked around the room again noticing the phone on a side table. She glanced at Theiv as he set his pack on the floor. "You can have the first shower. I just want to sit down for a few minutes, I'll order take out for us."

"Take out?" Theiv frowned, his translator not offering any translation.

"Something to eat." Brooke supplied, then bit her lip. "What sorts of food do you like?"

"Anything. Your human food is enjoyable." He looked at her intently as she shrugged off the jacket he'd given her. Her skin glowed in the dim light of the room revealing the iridescent pattern of the dainty flowering vine that he knew covered her body, even in the most intimate places.

His dick hardened, and he wanted nothing more than to tear off her clothes, revealing that magnificent body, highlighted by that pretty vine that marked her as his. He wanted to feast on her pussy, and suck on those sensitive nipples. He wanted to take her to the brink over and over again. He wanted to play with her, in the most erotic ways, do all the things he didn't have the time to do the first time. By the gods, wasn't he a sick bastard for wanting a woman whose injuries were a stark reminder of the danger they faced? He tore his gaze away from her, understanding that it was the Zeptos at work in him, and the scent of the exotic pheromone she was releasing now that they were in a safe place. It was a cold, hard fact of science that, after all the energy she'd expended, after the injuries she'd received, she would need sex to heal, to survive. Sexual starvation was a perversion of science, but in a Zemyneah slave, it was an unrelenting fact.

Their eyes met and held, tension building as the pheromone became a richer exotic scent that drifted through the air. Tearing his eyes from hers, he shrugged out of his jacket and toed off his boots, then turning he walked into the bathroom and shut the door.

Brooke stared after Theiv, her eyes wide. Her heart was thundering in her chest, her nipples were hard, and she was panting. And she'd known if he'd taken her as she'd thought he was going to, she would have been ready for him. She crossed her legs and took several deep breaths, stunned by how fast she'd become aroused. The shower turned on in the bathroom and she had to blink away visions of wet, hard, muscled flesh. She blinked. FFT. Blue was the new sexy. She laughed softly and forced herself to pick up the telephone and dial.

"Where the fuck are you?"

"Language." Brooke tried to sound stern. "I'm safe, Clay. Theiv found me."

"Where are you? I'll come and get you, or better yet, I'll call Jaxson to come and get you."

Brooke shook her head. "No, Clay. I'm safe and I need a little time. Just give me some time."

"At least call Jaxson and Dani. They need to talk to you."

"I'll––I'll try, Clay." She was silent for a moment, her emotions running riot. "Clay? I can't let that monster take me again."

Silence. "I know, Brooke." Silence. "We'll keep you safe. I promise."

"Don't promise, Clay. You can't possibly keep that promise." Her voice broke. Silence. She closed her eyes, trying to find her composure. She was his mother. She needed to be strong.

"Brooke? Mom."

It was so rare that he called her mom, Brooke fought the tears.

"Mom, I will do everything in my power to keep you safe."

"Thank you," she whispered. Oh god, she could not let him risk himself. She couldn't do it. She was his mom. It was her job to protect her kids. Even her grown up independent children. Helplessness overwhelmed her. How could she protect her family from a being who was so technologically superior? Her hand lifted to cover her mouth, as a sob threatened to break out. She forced herself to remember the fact that her kids were strong, resilient, capable, intelligent adults. Her job was to trust in that, and them. "After..." She took a breath. "After Theiv and I eat and talk, I'll put in a group call to you, Jaxson, Dani, and Nissa. We'll figure out the next steps." She heard the relief in his voice as they said their goodbyes, and she quietly hung up the phone.

The shower was still running, so she ordered pizza and then set about making herself a tea from the small supply in a basket on a table close to the tiny sitting area. The gas fireplace drew her. She couldn't seem to get fully warm. Shivering, she turned on the flames and curled up in a chair to sip her tea.

Theiv came out of the bathroom, wearing his pants, rubbing his hair with a towel. He paused when he saw her curled up by the fireplace. "Tea?" He stepped closer to her chair and leaned down to inhale the aroma coming from the cup. 'It smells like the achara tea that my mom and sister like. They claim it is the cure for everything." He gave her a bit of a smile. "Is it not strange, how we come from worlds that are light years apart, and yet, here there is this touching point." The pheromones hit him with the weight of a million dragons, and he reached out, his finger gently tracing the upward slope of her ear to the point.

Arousal flooded her as she stared up at this beautiful male and she swallowed, shivering at his touch. Something unrecognized and foreign, deep inside of her, wished to feel his touch on other exquisitely sensitive parts. His words played in her mind and she took a breath. "A touching point." She swallowed, her eyes meeting his, her mind filling with images of his fingers tracing over her skin. "Tea." She latched onto the word like a lifeline. "Tea is a meeting point in..." she rose to her feet. "In my culture too." Oh heavens, she was stumbling over her words. Where was her cool-headed counselor persona? *Buried under a wave of unrelenting lust.* The voice in her head spoke with a slight trace of humor laced heavily with hard truth. "I, uhm." She gestured towards the table. "The pizza came while you were in the shower. Help yourself." Turning, she hurried into the bathroom and shut the door, where she leaned against the cool wood taking deep breaths, mortified by the demands of this new body.

Theiv watched the door behind which Brooke had disappeared. He heard the shower turn on and visions of her naked and wet filled his mind. He took a step towards the door, his hand reaching out to rest on the wood, knowing that her need must be great to be projecting the images she'd been unknowingly telepathing into his mind. He opened the bathroom door. The interior was warm, steamy, and infused with the exotic scent that was uniquely Brooke. She sang quietly in the shower, absorbed in her ablutions her skin glowing softly in the dim light.

Theiv hesitated, his mind going back to the conversation he'd had right before he'd flashed away to find Brooke. It had been short, intense. The focus on doing whatever it took to save Brooke's life. The consensus being to call on the Zemyneah, rather than wait for an invitation that might never come. He'd argued against what he felt sure Brooke would take as a betrayal, but the Earth doctor, Reed, and Havyn reminded him of Brooke's continued refusal to accept the changes to her body. If the worst circumstances were how he found Brooke, if she was injured, then action would have to be taken if she were to survive. He would have to rely on the Zemyneah protocols to save her. And through all their arguments, all their logic, Theiv remembered his mother. Now, standing in this bathroom, with the naked woman that held the power of life and death over him, only a few short feet away, Theiv thought of his mother. His fierce, funny, loving mother, a woman forced to become Zemyneah, and he remembered how his father fought for the woman he loved. He knew he could do no less. He turned around and walked out of the bathroom.

Sitting down on the edge of the bed, he looked back at the bathroom, before reaching into his pocket for the device that had been given to him moments before he flashed. He touched the screen then activated the sole number the device contained. "Clay. This is Theiv. Brooke is safe." He looked over at the bathroom door again, knowing he lied. Brooke wouldn't be safe until they had sex, but there was nothing that would compel him to force that choice upon her. If she chose death for them both, then so be it. But he would ensure that she was at least in a safe place. "Can you come to us? I believe it is imperative to take Brooke home."

Chapter Twenty-Nine

EARTH DATE: JUNE 25 7:00 PM
    Canadian National Park, Rocky Mountains, Unknown Town

BROOKE CAME OUT OF the bathroom dressed in one of the robes that had been hanging on the back of the bathroom door, rubbing her wet hair with a towel. She would say one thing about alien medical technology, it was extremely helpful that their casting material could get wet.

Theiv stood up. "Do you trust me, Brooke?"

She paused and eyed him skeptically. What did he want? As she studied him, her mind went to the moment he caught her cutting her hair, and the way he encouraged her act of rebellion. The first fragile threads of trust had been born in that moment. Brooke tilted her head, staring into Theiv's unusual purple eyes as she reached out tentatively with the bond. Theiv froze at her first cautious touch, letting her into his mind, fiercely proud that she'd made this first step.

Unable to help herself, Brooke looked down the bond and felt Theiv open further to her, holding nothing back. She saw his memories of his mother. And felt his crushing despair when she was sentenced to be Zemyneah. Her heart ached for the young man he'd been even as she felt his utter rejection of doing that to any woman. Understanding seeped into her consciousness and swept her past his memories to the present and his internal conflict. He was a high-ranking Dragon Warrior, and he had a mission to complete, a mission now compromised by his decision to protect her at all costs. Her breath caught, horrified comprehension filling her, as she understood their lives were irrevocably joined. And Theiv was willing to sacrifice his life if she couldn't accept what that meant. He was determined to disappear if she rejected his bond, to allow the Zeptos in his system to fail. She could feel his desperate hope that the experimental Zepto technology in her system would continue to protect her, to mutate and overcome the bonding process. In that shocking moment, Brooke understood the true sacrifice this man was willing to make for her.

She remembered thinking she'd never known a man like him, and she was right. She could not be the destruction of this good man, and her heart, so brutally shattered by a violation so evil that she could not comprehend it, opened the tiniest bit. Healing just enough to allow this one being who counted her as worthy, inside. "Oh, Theiv," she whispered. "You should've come to me."

"I will not force you. If you choose to accept this bond with me, you do so of your own free will."

Brooke stared at him, her eyes searching his. To be with him was not a hardship. Hardship? That was the best sex she'd ever had. What scared her was the knowledge that Drace was still hunting her. Theiv's life was in danger no matter what choice she made. She took a deep breath. If Theiv was willing to risk his life to save her, then she must be brave enough to live. She undid the robe, heard Theiv's swift intake of breath, and then she shrugged it off completely, letting the material pool at her feet.

Theiv stood slowly to his feet. He was such a big man compared to her. His chest and abdomen rippled with muscle. "Are you sure, Brooke? Be very sure because I won't be able to stop once I start." His purple eyes looked deeply into hers.

How had she got to be forty-eight years old and never asked a man to be her lover? She'd hoped that dropping the robe and standing naked in front of him would do the trick. Except, Theiv was a man of honor. So, she took a breath and found the words. "I'm sure, Theiv. Would you be my lover?"

He reached out, and drew her forward against his chest, cupping her head. The other hand gripped her hip, as he stared into her eyes, before slowly lowering his mouth to hers. Their lips brushed. A breath of air. He licked her lips, then gently nipped her bottom lip. She opened and his lips moved over hers. She lifted her uninjured hand and clasped his shoulder, and he thrust his tongue in to slide against hers. Her arm slid around his neck as she moaned softly, then he coaxed her tongue into his mouth where he suckled it before taking control of the kiss again. His hand came up off her hip and cupped her breast. His thumb rubbed against a hard nipple sending fire streaking to her womb and clit. When he broke the kiss, they were both breathing hard.

"God, I love your scent. It's like some exotic perfume." Theiv's voice was rough with desire. He nipped at her neck, then licked at the sting.

Brooke gasped as a bolt of electricity shot through her. She moaned and arched against him. She could feel her pussy swelling, her juices easing through her folds. Her hand stroked down his chest, slid over the taunt muscles of his abdomen.

Brooke pressed a kiss to his jaw. He drew back from her. Brooke opened her eyes in surprise. He stared down at her, his cheeks flushed, his eyes glittering wildly with his hunger.

"Theiv?"

"Brooke, I want you, but not like last time. I know your body is pushing you to have sex. I know the Zeptos are working hard to drive up your desire, but I want you to be fully conscious of the choice you are making. There will be no going back from this. Your choice, but choose now, because I don't seem to have much control around you, and later will be too late."

Brooke bit her lip. She understood what he was saying, but there was far more going on here than the technology that had integrated into her system. She inhaled his wild clean scent and knew, as long as she lived, she would always wonder if she didn't say yes to this moment, to this man. "Yes." Her voice was a husky whisper. "Yes. I want you."

And then he was walking her backwards to the bed. He lifted her and she suddenly found herself tossed onto the bed, and he was coming up over her like a conquering warrior. Her hand came up to press against his chest even as her body flamed with lust. He captured her hands and pressed them up by her head, careful of her injury.

"Keep them there." It was a rough growl. A faint smile touched her lips at his command, but wow, she shivered feeling more cream easing from between her folds. He took her mouth in a rough kiss. His tongue demanding entrance, surging into her mouth, gliding against her tongue. She moaned when he broke the kiss, her hand lifting to clench in his hair, but he moved down her body pressing kisses and sharp little nips to her neck, then her collar bone. His hands filled with her breasts, his fingers tugging at her nipples, then he was licking at her painfully hard tips. His hand cupped one breast as he sucked the other nipple into his mouth. He sucked and licked, alternating hard suction with soothing licks. His fingers caught her other nipple and plucked at it, played with it. Brooke gasped and bucked against his hands when he switched nipples. Reaching up she grabbed a handful of his hair to hold his head to her breast. He nipped her in punishment and removed her hand from his hair pressing it back against the bed by her head. "Keep them there."

Brooke panted, her head moving restlessly against the pillow. She was on fire.

Theiv's hands moved down her stomach and over her mound. His fingers found her pussy and he slid between the swollen sensitive folds. He circled her clit and her hips shot up off the bed. "Please!" The word burst past her lips.

He caught her hips and pressed her back to the bed, his eyes meeting hers with glittering wildness as he moved down forcing her thighs to open wide to accommodate his broad shoulders. Lifting her knees, he pressed them apart until she lay open before him. His thumbs caught her lips and spread them. "So beautiful," he muttered, his voice a harsh rasp, and he licked her. Brooke's back arched, her head pressed back into the pillow, shocked at the intensity. Her hands clenched into the blankets. She was stunned to realize that she was making little pleading noises. His tongue circled her clit. Shudders raced through her. It was so good, so amazing, why hadn't she known how good this could be? He suckled her swollen clit then pulled back and drove his tongue deep inside her. She moaned, her fingers clenching the sheets. He went back to her clit and licked it vigorously. Her body tightened and she could feel her orgasm racing towards her. He pulled back and thrust his tongue inside her again. She gasped and arched desperate to have him back at her clit. He licked through her folds and circled her clit and then he sat back on his knees away from her.

Brooke gasped and stared at him. "No. I––I need..."

Theiv stared back at her through glittering eyes. His erection stood up hard and thick against his stomach glistening with pre-cum.

"Not yet. Turn over." Then his hands were holding her hips urging her onto her hand and knees. His hand pressed between her shoulder blades urging her chest down. She trembled at his dominance, but found herself submitting, her pussy aching to be filled, wetness easing through her folds, coating her. She felt the tip of his heavy erection pressing up against her slit. She shivered then moaned as he slid in an inch. She pressed back desperate to be filled, but he had a firm grasp on her hips, and she couldn't move. She could only feel his slow deliberate possession. Whimpering as every millimetre of hot hard cock slowly filled her, burning, stretching, until he was fully seated inside her. She writhed helplessly in his grip. "Please! Please! I need more!" she begged. But still, he didn't move holding her in place as her body adjusted to his. Finally, he drew back until only the tip was inside her then he thrust forward. She gasped. He withdrew and again thrust inside. And then she lost all track of everything except the intense pleasure of this man impaling her on his cock. She swept back up to that pinnacle. One more, just one more thrust and she would go over. She panted and tightened. He withdrew. "No!" she cried, shocked. "Please, Theiv, please!"

He flipped her over to her back. She frantically reached for his cock. He caught her hand and pinned it above her head. Then he was filling her again. Hard. Fast. His hips slamming into hers as his mouth came down over hers in a savage, wildly dominant kiss. Harsh breaths billowed out of his lungs, sweat rolled down his chest and dripped onto her. She wound her legs tight around his waist, and he held her wrist firmly pinned above her head. She was a wild panting creature of exquisite sensitivity. Her whole world narrowed down to the intense sensations pulsing through her, lifting her higher and higher, until she didn't know if she would survive.

"Come!" he commanded harshly, and she exploded. Shuddering and writhing, extreme pleasure sweeping through her in fiery glory, she screamed, her back arching as her orgasm soared impossibly higher.

She heard a male roar, his thrusts urgent, slamming into her, filling her with searing hot blasts of his seed. It seemed to go on and on. Sweeping her into a second orgasm, a whirlwind of emotion and colour and he was there, feeling everything with her, holding her, grounding her.

Finally, it eased, and she collapsed, gasping, panting. He followed her down. Her pussy milked his cock in a tight clasp sending shivers racing up her spine, and she felt the last of the hot spurts of his cum coating the inside of her sheath. His breath stalled, and he slumped over her, deep shudders racking his muscular frame, as he panted and swore quietly above her, his weight pressing her into the mattress.

A long minute passed before he rolled to the side, taking her with him and cuddling her against his body. And Brooke was afraid. Because this hadn't been a Zemyneah's commanded response. This had been a woman's response to her man. This involved feelings and her emotions, and that terrified her.

Chapter Thirty

EARTH DATE: JUNE 25 10:00 PM
   Canadian National Park, Rocky Mountains, Unknown Town

BROOKE WOKE UP TO THEIV drawing her into his arms. Holding her close, he idly trailed his fingers up her back and neck, then stroked the upward slope of her ear, his finger coming to rest at the tip. He'd done that last night too, she remembered.

Theiv lifted his head, and hesitated, before again stroking a gentle finger over the point of her ear. "Have you noticed that your ears have developed a slight point to them?"

Brooke blinked, then reached up to feel her ear. And right at the top she could feel a gentle slope and point where once there had only been a curve. She felt her other ear. It was the same. Elf ears? She had Elf ears? "Why... how could that happen?" She asked, confused.

"It must be the genetic material that was utilized in the experimental formula they administered to you. Drace was experimenting with DNA from several sources, and with the Zepto technology, he couldn't seem to find a formula that worked. Many women died," Theiv said, his voice grim, a muscle ticking in his jaw. "The Dragon Warriors were contacted by the Captain of the Exanthus, reporting strange and concerning events on his starship, and then they received an encrypted message by a trusted source that said the Emperor was at risk and naming Drace Aphelion. I was sent to investigate.

Havyn told me that Drace left the ship for a few weeks, after several test subjects died horribly painful deaths. That is the time when the Dragon Warriors were contacted, and I was installed as head of security.

Drace returned with more DNA samples. The experiments began again, in earnest. To activate his experimental formula, he combined the original Zemyneah serum, and a cocktail of genetic material and DNA taken from other species of humanoids.

We do not know exactly what was in the formula he gave you. He closely guarded his secrets, even from Havyn.

What you need to know is that there are many populations of humanoids in the universe. In particular, there are five alien hominid populations in this galaxy that are considered to be the most sexually driven. We believe that Drace harvested genetic material and DNA from each of those populations to create the base for his formula. We have always known that if he succeeded, his subject would have an extraordinary sex drive. We did not expect any of their physical characteristics to surface." He reached out and drew his finger lightly over the tip of her ear again. "Apparently we were short sighted."

Brooke, a flutter of arousal moving through her with Theiv's gentle touch, pulled away, sitting up and holding the sheet to her chest. A sense of foreboding filled her as she waited for Theiv to continue.

"Drace has committed countless murders in pursuit of his experiment. Any genetic material he obtained came at the cost of someone's life." Theiv sat up and leaned back against the headboard before speaking again, his next words careful. "Brooke, you have to realize that you are the living evidence of his crimes. His eyes met hers, his expression grim. "Your ears show that he murdered a woman under accord protection. Her planet is called Sarisia. Her people are a fierce race. I have no doubt that she would have fought to the death."

He could see Brooke's shock, but he knew that she needed to understand the full magnitude of the situation. "Your purple hair is of Althanean origin, probably from a Zemyneah. It is a rare colour, even for us. My mother has such hair." He kept his expression blank as he looked at Brooke. "She was forced to become Zemyneah when I was sixteen years of age."

Brooke gasped, horrified. "But... I thought wives were protected?"

"Unless they commit a crime. My mother discovered that my sister Iandra and her friend Ashiae had gone to a Zemyneah compound. They were attempting to find Ashiae's little sister, who had been recently relegated to become Zemyneah, after a physical exam showed a slight anomaly in her hearing. My mother went after them and got them out, but she was caught."

Brooke stared at Theiv, tears welling, her hand lifting to cover her mouth. She took a deep breath trying to force back the nausea churning in her stomach.

Theiv remained silent, swallowing against the brutal lump in his throat. He stared at the wall in front of him as he went through a mental exercise he'd learned as a new dragon warrior. When he finally spoke again, he'd managed to shut off all the dark emotions he'd almost let slip. "You're an astonishing being, Brooke. What Drace did, shouldn't have worked. Yet here you are."

He looked at her, and a frown crossed his face as he studied her before climbing out of the bed. He walked over to retrieve a small light from his pack beside the door. Sitting down on the edge of the mattress, he shone it on her hand. "The Amberisian mating mark we discovered earlier."

Brooke glanced at her hand. Her skin seemed to almost shimmer with a beautiful iridescence, the vine pattern glowing a pale blue in the darkness. She blinked at the soft iridescent colors shimmering over her skin, then looked at Theiv uneasily.

"I recognized it when you showed me, but I wanted to discuss it with Riak and T'lain. You seem to be good at shocking our scientists, Brooke. How is your night vision?"

"I can see better in the dark than I ever could before." She rubbed the arm with the cast and looked worriedly at the man who seemed to know far more about her than she did.

"Amberisia coming up again." He muttered. Moving behind her, he ran his hands down her back, felt her spine, felt her shoulder blades. Manipulated her uninjured arm while feeling along her upper back.

"What're you doing?"

His hands stilled, then he carefully ran his fingers down along the shoulder blade again, moved a few centimetres, and felt again. He let out a long low whistle. "Karis. By the Emperor. Karis as well. How did he get his hands on Karis DNA? Is he trying to start an intergalactic war?"

"Theiv?" Brooke's eyebrows drew together, and she leaned in closer to him.

"Tell me of any other changes you've noticed with your body, your abilities."

"I don't know what to tell you. Everything is different." She crossed her arms tightly over her chest and laughed bitterly. "I had a nightmare before I escaped the base. Except, it felt... real. I don't... It wasn't a nightmare, Theiv. I don't understand how, but Drace was communicating with me. Telling me his plans. He is," she shuddered, "a disgusting, evil creature." Her eyes lifted to Theiv's. "I couldn't let him find me again!" A sob escaped her. "Please, Theiv, just let me go home. I'm not just an experiment. I'm a human being, and I need to heal. Please." Her voice shook, and it was a punch to the gut hearing her anguish. He turned her to fully face him, his face carefully wiped of emotion, his hands firm on her arms. He couldn't save her if he gave into the compassion he felt in his heart. "Tell me about this incident with Drace."

Brooke shook her head. "I––I can't." she swallowed against the nausea rising in her throat.

"It's important." A muscle flexed in his jaw, his eyes staring into hers.

Brooke looked away, swallowing hard and fought the fear that choked her. "I was on the ship again. I heard his voice." Brooke shivered, "He said it wasn't a dream, that it was the continuation of his experiment. He said that he would retrieve me and harvest the women from earth." Tears spilled down her cheeks. "He said I am meant for two men." She shuddered and shook her head violently.

Theiv tightened his grip on her. "Brooke." His voice was grim, and he gave her a little shake when she tried to break away from him. "I do not believe this was a nightmare either."

Brooke froze. A terrible dread rising sharp and painful in her. "What do you mean?" she cried.

"I think Drace is deliberately tormenting you. It should not be possible, but as we've learned, he has achieved the impossible."

Brooke tried to move away from Theiv. "Let me go!"

He shook his head and pulled her fully into his arms, "No, little Dragoness, we will make this journey together."

Brooke began to shake her head. "I am going home. I won't let him do this to me!"

"How will you stop him, Brooke? He can reach you even from the vast distance of space. We must work together if we're going to end his madness." The look on Theiv's face was fierce. "We must stop him, and by the dragons, you will help me. Your world is at risk and so are others. I suspect the bastard used genetic material from a species called the Giastean. It's the only way he could've changed your genetics enough to telepathically communicate with you, and to create a physical need great enough that it could only be fulfilled by two males. Giastean genetics dictate that for procreation to happen, there must be two unrelated male sperm, and a single female ovum. They have an instinctive need to mark their mates. Often with a bite to the neck." Theiv grew silent and stared past Brooke. *No wonder, by the most ancient of creators, no wonder his attempt to track her resulted in a bond.*

Brooke shook her head, her mind racing with all the information that Theiv was telling her. "I don't... understand any of this."

"You do, Brooke, you just don't want to accept it, but you must. It is imperative for your survival that you understand what's happening to you. I think, from what I'm seeing, that you share DNA with five unique races. Much more than the small amount we thought Drace harvested. I believe that Drace created a rich cocktail of genetic material. It makes sense since he was seeking characteristics from each of these races for his ultimate Zemyneah. Your humanity seems to be the perfect medium to accept the DNA from the women he captured. If what I believe is true, then you contain genetic material from a woman from each of these worlds: Althanea, Sarisia, Amberisia, Karis, and Giastea.

How you survived, let alone adapted, is a miracle. Your body is evolving, Brooke. The different DNA combined with the Zepto technology is changing you. We need to get you to Havyn as soon as possible. This must be documented. And...." He paused, his voice growing hard. "The murder of five Accord-protected women must be made known."

Brooke stared at Theiv, her head slowly moving back and forth in denial. Her mouth opened, but no words came out.

She tried again. "He killed five women so he could do this to me?" Her voice was an anguished rasp as she fought to reconcile this terrible fact.

Theiv stared at her for a moment, seeing the horror in her eyes, then he pulled her into his arms. "Ah, Brooke, little one."

"Why? Why would he do this? He is evil!" Her voice was a broken, tormented wail.

Theiv continued to hold her. "I have you, little one. I have you." His voice was rough.

The pain, the agonized grief welling up inside of her was too much. There seemed to be no escape from this nightmare. How could she accept this terrifying truth? She struggled, tried to break free. Her screams were a terrible thing. Inconsolable. Tormented. Enraged. Theiv shuddered and held her tightly. And outside their room, the storm returned, raging along with them, roaring out its fury, shaking the building, and hiding the anguish in its midst.

Chapter Thirty-One

EARTH DATE: JUNE 26 6:00 AM
Canadian National Park, Rocky Mountains, Unknown Town

THE SKY WAS FILLING with the first greyish pink touches of sunrise and Brooke was numb. She swiped at the tears and looked at the alien who held her so protectively while she broke apart. There was a strength in this man that not many possessed. "Is there more?" she asked, her voice ragged.

Thciv felt as if he was an ancient being who had lived through too many horrors, but he nodded, then handed her a glass of water.

She gratefully accepted the water and took a long drink.

He watched her silently for a minute, then looked down at his hands. "The Amberisian DNA has consistently been present in the pheromones you produce, and our belief has always been that the pheromone was his goal. We did not expect your night vision to change, nor the iridescent glow to your skin, and the mating mark."

He took a drink from the glass she handed back to him before continuing. "The Amberisian race is nocturnal, which explains your night vision. They're beautiful in the moonlight, with their glowing skin. A trip to Amberisia is a trip of extraordinary sexual pleasure. Even the night flowers that grow on that planet produce aphrodisiacs. It's like sexual desire is in the very air you breathe."

Brooke stared at him speechlessly, her eyes wide. *There was such a world and such people?*

"The Karis are a very dangerous species. They are part of the accord, but they do not associate with any other race. They are isolationists, and never mate outside their own people. They have wings, Brooke. Their males are very dominant, their females are submissive, and they mate for life. Drace wanted that submissive quality in his experiment."

Brooke stared blankly at Theiv. "Am I going to grow wings?" she asked faintly.

"I don't know." His face was grim. "You've developed the bone structure in your back that would suggest wings are a possibility. I'm sorry, but I can't give you the answers you need. There simply has never been anyone like you. Havyn may be able to tell us more." Theiv watched Brooke silently as she processed the information.

"My main concern, at this moment, is that Drace has developed the ability to communicate with you, and the ability to be in your mind, accessing information that could lead him to you. As I am assuming you accessed information from him during that nightmare. I saw the video feeds. You did things you should not have even known you could do."

Brooke nodded stiffly, even as her veins seemed to fill with ice, and she struggled to breathe. *No. No. This can't be happening.*

Theiv tilted up her chin. "Breathe." He couldn't change the hard edge to his voice. Not if they were going to survive and evade Drace. This was not the time for panic. "The storm is subsiding, Brooke, and we need to go, Drace could be close."

"He's here? How do you know?" Brooke swallowed and grabbed Theiv's arm. "Can you use that light thing to get us out of here?"

Theiv shook his head. "I had to sabotage my own flash technology so that I couldn't be traced. I couldn't risk leading him right to you."

"How did you find me?"

Theiv shrugged. "Do you remember when I came to the room you were in on the Exanthus? I initiated a telepathic bond to you, and in case it failed, I put a tracker on you. The tracker itself is a type of Zepto Technology. It's far too small for the human eye to see and it migrates around the wearer's body, imitating the energy signature of the zepto's in their system, making it very hard to detect."

Brooke glared at the alien. She didn't care if he was one of the most beautiful men she'd ever seen. That was damned sneaky, and she was pissed. "Is that how Drace is tracking me?"

"No. That tracker is Dragon Warrior technology. As I said, he has access to your thoughts. The longer you remain in one place the closer he is getting."

"How do you know so much about this telepathy thing from the Gi-, Gee-"

"Giasteans. I know so much because my sister is mated to two men from Giastea."

Brooke stared. "I'm getting a headache," she muttered.

Theiv raised an eyebrow. "I told you my mom was forced to become Zemyneah to protect my sister. My father was devastated. He was one of the greatest warriors of the Empire, and no one was going to take the woman he loved. He went after her. Before he left, he made me promise to protect Iandra. I told the council my father had betrothed her to a wealthy man on another planet. They allowed me to take her, when she turned twenty-one, to her 'betrothed's' planet. We ended up stranded on a rough trader's world called The Forge. My craft was nothing but a patched-up bucket of sprockets, bolts, and injectors, but it was all I could afford. We were in serious trouble and I didn't know a lot about fixing a flyer.

There were many dangerous men on that planet. I went out to find some parts, and some men got the jump on me. They were in the process of beating the living hell out of me, when these two Giasteans showed up and kicked their asses.

They helped me back to my flyer." He shook his head, a faint smile curving his lips at the memories. "They took me under their wing so to speak. Taught me how to repair my ship. But they took one look at Iandra and fell in love with her. She was furious, of course, absolutely refused to have anything to do with them. They seemed to take that as a challenge.

Interestingly, somewhere in all their fighting, my sister managed to fall in love with those two idiots. They mated with her and took her to their world. Before they left, they formed a bond with me so that we could communicate."

"How did they do that?"

"They bit me."

Brooke glared at him, suddenly understanding how he'd formed that telepathic bond to her. "You bastard."

Theiv laughed. "I am a warrior, and my priority is to protect the Emperor. I feel no guilt over what I did. Now listen. You might need this information in the future. The Giastean, in a strange twist of fate, shares DNA with the large cats on your planet. They are human in appearance... mostly. They have larger canine teeth than a human and some of them have stripes and spots. They also have a strange need to build their houses in the tops of the trees of their world.

I do not fully understand the Giastean people, their ways, or why a bite forms a bond, but our scientists have long theorized it has something to do with a DNA exchange. It looks like we have proven that theory to be correct."

Brooke frowned, shaking her head. "This is insane. You must be making this up. I don't... I can't believe this stuff."

"We don't have a lot of time, Brooke. We need to get out of here." Theiv reached out, and hauled her against him, intending to help her out of the bed. Brooke gasped, and in a reflex so fast that she never would understand how she did it, she raked her nails down his face and leaped away from him.

Theiv lifted a hand to his bleeding face, and eyed the growling woman crouched back against the wall. Her eyes were glowing green, and he could smell the exotic spice of her pheromones. "Definitely Giastean."

Brooke's eyes were huge. She'd... She looked at her hand... claws. Claws! That disappeared before her eyes. Just like before. She lifted confused eyes to Theiv.

"Giastean. I told you." He pulled one of his medicated wipes from his backpack and swiped it over the long furrows in his cheek.

Brooke winced. "I'm sorry. I didn't mean to..."

"I deserved it. I shouldn't have grabbed you like that. I think we can safely say that Drace's attempt at coding your genetics for submissiveness has failed."

Brooke glowered at him. "The Giastean people have claws?"

He sighed and rubbed his forehead. Why was this woman so noncompliant when she had a ton of DNA from races that had very submissive women? He took a deep breath, and the scent of exotic pheromones stormed his senses. By the Emperor, this was not the time. He knew it was her fear, and probably that sudden reaction she'd had when he grabbed her. Dragons have mercy on him, he could not lose control. "Brooke," he said hoarsely, trying to regain control.

Brooke fought against the arousal coursing through her body, shocked and horrified. *Stupid, weird, alien ways.* Her body was betraying her, responding with more heat as panic increased her heart rate. She could feel her most intimate flesh swelling, dampening.

Theiv gritted his teeth and fought against the staggering arousal coursing through his system. The scent of the pheromones she was releasing nearly overwhelmed his control. He was sweating, trembling, and his dick was so hard he swore it was going to explode. Clenching his teeth and drawing on every bit of self-control he'd ever possessed, he stomped over to the bathroom, grabbing his shirt and boots on the way by. "By the Emperor!" Theiv's rough voice was a snarl of fury. He slammed the bathroom door, creating a barrier to keep himself away from temptation.

Brooke stared after Theiv warily, arousal still rushing through her in hot pulsing waves. She swallowed, filled with a deep shame. What kind of woman was she? They were in danger.

Chapter Thirty-Two

EARTH DATE: JUNE 26 10:00 AM
Canadian National Park, Rocky Mountains, Unknown Town

THERE WAS A KNOCK ON the door and Brooke looked at Theiv, frowning. They moved to the door, and Theiv took up position beside it with his phase pistol in his hand, whispering, "It should be Clay." Brooke looked at Theiv in surprise before she reached for the doorknob.

"Clay?" She couldn't contain the relief in her voice. "Thank goodness you're here!" She paused, a tiny frown creasing her mouth. "Why are you here? How did you know where to find us?" Theiv's hand closed firmly over her arm, and tugged her back, as Clay stepped into the room. He nodded at Theiv and took a quick glance around before pulling Brooke into a gentle hug. "Theiv called me. He warned me that you were injured, but fuck, Brooke. What the hell did you do to yourself?"

"Theiv called you?" She turned to look at Theiv in confusion, ignoring Clay's question. "What? Do you have a telepathic link to my son too?"

Theiv laughed and took a cell phone from his pocket. "Clay gave me this before I left to find you."

"We need to get going. There have been reports of strange lights in the area," Clay said as he handed Theiv a hoodie and sunglasses. "Put this on, hood up. I've parked the van just outside the door. We should be able to leave without anyone noticing you." He paused to look at his mother. "We are going to talk later."

Van? Brooke peeked out the door. There was a grey mini van with five people in it. She quickly shut the door and looked at Clay. "Who are those people?" She wasn't touching that "we are going to talk" comment.

"Who do you think they are? That's Havyn, Riak, T'lain, Storm and Sev. It's not like the government was going to let us just go anywhere we wanted with a few aliens in tow." Clay's voice was a bit growly, and Brooke had a feeling he'd argued against his entourage. "A military unit has been deployed to your land, and I'm hoping like hell they at least went in civilian clothing. It's going to be all over the gossip lines if we have a military convoy showing up at your house. Especially, after the search was called off."

Theiv snorted and slung his backpack over his shoulder as he exchanged a look with Clay in the way of military men.

Brooke frowned, knowing some kind of silent communication had taken place between the two men, and put on the jacket that Theiv gave her. "We're going home?"

Clay nodded knowing that, while he agreed with Theiv that they needed to get Brooke home, it was not going to be a simple thing to protect her there. That alien bastard found her there once. There was every chance he would again.

As soon as Theiv helped Brooke into the van, Havyn tugged her into the seat beside her, and pulled out her scanner. "What has happened to you? Do you have pain?" She was already running the scanner over Brooke.

"I managed to crash the vehicle I was driving."

Havyn nodded. "The scans are showing there was significant damage." She tapped her scanner, frowning, then ran it over Brooke again. "Riak, give me your scanner. Something is wrong with mine." She took the device when it was handed to her and ran it over Brooke, as her frown grew bigger. "This is not possible," she muttered and adjusted the scanner before looking at the read out again. "How?" She paused and tilted her head as she read the data again. Finally, she looked at Theiv, then back at Brooke. "Tell me where the pain is."

Brooke shook her head, "I'm not in any pain this morning. Even my arm is not hurting. That's weird, right?"

Havyn regarded Brooke for a long moment, then reached up and gently removed the bandage from her forehead. "There is blood on the bandage, but the wound looks as if it's a few days old." She frowned again and did a slower scan, shaking her head, and muttering the whole time. "I can't believe how fast that cut is healing. This is not normal. And these pheromone readings are off the charts." She tapped again on the screen of the device she held. "We did not anticipate the Zeptos forcing the increased production of pheromones in an attempt to save your life."

Brooke's eyes grew large, and she looked at Theiv, her face warming.

"Havyn." Theiv spoke up in an attempt to change the subject. "You need to do a complete scan on Brooke. There have been significant physical changes."

Havyn paused and looked at Theiv. "What have you noticed?"

"Look at Brooke's ears. Look at her skin with a light. Her night vision is exceptional, and you really need to assess what is going on with the bones in her back. Havyn, this must be documented." His eyes met the scientist's, and he could see she understood what he had not said aloud.

Havyn nodded grimly and started scanning Brooke once more. She frowned over the readings. "Riak. T'lain. You need to go over these findings. I've sent the data to your devices."

The two scientists were soon immersed in the readings coming off the scans. "Brooke's injuries seem to be healing at an accelerated pace. The bone in her arm is healing as we're watching the data flow." T'lain shook his head slightly, his voice puzzled.

Riak moved up beside Brooke and Havyn, ignoring Storm and Sev's glares. "There was evidence that you sustained internal injuries," he said as he ran his own scan, "but you've healed. I've never seen anything like it." He turned troubled eyes to Havyn. "There is certainly some kind of evolutionary adaptation process going on with Brooke."

Theiv was done with his mate being examined. He growled, and when Riak turned startled eyes to him, he stood up, at least as far as this infernal earth vehicle allowed. "Move."

Riak moved. You did not get between a Dragon Warrior and his mate.

Brooke felt relief as Theiv sat down beside her and put his arm around her. She wanted to bury her face in his chest, terrified and overwhelmed by what the alien scientists said, but how would he react to that? She had so much to learn about this man.

Chapter Thirty-Three

EARTH DATE: JUNE 26 3:00 PM
Gardenside Alberta, Brooke's Home

AS THE VAN CAME TO a stop in the parking area of her home, Brooke saw Jaxson, her son, standing with his arm around his sister, Danielle, who held her baby daughter. Danielle's small son stood beside her, and she held hands with Brooke's best friend, Nissa.

Brooke jumped from the van and ran to her family before the vehicle fully stopped. They crowded around her, and the love they felt for each other swept over her. She'd been terrified that she'd never see them again. Shaking, tears running down her cheeks, she couldn't stop touching them, hugging them, until her grandson tugged on her shirt. "Grandma, who are the funny looking people with Uncle Clay?"

The silence was abrupt, as everyone turned to look at the people standing outside the van watching them curiously. Brooke took a deep breath, and her eyes met Clay's. She wasn't surprised that he'd stood back. It was simply his way, but she sent him a gently scolding look. He was part of her family. He shrugged, but she saw the smile in his eyes. He understood. She turned to look at her family and wondered how they would take this. "Jaxson, Danielle, Nissa... this is Havyn Aphelion, T'lain Netron, Riak Valkor. They are..." she bit her lip and took another breath. "They are from the Planet Althanea." She felt the cool breeze on her face, heard the birds chirping in the trees, her heart beating hard as she waited for their reaction.

"Hello." Jaxson said, and stepped forward, his hand outstretched. Brooke felt relief coursing through her. The scientists came forward, and shook hands with him, Danielle and Nissa.

Part one accomplished, she thought, and turned to the two military men who were silently watching. "This is Sev Conder and Storm Kenyon." The two men nodded at her family and Clay spoke up, "Storm and Sev are working with me to provide protection for Brooke. There was a unit sent here to secure the area. Have they arrived?"

Jaxson nodded. "Arrived and deployed. Somewhere in the forest I believe. Their vehicles are in the barn."

Clay nodded. "Nissa, I hope you have coffee on. I could really use one." He turned to look at Brooke. She swallowed, and walked over to Theiv, her hand slipping into his. "This is Theiv Draakon. He is my..." *Oh heavens, how did she introduce this man to her kids? Her friend didn't even come close. Her lover? Heavens, she couldn't introduce him as that! Boyfriend? Too juvenile.* She opened her mouth, and Theiv stepped forward, tugging her along with him.

"In my world we have an ancient phase that roughly translates to, her chosen."

Brooke saw the shock on the faces of her family. She opened her mouth to try to explain, but Clay jumped in.

"This situation is going to take some discussion. What's important is that we have Mom home safe. Theiv is trustworthy, and... we need him to help us protect Brooke.

Theiv watched the play of emotions across the faces of Brooke's family, and understood their shock. Even in his world this was an unprecedented moment. His eyes moved from the tall man with light hair and green eyes as vivid as his mothers, to the young woman holding a little baby girl. Danielle. She was the spitting image of her mother, and the baby she held, promised to bear a striking resemblance to her grandmother too. His gaze moved to a slender middle-aged woman with grey eyes and dark hair. A hand tugged on his jacket and he looked down. The small human male child, with green eyes full of energy, mischief, and daring was staring up at him. "Why is your skin blue, and your eyes purple?" He heard Brooke's horrified intake of breath, and he laughed. Hunkering down in front of the little human male he replied. "On my planet we are all blue, but our hair and eyes can be many different colors. Is that the same for your world?"

The little male shook his head. "Grandma says in our world we have lots of different colors of skin and eyes, but I've never seen blue skin or purple eyes." He shrugged his little shoulders. "Color doesn't matter, we are all unique." The little boy stumbled over the word and Theiv smiled. "That means special. Grandma told me. Did you find my Grandma? She got lost, and my mama cried lots."

Theiv nodded solemnly. "I did find your Grandma, and with my friends' help we brought her home."

"Thank you. I missed her. My name is Ethan. Where do you live? On Mars?"

"No, I live much farther away than Mars. My world is called Althanea."

Ethan nodded as if he knew everything there was to know about foreign worlds. "I'm going to be an astronaut when I grow up, and I'm going to live on Mars. Can I come visit you on Althanea?"

Theiv was totally enchanted by this little boy and his plans. After a long discussion about space, stars, and other life forms, they came to an agreement. Brooke was the most beautiful grandmother in the universe, and he would help Ethan to protect her and keep her from getting lost again.

Chapter Thirty-Four

EARTH DATE: JUNE 26 11:00 PM
Gardenside Alberta, Brooke's Home

IT WAS QUIET HERE, he thought as he stood on the porch of Brooke's home, staring up at the midnight blue of the sky. The star-studded darkness was breathtaking, and left him with a sense of wonder, but it was his realization that he had grandchildren that filled him with awe. What a strange feeling, to have grandchildren before he'd even had children, and they were beautiful little beings. When they'd finally made it into Brooke's home, the baby, Mia, took one look at him, batted her lashes over her big green eyes, held out her chubby little arms to him, and he fell in love. Grandchildren. He grinned. Of course, that meant he also had grown up children, and that was a bit harder to wrap his brain around. He wondered what Brooke would think of him claiming her children and grandchildren as his own. He really didn't think she was ready to hear that yet.

He watched a meteorite streak across the dark sky before his eyes turned to the single glowing crescent moon hanging in the darkness of this alien world. He admired Brooke's strength, the way she kept bouncing back. His woman had the courage of a Dragon Warrior. He wondered what his dragon would think of her. Then he laughed, Hell, F'tal would encourage her rebellion and cuff him across the head for even thinking he was capable of owning a dragon. He could almost guarantee that they would turn his hair white with the shenanigans they would get up to. Creators, he missed that scaly beast. He could really use his advice right now because he had some work ahead of him if he were going to win Brooke's heart. He paused and thought about that. Neither of them chose this bonding, but he knew to the depths of his soul that, if he met her without all this insanity, he would go after her with everything he had inside him. She was everything he wanted in a mate. Everything––fire, passion, strength, courage, and kindness. Women like Brooke were rare, and by the Creators, he was not such a fool that he would let anything stand in the way of having her in his life—certainly not the small physical things she worried about.

"Theiv." A soft hand touched his back, and he turned and instantly noted that she no longer wore the cast on her arm. He raised his eyebrow. "Havyn removed the cast."

Brooke nodded. "Advanced healing is apparently a bonus of the Zepto technology. Who knew?"

"Certainly not the scientists who invented them." Theiv said, his voice dry, and Brooke laughed.

"Please tell me there is good in the universe, Theiv. That there are kind and caring beings out there."

Hearing her words, his heart contracted. How frightening it must be to her. "There is so much goodness, Brooke. So many beautiful things, and wonderful beings who are courageous, and kind. Beings who will care deeply about what has happened to you. Beings who will rise up to stand with you." He gave her a crooked smile. "They will have to stand behind me of course." She laughed as he intended.

Brooke looked up at the sky and smiled. "Were you stargazing?"

"Yes." he nodded and took her hand in his. "Your skies are different from my home world's and you have only one moon. Althanea has two. They glow a pale blue in our night sky, Charon is the bigger moon, Zaraida is the smaller one. And they are usually close together. We say that their love dances across the sky for us to see.

"That is a lovely story." Brooke said and smiled, looking up at him. Their eyes caught and held. The night seemed to still. Slowly, Theiv lowered his head. His lips brushed hers, lifted a bare whisper, then brushed them again, before settling. A gentle sweet kiss that made her long for more. They stared into each other's eyes in silence, still holding hands.

"It's late." Brooke whispered as she reached up and brushed back his hair where it had fallen over his forehead.

He nodded, his eyes searching hers.

Brooke took his hand and led the huge alien back into her house and up to her bedroom. She bit her lip as she opened the door, wondering what he thought, as she gazed at her room with new eyes. It was painted a soft cream color with the huge iron antique bed she found at an estate sale about a year after her husband died—a bed that she'd never brought a man to until this moment. She took a deep breath and turned to face him, pulling her shirt over her head.

Theiv stood silently in the beautiful bedroom, the bed was the biggest he'd ever seen, crafted by an artisan. A bed he'd been invited to share. He watched Brooke bare her beautiful body to him, swallowing as his gaze moved over her breasts with their dark dusty rose nipples. She wiggled out of her jeans and stood naked in front of him. He tugged off his shirt, and toed off his boots and socks, his hand releasing the fastening on his pants. She walked over to him, took his hand, and led him to the bed. He stripped off his pants, and when he was naked, Brooke bit her lip, and shyly looked at his body. She never seemed to get tired of looking at him.

She felt so small compared to him. She reached out to touch his chest, her thumb grazing over his nipple. And she paused to examine his tattoo. The ruby red dragon tattoo rested its scaly head over his left shoulder, its tail curled around his waist, then wound its way down over his hip and around his right thigh. It truly was a work of art. It seemed so life-like that she caught her breath and let her fingers trail over the image. His cock rose against his belly, fully erect, the head a darker blue than the shaft, gleaming with precum, and Brooke wanted to taste him. She knelt in front of him and drew a finger the length of his shaft. He groaned, and Brooke smiled, feeling a blaze of feminine power. She closed her hand around the hard shaft, and stroked. His hips shifted forward in a slow thrust, and Brooke couldn't wait anymore. She leaned in and took him into her mouth. His flavor burst across her tongue, and she hummed her approval.

Theiv sucked in a hard breath, his mind short-circuiting, her mouth was heaven. It was enough to drive him insane. He groaned when she drew back, stared into her deep green eyes, and forgot everything except how she looked all flushed with desire, her lips swollen from sucking his cock. He swallowed, and thrust his hands into her hair, urging her to her feet. His mouth came down on hers, his tongue demanding entrance. The exotic bite of spices was something he knew he would always associate with her. He kissed her until they were both gasping for air, backing off only long enough for them to gasp a breath before his mouth was on hers again devouring her, ravishing the lush dampness of her lips.

His hands left her hair and settled around her waist. He lifted her easily, setting her on the bed, and stepped back, his chest heaving as he drew in air. Grasping her ankles, he slowly spread her legs until he could see her beautiful pussy, see the glistening wetness of her desire coating the plump folds. "Beautiful." His eyes met hers, and he leaned forward, his eyes never leaving hers, and licked through her folds, his tongue circling her swollen clit, the exotic flavor of her desire bursting across his tongue. She cried out, her hips arching, and he smiled against her. She liked that. He did it again, and again, as she arched and cried out. Then he began to alternate sucking with licking, and she went wild beneath his mouth, coming hard, her body convulsing over and over until she lay limp. He lazily licked her again and she gasped and jerked. He smiled at her grumble about sensitive bits and moved up her body, between her parted thighs, catching her hips, lifting, and thrusting his cock deep into her welcoming clasp. Heat enclosed him and he began to thrust, hard and heavy inside her.

Brooke moaned as he filled her in one hard thrust, she stared into his eyes, feeling their bond swirl around them. Incredible pleasure rippled through her as he began to hit that spot inside her. She gasped and twisted in his grasp, moving with wild abandon. The pleasure she found with him was a wild untamed thing. She wanted more, moving with Theiv in a frantic dance that lured them ever closer to the flame that threatened to burn them alive and into a climax so intense she felt seared to the depths of her soul. She heard Theiv growl as she stared into his amazing amethyst eyes, felt his hot seed flood her womb as her body convulsed over and over. Panting, he collapsed over her and she hugged him to her, hanging on to the beauty of this moment.

Chapter Thirty-Five

BROOKE WOKE UP EARLY. Theiv was wrapped around her like a warm blanket, dawn just peeking over the horizon casting a slight pink glow to her room. It felt amazing to waken in her room, surrounded by her things. She moved, and Theiv moved with her. Smiling she wiggled away from him until she could sit up and leave the bed. Theiv opened one eye, his voice a sleepy rasp. "What are you doing?"

"Taking a shower."

"Wake me when you're done."

Brooke shook her head and turned to walk into the bathroom. She turned on the shower. Her shower. It had a big rainfall shower head, and her body wash, her shampoo and conditioner lined the shelves. She adjusted the temperature and flipped on the towel warmer. By then, steam was rising from the shower. She tugged off Theiv's tunic that she'd slept in and stepped inside. The hot water washed over her, and she simply stood there letting it pour down on her. Finally, she opened her body wash, and began to lather herself. The fresh scent of peaches wafted around her, and she inhaled deeply. Tears pricked at her eyes. It was so good to be home.

An hour later she came downstairs to find a note on the table. Theiv had got up while she was showering and was with Storm and Sev, walking the perimeter of her land, checking out the defensibility of her property. Havyn, Riak, and T'lain were with them. She was supposed to stay here until they returned. Yeah, right. She laughed softly. Not happening.

Her purse was where she'd left it, that fateful day when she'd been kidnapped. She picked it up and slung it over her shoulder. It was hard to believe that it had only been weeks. She felt like she'd lived a lifetime. Her whole world changed. Grabbing her soft brown leather jacket off the antique coat tree that stood by her front door, she stepped out of the house.

Crossing her yard to the garage, she walked inside. Her retro mustang gleamed softly in the sunlight. Brooke stroked her hand over the glossy black paint and got into the driver's seat. It started with a deep-throated rumble. She reversed out of the garage.

Theiv stepped off the wrap around veranda wondering where the hell Brooke was, when he heard the throaty rumble of an engine. She wouldn't dare. He stalked towards the noise and paused when he saw a gleaming black earth vehicle unlike any he'd ever seen.

Brooke grinned, shifted into first, and stepped on the gas. The car shot forward, and she waved as she passed Theiv. She was going to be in trouble when she got home, a tiny shiver of arousal ran through her and she smirked. Better make her getaway worth it then. There was chocolate calling her name.

She glanced into her rear-view mirror and saw him lift his cell phone to his ear, staring after her. Calling Storm or Sev no doubt.

She drove down the long winding driveway, and just as she pulled up to the lane, she heard a faint shout, and saw Storm and Sev burst out of the woods to her left at a full run. She turned up her radio, and lowered the window, letting the pounding music of Troopers 'Raise a little Hell' pour out of the car. Waving, she gunned the motor, and the car shot out onto the gravel lane, the back end slid to the side, she grinned, smoothly brought it back to centre, and stepped on the gas, leaving Sev and Storm standing in a cloud of dust. Five miles later, she was on the highway, the radio cranked, windows down, and the gas pedal floored. Seven miles further, and she flew past the hidden area where Clay often waited to catch speeders. Red and blue flashing lights appeared in her rear-view mirror seconds later, and she grinned.

Brooke roared into town with the red and blue flashing lights still behind her. Pulling into a parking spot in front of Nissa's diner, she hopped out of the car just as Clay strode up to her, and immediately launched herself into his arms.

He caught her in a tight hug. "Damn it, Brooke! You're supposed to pull over the minute you see my lights, not when you get to your destination! This wasn't a fucking police escort!" His voice was gruff, thick with emotion, and Brooke clung harder to him. He finally set her back on her feet and stepped back, studying her face intently. Reaching out he ruffled her short purple hair, "You look so much like Dani, it fucking shocks me every time I see you."

"Language!" Brooke shook her head and swiped at a tear at the sheer normality of the moment.

"You ditched your protection detail? Where's Theiv?" Clay looked at her knowingly.

Brooke bit her lip, then nodded. "I needed to do this on my own. Needed to see all of you."

Clay nodded slowly, his eyes searching her face, seeing her fears. He struggled with his rage, with the fact that he hadn't been able to protect her. It was his job to protect the people of this town, and he'd failed with one of the most important people in his world. He hauled her close for another bone-crushing hug.

Brooke hugged Clay tightly. "It's not your fault, you know. There was nothing you could've done." She stepped back from his embrace. "They are so advanced, Clay. There truly is nothing you or anyone else could've done." Brooke reached out and stroked his jaw, remembering all the times he and her son came racing into the house after school looking for cookies. "I don't want you beating yourself up about this anymore."

Clay stared at Brooke. "People are going to freak out when your alien comes looking for you." He stated, instead of answering her directly.

Brooke laughed, "A little excitement is good for people. I'm going to go into Nissa's Diner, why don't you go and get Jaxson and Dani and bring them here."

Brooke turned away and strode over to the diner. She hesitated outside the door, wiped at the tears that were threatening to spill over, and straightened her shoulders. Taking a deep breath, she stepped into the diner. The immediate smell of home-cooked food washed over her. She inhaled and glanced around the interior. It was cozy and warm, with rough log walls and a huge stone fireplace. Several bench tables and a long counter with stools made up the interior.

"Brooke?"

She turned, and there was Nissa, wearing her usual tight blue jeans and low-cut top.

"I was hoping you would come by today. We didn't get to really talk yesterday with all those people around." Nissa's voice trembled, then she was hugging Brooke. Brooke wrapped her arms around her friend and held on tight. When Nissa stepped back, she was sniffling and brushed her tears away with the back of her hand before she reached into her apron pocket. She pulled out some napkins and handed half of them to Brooke.

"I told Clay to bring Jaxson and Dani here, Nissa. I hope you don't mind." Brooke said in a husky voice, wiping her eyes.

Nissa squeezed Brooke's hand; "Where else would we meet? We've been having our family meetings here for years." she smiled. "Just hang on a second, Hun." Rising to her feet, she faced the early morning coffee drinkers who were openly staring at them. There were quite a few raised brows and a few who had paused with their cup halfway to their mouths. "I'm closing shop for the day." Collective groans. "Fred's place is open. He'll be glad for the extra business." More grumbling, but they slowly got up and headed out. Nissa flipped the sign on the door to closed.

Brooke took advantage of the few moments of quiet, while Nissa hustled around organizing things to reach out telepathically to Theiv. As soon as she connected, she was aware of Theiv, and realized he'd been monitoring her. *I just need to do this on my own*, she sent. Immediately she felt his smile, his confidence in her, his reassurance that he understood.

Nissa disappeared into the kitchen, returning with a plate of her famous pastries as Clay arrived with Jaxson and Dani.

They worked their way through a pot of coffee before Brooke found the courage to talk about her abduction. Her voice shaking, she talked about being abducted by aliens. Tears slid down her cheeks as she spoke about the experiment. Her voice, a whisper, she stared at the table as she confessed the changes to her body and tried to explain Theiv. Trembling, she waited for their scorn, their rejection.

"Mom." Danielle's hands covered hers. "The important thing is that you survived. We can deal with everything else. I promise, Mom." She began to cry. Brooke lifted anguished eyes to her daughter, and Danielle moved over to sit beside her, wrapping her arms around her. "Mom, you're home, and I don't care what color Theiv is, or what planet he's from. I don't care if you came with a whole shipload of aliens, and their crazy devices. I just need you home."

Jaxson reached across the table and took his mom's hand. "All those years of Star Trek prepared us for aliens, Mom." Everyone laughed, and then, he met her eyes. "Dani is right.

The important thing is that you are with us. And if Theiv pulls any bullshit, we have a lot of land to hide a body on."

Brooke gasped. "Language! And don't say things like that! You would not look good in prison orange."

Jaxson laughed and traded a look with Clay. "I've got an in with the cops."

"Stop trying to get me in trouble with Mom," Clay said, and everyone started to laugh.

"We can trust Theiv." Clay looked around the table at everyone. "He chose to put his life on the line to protect Brooke and to get her back home. And honestly, he's just as trapped by this situation as Brooke is."

Deep inside, Brooke cringed at Clay's words. Trapped. God, she never wanted that.

"I, for one, wouldn't mind an alien lover if he looked like your Theiv." Nissa said, having picked up on Brooke's reactions. "So, what if you have a lover? Hell, so what if you have ten? If that man is the hero you say he is, then we will love him. It's that simple, baby."

Chapter Thirty-Six

EARTH DATE: JUNE 27 1:00 PM
Gardenside Alberta, Brooke's Home

PULLING THE CAR INTO the garage, Brooke was surprised to see Theiv sitting on her ride-on lawnmower. He straightened as she put the car into park. Brooke nervously bit her lip as she saw the look on his face, then turned off the motor. *Oh, hell.*

He opened the door for her and helped her out of the car. After shutting the door, and making sure the vehicle was securely locked, he calmly picked Brooke up and tossed her over his shoulder, then strode towards the house.

"Theiv!" she gasped, "What are you doing? Put me down!"

A large hand landed heavily on her ass, and she squeaked in surprise. "I keep threatening you with a spanking, and you keep right on defying me. I guess it's time for you to learn that there are consequences."

A shocking spark of arousal streaked through her body, leaving her wide-eyed, and a bit breathless. "Where... where are the others?" she stuttered, dismayed by her body's reaction to Theiv's dominance.

Theiv shrugged, "They're holed up in your office, going over the scan results, and talking to Dr. Reed on the computer. Don't worry, they won't interrupt." Entering the bedroom, he shut the door and tossed Brooke onto the bed. She scrambled to her knees and watched Theiv warily.

"Take off your clothes," he ordered, his voice firm.

Brooke shook her head. Theiv caught her arm, his voice brooked no refusal. "Brooke, take off your clothes."

"Theiv, be reasonable."

Theiv lifted an eyebrow, "I'm very reasonable. Now, take off your clothes. If I take them off you, they're going to get ripped."

Nibbling on her lip, Brooke considered her options. She'd known when she drove past Theiv that she was playing with fire, but this? "Uh, Theiv..."

He pounced so fast that she never had a chance to move. One second, she was kneeling on the bed, the next Theiv ripped her T-shirt right off her, and was unlatching her bra. She automatically caught the front before it fell and found herself flat on her back as Theiv grabbed her yoga pants and stripped them, and her underwear, down and off her legs. Gasping as she suddenly found herself flipped over his knee, she put her hands out to catch herself, and her bra slid down her arms to the floor. A hot male hand smoothed over her buttocks and she froze.

"There is something you should know about me, Dragoness" Theiv said, his voice utterly calm. He cupped her mound and she almost moaned as he slid his fingers between her lips and circled her clit. His other hand continued to stroke and pet her buttocks. "I never joke about spankings."

He slid two fingers through her wet heat, and then plunged them deep, she gasped, bucked, and he began to rub his thumb back and forth over her clit. She moaned desperately as fire surged through her body and every nerve flared to hot erotic life. He continued to fuck her with his fingers, rubbing at her swollen clit, as he brought her right to the edge of a powerful orgasm. Then abruptly, he stopped, and his other hand descended on her ass firmly delivering a sharp smack.

Brooke gasped and tried to jerk away, but he held her firmly and delivered three more sharp smacks that burned, and at the same time sent more of her silky wet cream sliding through her folds and dampening her thighs. Then those tormenting fingers were back, plunging inside of her. She moved helplessly back against the marauding digits, moaning as his thumb swiped over her distended clit. An orgasm again blossomed inside of her, and again, it was jerked out of her reach as he delivered more of the sharp slaps to her bottom. Panting, she jerked helplessly in his grasp. She could feel her arousal ratcheting higher and higher and was shocked. Abruptly she found herself upright and facing the mirror on her dresser as Theiv lifted her, and then brought her down, impaling her on his rock-hard cock.

It was a shocking sight, Theiv fully clothed, her naked and impaled on his lap, her back pressed to his chest. His hands came around, and he caught both her nipples and tugged. She moaned, caught up in the sight of his big hands working her nipples, her buttocks burned against the denim of his jeans and somehow that slight pain increased her arousal. She writhed against him unable to tear her eyes away from the mirror. Her pussy felt stretched, filled to the limit. He thrust up against her, and she groaned as fire streaked through her. His big hands suddenly moved to her knees, and pulled her legs apart, she stared dazed into the mirror at the sight of his cock disappearing into her pussy, her outer lips were pink and swollen, glistening with the evidence of her arousal, and her clit stretching out from under its hood. He caught her hips with both hands and began to power into the hot silky depths of her pussy. The wet slap of flesh against flesh filled the room. Brooke panted, she was close, so close. She reached down and slid her hand over her mound to her clit. She rubbed her clit, feeling the fire race up her spine. "That's it. Play with your pretty little clit," Theiv panted in her ear. She jerked her gaze to the mirror and saw that he was watching her with rapt attention. "Make yourself come," he whispered, and that suddenly, her orgasm swept through her and she tightened around him. He shouted as the deep shudders of her orgasm swept over her, and she felt his hot seed spurting deep inside of her.

Collapsing back against his chest, he wrapped his arms around her, hugging her back against him. "Next time, talk to me before you take off." He whispered against her neck.

Brooke shuddered as his warm breath blew over her hypersensitive skin. "I can't promise too always be good. What would be the fun in that?" She felt his laughter against her neck.

Chapter Thirty-Seven

EARTH DATE: JUNE 28 7:00 AM
Gardenside Alberta, Brooke's Home

SHE STOOD OUTSIDE HER house in the early morning sunshine and stared up into the blue sky. Her smartphone was in her hand, earphones plugged in, her running playlist pulled up on the screen. She stared at the path, and her mind kept replaying the events of the last time she'd run on that trail.

It struck her that she no longer had to run, because her ass wasn't a size sixteen anymore. She could eat as much chocolate as she wanted, forever. No running involved.

She swallowed, her heart and thoughts racing, her breath sawing out of her lungs even as she logically understood that she was experiencing an anxiety attack.

She took a step forward, her heart pounding, and stopped. *I don't have to run. I can turn around, go back in the house, and have tea. Maybe a cinnamon bun.* Looking back at the house, she thought of how she'd longed for life to return to normal. How having her routine and purpose back filled her thoughts. She leaned down, putting her hands on her knees, breathing deeply, willing the anxiety to leave, unable to make a decision that would either send her home or on a run.

A warm hand settled on her back, and Theiv crouched down in front of her. "Breathe, Dragoness."

She looked up at him and took a deep breath. "I don't need to run."

Theiv tilted his head slightly, watching her. "No, it's not necessary for you to run."

"I used to run because I was a bigger person. I ran to lose weight." She sat down abruptly and began to frantically flip through the pictures stored on the device. "Here! See." She practically shoved the device into his face. Theiv caught her hand and looked down at what she was trying to show him. He smiled as he recognized Brooke. "I like this picture."

She stared at him, then pulled her hand back, and stared down at the picture, her thumb gently rubbing the image. "I hated it. I rarely allowed anyone to take my picture."

"Why?"

"I was too big."

"Too big?" Theiv frowned and looked at Brooke. "People come in all shapes and sizes. Is it not the person you are inside that counts?"

Brooke laughed, a brief harsh bark of sound. Even on Earth, Theiv, women seek the illusion of perfection. She looked up into Theiv's concerned eyes. "I was a counsellor. I taught that truth to young women and teenagers. And yet, I see that I did not understand it for myself."

"Your beauty is not in the perfection of this Zepto-created body. It is not the sensuality of the Zemyneah." His hand slid into her hair, and he tilted her face up to his. "It is the light of goodness in your eyes. It is the energy of hope that pours out of you. It is the resilience of your soul, and the compassion of your heart. In any dimension, on any planet that I encountered you, Brooke, I would've chosen you. No matter your shape or age, I would've chosen you, and I would have pursued you and made you mine."

She started to cry and Theiv reached for her. "Why am I crying? This is so stupid. I should be happy. I've got a body that so many would do anything to achieve and the sex drive to go with it. I can produce pheromones that drive a man into insatiable lust for me. Heck, I get to have sex whenever I want with the most beautiful man in the universe. Why am I crying?"

Theiv gave her a slight crooked grin before tightening his hug. "You did not choose this new body or way of being, Brooke, or even me. Tears and rage seem reasonable when you understand the violation you endured at the hands of an evil being. Healing, under the best of circumstances, is a tangled messy procedure. There is no star map, no coordinates. You must find your way on a journey you have never been on before. The way of healing, meanders through many star systems, explores many planets, communes with hidden galaxies, doubles back on itself many times, and you must pause often for repairs, to consult with experts, and to rest.

"Do you do counselling on your home world?"

Theiv looked startled. "I'm warrior class."

Brooke smiled. "You are a wise warrior. I shall take your counsel under consideration." She stood, stretched, then stared at the path that led into the thick forest, wiping her suddenly damp palms on her leggings. Pressing her lips together, she shrugged her tight shoulders.

Theiv watched her silently, then picked up a large straight stick. He began to slash it through the air, his movements smooth and coordinated, and she thought it like a graceful dance. When he was done, his skin glistened with sweat, and he was breathing heavily. He handed her the stick and nodded, stepping back. "Now, you."

Brooke stared at him in surprise. "I can't do that."

"Why not?"

"You obviously have years of training."

Theiv nodded. "I am a warrior. My job is to protect. We fight with modern weapons, and hand to hand combat, if needed. I am proficient in many weapons and fighting styles. It is necessary. Control is also essential. Fear could render me unable to do my job, unable to protect those who need me. Fear could leave me vulnerable to attack. There is no lack of fear as a Dragon Warrior, there is only control. A thin shield of protection, indeed."

Brooke's eyes met his.

"What I just demonstrated, is an ancient form of combat called Najaesh. Najaesh is not a practical form of combat any longer. Our weapons are far superior. It is not necessary for me to know this form of combat." He watched her for a long moment. "I practice Najaesh, because when I learned about it, I was intrigued. It takes control, discipline, and many years of training to become proficient at it. You must travel to the dangerous Najaeshian Expanse to find a master to teach you. You take your life in your hands just by going to that region. The Expanse is dangerous to navigate. Massive asteroid fields, rogue planets, unpredictable space vortexes. The lessons are taught on Jaeshia, a planet that is all plunging gorges and soaring rock spires. Every zepto-second could mean your death. One wrong step, the momentary loss of concentration, the loss of balance, could send you plummeting to your death. Many died in times past. I have never experienced such fear as I did learning this form of combat. But I also learned to not let the fear control me. I had to face it. Accept it. Move past it, and finally control it." He reached out and tipped up her chin, until her eyes met his.

"I keep training because it is good for my soul. It helps me to sort through many things. It relieves stress for me, and it is good for my body. I think that I am a better fighter because of it, and I am a better man. Sometimes things are not necessary but are essential for our souls. Do you understand?"

Brooke nodded, and looked again at the path before her. Fear beat at her, and this time she recognized it for what it was. Of course, she was afraid. It was this path that led her to a monster. She'd barely survived the encounter. But this was her land, and this was her life. She would not cede it to the evil that sought to destroy her. So, this was her Najaeshian Expanse—her Jaeshia. She could make the journey, or she could run away. Courage is not the lack of fear, but the strength that overcomes it.

She was shaking, but she took a step, and Theiv stepped up beside her. She looked at him questioningly.

"This is the path you ran, when you were taken?"

Brooke swallowed, and nodded.

"Then I go with you."

Chapter Thirty-Eight

THE IN-BETWEEN
  Earth Date: June 28

HE HAD SHOULDER LENGTH blond hair and eyes of such dark blue that they appeared black—and the body of a god. She sighed, remembering that body, remembering all the times she had touched it, loved it. Loved him.

Walking over to the transparent wall that allowed her to gaze out over the multiverse, Eliana stared morosely out at the stunning beauty spread before her. Beautiful, like Ash was beautiful. Except Ash would never have the purity of the multiverse. Ash was charming, and intensely sexual. He carried the magnitude of his power so casually, that it was always a shock when you felt the punch of that power in the air that surrounded him. And he was evil.

Shivering, she turned away from the cold vista of space, and curled up on the couch, pulling a soft hand knit blanket up over herself. She looked over at the fireplace, and flames instantly sprang up inside it. A delicate cup of fine pale blue china, dainty flowers hand painted on its fragile surface, appeared on the low table in front of her. Eliana lifted the cup and inhaled the steam of her favorite spiced tea before taking a sip.

It was hard to think of the man she had once loved with all the fire in her heart. He hadn't been heinous then, but the warning signs were there. She'd thought of him as dark, a little wicked, maybe a bit depraved, but in all the best ways, not evil. Never evil. She'd been blind to his true nature. She ignored warning signs, her own instincts, and believed that if she loved him enough, he would love her in return. Love her enough to turn away from anything, that could cost him their relationship. And even millenniums after they ended their affair, she'd wanted to believe he was... somehow, simply misunderstood.

How many times had she lain in her bed, and thought about all the "what ifs" surrounding their relationship? What if she loved him deeper? What if she argued less? What if she did... more? Not that she ever understood what the more could be. It destroyed something inside her to know that she wasn't enough. Round and round it went in her mind until she finally realized that she was breaking her own heart. Ash was what Ash was. An astonishingly beautiful angel, whose heart was dark with the vileness of his deeds. His fall had been inevitable. And there was nothing she could have done to change it.

The missive she'd received this morning from the angel Levi, whose host guarded the planet Earth in all the dimensions of the Milky Way Galaxy, irrevocably set them on a course for a showdown. Rune needed to be told, and Ash needed to be stopped.

Chapter Thirty-Nine

EARTH DATE: JUNE 29 7:00 AM
Gardenside Alberta, Brooke's Home

THE RICH SCENT OF COFFEE, and freshly made cinnamon buns gave the kitchen a homey vibe as Brooke and Havyn sat at the table, the ticking of the wall clock the only sound in the otherwise quiet room.

Brooke sipped from her cup as she watched Havyn. The scientist was busy on her scanner, a look of intense focus on her beautiful face. It was a look Brooke was beginning to associate with Havyn, she thought with some amusement.

The house was quiet around them, Jaxson and Danielle had taken the children to town, and the other men were out doing a security sweep. It was a moment of peace in the midst of the chaos her life had become.

"Brooke, the Zeptos appear to have entered stealth mode, and your pheromone levels are balanced." Havyn spoke as she tapped data into her scanner. "It is important to keep them at this level." She looked up from the test results.

Brooke nodded, and took another sip of her coffee. She reached for another warm cinnamon bun, then nudged the plate closer to Havyn. "My grandmother's recipe. You should try them."

Havyn frowned but reached out to take one. It smelled good. That had to be a sign that it was edible. Just as her fingers closed around the sweet bun, a blinding flash of light filled the room and two men appeared.

"Drace!" Havyn shot to her feet, her chair crashing to the floor.

"Hello, wife."

Brooke froze. That cold, emotionless voice raked over her, and she could almost feel the color leaching from her face. He was here. Oh God, the monster had found her!

She rose silently, her gaze shooting toward the door. Help was so close, if only she could get to the door. But Drace turned toward her, his eyes hard, and he was far faster than she would have believed.

He grabbed her by the hair and yanked her back, a gasp of pain cutting through the room as she stumbled into a chair and landed on the floor at his feet. The hand in her hair was merciless as he hauled her up to her knees in front of him, tears springing to her eyes as she grabbed his hand with both of hers, attempting to pull him off her.

"Hello, my beautiful little Zemyneah." He stroked his hand along her cheek, a cruel smile spreading slowly across his lips at the fear he read in her eyes.

Brooke felt her soul freeze as their gazes held, her breath trapped in her throat. He had her. After all their running, he had her. She watched the victorious pleasure in his eyes harden as he turned to Havyn, and a feeling of dread consumed her as she followed the path of his gaze.

"Did you really think I would allow you to interfere in my plans?" He backhanded Havyn, the force of it slamming her into the wall.

The suddenness of his violence shocked Brooke, and she tried to tear herself out of Drace's grip. He tightened his hold on her hair, almost ripping it from the roots. She cried out, and he grabbed her throat, his fingers digging into her windpipe until the room began to swim in her vision. He shoved her back to her knees! "Be careful, Zemyneah. I will not lose you again."

Deep blue blood trickled from Havyn's lip as she pushed herself up against the wall, blinding pain and dizziness clouding her mind. She had to get up. She had to get up, now! She struggled through the mists clouding her thinking knowing only that she could not let Drace take Brooke again.

Air rasped into Brooke's oxygen starved lungs, *Oh God! Oh God!* She had to get help. Desperately she reached out along the telepathic bond she shared with Theiv, her nails digging bloody crescents into Drace's skin. *Oh god! Please, Theiv! Please, please hear me!*

Instantly, she became aware of Theiv's presence in her mind, her terror flowing out to him. She glanced sideways at Drace, trying to warn Theiv. Was this how this bond thing worked? Could he see what she saw?

Drace watched Havyn with cold satisfaction as she finally gained her footing. "I've reformulated one of the extra vials of Zemyneah serum just for you, my dear wife. Did you really think that I wouldn't have a backup plan?" A sick smile of amusement blossomed on his face as he seemed to savor the moment. "When we return to the ship, you will join the Zemyneah ranks. I have a special plan for your initiation."

Dragging Brooke with him, her hair caught in his merciless grip, he leaned toward Havyn, his voice a cold hard sneer. "Since I refuse to touch you again, you will be turned over to my loyal warriors. We'll see how much you like being a Zemyneah since you do not appreciate the privilege of being a wife." He backhanded her again, sending her reeling into the silent, second man.

The man, his face a mass of fading bruises, almost fell before catching himself at the last minute and standing tall. Havyn crumpled at his feet. His hands bore the evidence of a fierce battle. There was a healing scrape across one high cheekbone, a smear of dried blood on his chin from where his lip had been split. His eyes, an unusual shade of pale green, glittered with an almost insane fury made worse by the ravages of grief. Long hair fell down his back and, even though it was a tangled mess, the blue-black hues were striking. He stood a solid six feet tall with a powerful muscular build, his skin a golden brown. Dark bruises, scrapes and cuts marred his ribcage, and a deep burn seared across the front of one shoulder. A black collar tightly circled his throat, his hands were cuffed in front of him, and he was dressed only in torn black pants. Even his feet were bare, and shockingly, black iridescent wings rose high from his back.

A growl rumbled low and deep from his throat as he flashed razor sharp canines at Drace, and he positioned himself to crouch protectively in front of the fallen female.

"A Karisean!" Havyn whispered at his back in shock.

Drace laughed, an ugly sounding chuckle, that caused shivers to run down Brooke's spine. "Where is your master, Zemyneah?" The hand in her hair forced her head back until she stared into his cold dark eyes. "Call him to you. It will make this much easier."

"He will kill you." She ground out.

Drace laughed again. "No, my little Zemyneah, the Karisean will kill him. The males of Karis are very possessive of their mates, and you are covered in the scent of another male."

Brooke's eyes widened, fear trickling up her spine.

"A little intergalactic lesson for you. A male from Karis will only mate with one female in his lifetime, and, until now, until you, only with female Karisean's." He grabbed her chin brutally, forcing her face up before his hand closed around her throat. He leaned in and sniffed her. "Mmm, little Zemyneah, you still smell delicious, like lust and sex. And what is this?" He stroked a finger across the faint scar left by Theiv's bite. "Interesting. The Zeptos left a marking scar. I'll have to remove that." Brooke's skin crawled and she felt Theiv's fury flowing along the bond she shared with him.

The Karisean slowly rose, turning to reach down to help Havyn, and moved so she remained slightly behind him. Havyn held in her irritation and watched for an opening. She would probably only have one chance at this. Carefully, she eased a syringe from her pocket.

The Karisean growled and Brooke's attention snapped back to him. He was huge, terrifying. She could almost feel the unrestrained violence within him. He was the most frightening thing she'd ever seen.

She had to warn Theiv. Karisean, she whispered across their telepathic bond and she pushed the image she was seeing of the enraged alien to Theiv, and felt his shock flowing back to her.

"Where is Shara? You said you were bringing me to my mate." The winged man's voice was a low snarl that made hair rise on Brooke's body.

"Drace, be reasonable, you cannot hope to control a Karisean." Havyn voice held only contempt for the man who was her husband.

Drace laughed a horrible, mocking sound. "I can. I do. We caught the Karisean and his female in their mating dance. He was in full heat. The perfect opportunity. I've had him for weeks. I harvested what I needed from the female, added it to the formula we used on the Earth woman, before having her body disposed of. And you never even suspected." He sneered.

The winged man became ominously still.

"You're not quite as smart as you think you are, Havyn." Drace released Brooke and turned to face Havyn fully. "And what better chance to correct this situation, to salvage my plans, than this. Perhaps I should thank you, Havyn. After all, if you had not stolen my experiment, I would never have considered injecting him with the Zemyneah serum." Drace shrugged, and a horrible caricature of a smile twisted his lips. "This Karisean is mated to my Zemyneah."

Havyn said something violent that Brooke's translator did not translate. Brooke swallowed against the lump suddenly burning her throat, her fingers rising to her chest, and felt a tear fall as she watched a barrage of emotions cross the unknown man's face.

A roar filled the room as the man strained against the cuffs that held him, his eyes filled with a killing rage that terrified Brooke. His muscles bulged as he turned toward Drace, his face contorted into a terrible grimace of hatred and agony. The snap of metal breaking was loud in the sudden silence, then the creature was falling to his knees, screaming in agony as the black collar around his neck lit up.

Drace took a hasty step back, almost stumbling into Brooke before releasing the button on the small device he held in his hand. The Karisean's scream cut off and he collapsed forward, still on his knees, his head resting on the floor as he panted for breath, his skin glistening with sweat, his wings fluttering.

"Get up!" Drace screeched at the man. "Get up!"

Havyn threw a contemptuous look at Drace, then reached out to help the male rise. "I'm sorry." Her voice tight, she swallowed and turned slowly to face Drace.

"This is your mate," Drace hissed, ignoring Havyn. He dragged Brooke forward, and threw her towards the Karisean.

Brooke landed hard on the floor in front of the growling man. She started to scramble away, but Havyn grabbed her arm. "Don't move!" She hissed. "Karisean's can be very dangerous. Especially one in the mating heat."

The man turned his gaze to the two women. He struggled to contain the demand for vengeance surging through him, recognizing that the mating heat was upon him. The scent of the two women washed over him as he watched the

Athanean help the other one to her feet. His eyes glittered in fury at the knowledge that he was mated to an alien species, that his beautiful, gentle Shara was lost to him forever.

He would have his revenge. They would pay for what they'd done to Shara, for what they were now forcing him to do.

Pacing around the women, a low growl rumbling through his chest, he came to a halt directly in front of them. The one with the short spiky purple hair and the pale skin was of a species he'd never seen before, but something was strangely familiar. He studied her. She was tiny compared to the women of his planet, with large eyes, a deep green like the forests of his home world. Her ears sloped gently into a delicate point and she smelled wonderful like the rare flowers of Amberisia, but her scent was overlaid with the scent of another male. He inhaled again and caught another scent, something that should not be there.

He shifted his gaze to the Athanean female. She was lovely with her large golden eyes, and long, pale purple hair. *Exotic*, he thought, his eyes drifting over her again. Her lips were a darker blue than her skin, a thin trickle of blood flowed down from her lip, and her eye was beginning to swell. In his world, any male who dared to damage a female in such a way would have been put to death.

What had Aphelion called her? Havyn. She was slender with gentle curves. He thought. *I could easily circle her waist with my hands.*

His nostrils flared as he took in her scent. Looking from one female to the other, he inhaled again before turning to look at his enemy. "Release my hands so I may kill the male who defiled my mate." His voice was a hard, dangerous rumble.

"You're not my mate." Brooke's voice shook, but she held the gaze of the terrifying creature before her, even as she once again reached for the bond she shared with Theiv. The Karisean growled at her as if he sensed her reaching out to Theiv. His wings stretched out in a massive wingspan then settled against his back again. A second passed as he and Drace stared at each other, their hatred far from hidden, then with a click, the cuffs released, and his hands were free.

He reached out and lifted the little shorthaired one to her feet and tucked her against him. Brooke stiffened and tried to push away. A low warning growl filled the air by her ear, and she froze. He smelled her neck, and she swallowed, but he turned slowly to face Drace.

Havyn had managed to ease from behind the huge male, while he was distracted with Brooke, and inch her way closer to her maniac husband. Hidden in her hand was the syringe.

"Drace!" Havyn whispered urgently.

"Shut up!" Drace hissed and reached out to grab Havyn, jerking her towards him. "I am going to enjoy watching my men use you."

Havyn didn't resist as he yanked her close. She had one chance, and by the Empire, she intended to take it. Gritting her teeth when he grabbed her hair and forced her to her knees, she lifted the hand with the syringe as he fumbled with something in his pocket. Her hand was coming down, her intent to jam the syringe into his thigh. She never saw the device in his hand.

He smashed it against her head, and she screamed, her whole body going stiff, her eyes widened, almost glowing with her agony, as the device activated. The syringe she held dropped to the floor and rolled away unnoticed. "You are no longer my wife. The marriage bond is broken!" He jerked the device away and in the same motion backhanded her. She was thrown backwards into the Karisean, who shoved Brooke behind him the instant that Drace grabbed Havyn and was growling furiously.

Brooke's blood ran cold at the sounds erupting from his throat.

The Karisean carefully lifted Havyn to her feet. She was shaking, a cut seeping blood along her jaw, where the device had gouged her. She lifted her eyes to his, defiantly bracing herself for the death she read in his eyes.

Brave little enemy.

He handed her to the other woman and turned back to face Aphelion. He snarled at the Althanean male who dared to think he could control a Karisean, who dared to force an alien mating on him. His rage was boundless, his need to kill, to bathe in the blood of his enemy, almost beyond his control. "This is your wish?" he growled, his words barely understandable. "That anyone who endangered my mate, would die?"

Drace laughed, cocky, sure of his plan. "That is exactly what I wish."

"Release the collar, then, and I will hunt."

"I'm not that foolish, Karisean."

"You hold my mate. You control me." He stared at Drace Aphelion, bitter hatred in his eyes. "If you wish me to hunt, you must release me."

Drace skirted him, watching warily as the man turned with him, keeping him always in his sight. He positioned himself on the other side of Brooke.

The collar released and dropped to the floor.

"No!" Havyn screamed. "No! Drace, I switched the vials of Zemyneah DNA!"

Drace turned. "Whose DNA?"

"Mine."

Drace made a desperate grab for Havyn.

The winged male jerked Havyn out of Drace's reach and leapt, death in his eyes. Drace stumbled back fumbling for his weapon and fired a wild shot. The Karisean took the hit and never slowed down. He grabbed the hand that Drace held the weapon with, and a sickening crack filled the air as bone snapped. Drace screamed and went down to his knees. Hard fists slammed into Drace's jaw, his temple, blood spurted as his nose broke. As Drace hit the floor on his hands and knees, the male yanked him up and held him above his head then with a mighty heave, sent Drace flying.

Drace hit the wall hard as bones cracked and broke, then fell to the floor. He moaned, blood seeping from his mouth. The Karisean leaped forward, intent on ripping his prey limb from limb, eviscerating him. The room flashed bright and Drace disappeared.

The man roared his outrage and turned to the women, who shrank back against the wall. He stalked back to them, low growls rumbling from his throat, incensed that his enemy had escaped. He grabbed Havyn's arm. "Do you know what happens in a Karisean mating?"

Havyn shook her head and tried to pull her arm away. "Let me go!" *What I wouldn't give for a stun gun right now. Bastard!*

He could read the fear, the knowledge in her eyes that she was in terrible trouble, but the hell cat still stared at him with utter defiance.

"Submission. Obedience!" His voice was an enraged snarl, his eyes, cold merciless green gems.

Havyn shook her head and tried to twist away from the looming brute. "That formula shouldn't have worked with my DNA! I am not mating with you! You can forget any thoughts about obedience from me. If I didn't submit to that bastard I was married to, you can bet I won't submit to a barbarian like you!"

The Karisean male tilted his head and smiled coldly "But it did work." He paused. "Mate." Staring at her, he circled her slowly as she turned with him, keeping him in her sight. "The moment he injected me, I was mated to an alien. You!" His voice was a terrible growl of rage. "I am Raine. King of the Windborn. You and that foul being have forced me to destroy the purity of the Windborn. You killed my chosen mate. You will pay for this."

Havyn glared at the man in front of her. "Drace killed her. I had nothing to do with it. If I had known she was there I would have tried to save her!" Raine reached into an invisible pocket and tugged a golden cord from it. Havyn tried to jerk away from him. "Let me go!" He ignored her struggles and futile threats, forcing her arms behind her back and wrapped the cord around her wrists.

"Raine." Brooke touched his arm.

He whirled on her, a growl erupting from his throat.

She backed up against the wall. "It's not her fault!"

He advanced on her, grabbing her arms and yanked her closer to him, sniffing her neck. "Your scent is of Karis" He turned her around, pressed her against the wall then ran his hands over her back, pausing when he felt the wing base in her back. "How is it possible for a Zemyneah slave to smell like a Karisean and have a wing base?" He pressed her harder against the wall. "Answer me!" he snarled.

"Drace." Havyn ground out as she struggled against the cord he'd bound her with. "She was an experiment. We did not expect her to survive!"

Raine turned hard eyes on the woman he was mated to. "Your crimes are many." He started walking back over to Havyn, pulling Brooke along with him. "You will come with us. My scientists must examine you."

The door to the kitchen slammed open.

Raine grabbed Havyn, tucked her behind him. His wings stretched out to shield her.

"Get away from the women!" Theiv burst in, his weapon drawn.

"You may keep this one, Dragon Warrior." Raine released his hold on Brooke and touched the transporter hidden in the feathers of his wing. The room flashed with light and Raine and Havyn disappeared.

"By the Emperor, what was a Karisean doing here!"

Chapter Forty

EARTH DATE: JUNE 29

Unknown Planet, Unknown Galaxy, Unknown Dimension

ASH MORANA SWORE, AND hurled his heavy crystal cut glass across the room. Whiskey splashed out in a golden arc, and the glass shattered against the stone wall of his private den. He'd given the fools all the tools they would need to accomplish his plan. Striding over to the side table, he poured himself another whiskey. And yet, here it was, centuries later, and they still had not accomplished the simple matter he asked of them. He thought about what the High Elder of the Protectors of the Sacred Way said to him three hundred years ago. "*Lord Morana, I received a dream last night, that I believe you should know about. A great being with long white hair, and fathomless eyes came to me. He said that a Dragon and a Lady would destroy everything you've built. He called you a deceiver and warned of terrible sorrow if we did not turn from this path.*"

He'd wanted to kill the cretin, and if he hadn't exercised his formidable control, he would've done so immediately and with violence. Instead, he smiled at the High Elder, and invited him to stay for dinner so they could discuss this dream, and its possible interpretations. Rune. It could be no other. Rune would not destroy his plans. And since Rune so foolishly showed his hand, Ash shrugged, it was only reasonable that he would outplay that particular Creator. He smirked a bit and thought about how he would like to play with the other creator, force her to her knees. Make her pay for rejecting him. And that, too, was on his agenda. But first, he had to come up with a plan to prevent that fool's dream from coming true. He made sure there was plenty of wine and women available as they dined, and he coaxed that High Elder right into his plan.

Ash stared broodingly at the wet mark on his wall and took a drink of whiskey, relishing the burn. It was time for a new plan.

Chapter Forty-One

DRACE LAY IN HIS DARKENED cabin seething in rage. He shuddered in agony when the Exanthus entered hyper warp. The Zeptos were working to keep him alive, and while they were state of the art, there were some injuries that only the advanced medical class of surgeons waiting to operate on him could deal with. The Karisean would pay for that and for stealing his wife. The full might of the Althaneans' warrior class would be brought down on that barbarian's home world. Poor, sweet, naive Havyn. He had to rescue her.

And his Zemyneah, his beautiful exotic Zemyneah. He needed to work on her training, teach her, beyond any shadow of doubt who her master was.

They thought they had defeated him. He sneered at their stupidity. They would learn that Drace Aphelion owned them all.

A quiet chime sounded and Drace looked at the communication station that had been set up so he could access it from his bed. Who was calling him now? He was tempted to ignore it, but then the seal of the Protectors of the Sacred

Way lit up the screen. He glared at the seal for a moment debating the ramifications of missing this call. A second quiet chime sounded and he almost snarled. "Soft light." He said to the computer, then ran a shaky hand through his hair, before touching the symbol to enable the call.

A distinguished looking man, with piercing black eyes, appeared on the screen. "Drace, we were informed of your injuries and that you are returning to Althanea for treatment. Do we need to send in a replacement?"

Drace glared at Auberon Cosmo, the High Elder of the Protectors of the Sacred Way. "As soon as I have received treatment, I will continue my mission. There is no reason to bring in anyone new."

Auberon's features tightened, as he stared coldly at Drace through the view screen. "That is for me to decide. What is the status of the experiment?"

Drace pressed his lips together and bit back the comment he longed to make. "The experiment was a remarkable success. Subject 459 not only survived but she has gone on to display all the qualities that we hoped to achieve with the genome therapy."

The man on the other end of the call, leaned back in his chair, his fingers steepling together. "I would like to see Subject 459. Have her brought to your quarters. And Drace, Ash, himself, came to me last night. He has ordered that the Dragon Warrior you have working for you be brought to him. He also expects you to deliver the dragon that Draakon rides."

Drace could have sworn. Why in the seven hells was Auberon taking such a personal interest in his experiment.

"High Elder Auberon, I will of course bring the Dragon Warrior to you, but I do not have access to his creature. As for Subject 459, she is highly erratic currently. Once I have been treated, and have completed the handler bonding with her, then I will of course be happy to introduce her to you."

Auberon shook his head. "From the medical report that came to me, you are in no condition to complete a bonding with Subject 459. We cannot risk her death at this critical time. I will become her handler. It is critical that this mission succeed. Have the subject brought to your quarters immediately."

So, that was his game. Drace was not impressed. He would not be so easily replaced and dismissed. "I'm sorry, High Elder Auberon, I cannot do that. It is my duty to protect the experiment, and the mission. Subject 459 is in no condition to be paraded around for someone's viewing pleasure. She is a highly classified experiment, and her health must be protected if we are to succeed." Drace clenched his jaw against a wave of pain that had blackness encroaching upon the edges of his vision. "I apologize, High Elder Auberon, but I must rest now. I will contact you after my treatment." He ended the call.

Collapsing back on his bed, he knew that it was imperative that his Zemyneah slave be recaptured. His men were searching for her whereabouts even now. *Soon,* he thought. *Soon, you will be in my possession and I shall teach you a lesson that you will never forget.*

Chapter Forty-Two

EARTH DATE: JUNE 29 4:00 PM
Star Stealth Cruiser: Sol Star System

THORNE WAS APPROACHING the Sol star system, solar winds buffeting his ship as he crossed the bow wave. His fingers flew across the console adjusting for cosmic rays, pressure, and the magnetic field as he entered the heliosheath. An hour more and he would be in orbit. His thoughts cut off as three people appeared on his bridge. "What the ever-loving fuck?" His hand was almost a blur as he drew his weapon.

Eliana frowned, and glared at the man, her colorful hair swirling around her body. "Excuse me?"

Thorne swore again. The other Creator. "Eliana, I presume. Did Rune send you?"

Eliana lifted a brow, her eyes the many colors of a swirling nebula, watched him steadily. "Rune? Is my brother here?"

Thorne shook his head and folded his arms as he watched the three people carefully. He knew one of them, and it was not the Creator Eliana. "Your brother sent me on this mission to rescue a Terran, and then he said he could not interfere with 'the normal course of events' and disappeared.

Eliana nodded. "Of course." She sighed, then shrugged. "Fortunately, I am not of the same persuasion. This is Eli Draakon and his wife Ziva. You will need them if you are going to succeed in your mission. Actually, you will only need Ziva, but Eli was not pleased with the idea of his wife going on a mission without his protection."

Ziva laughed, her dark purple hair shining in the lights of the bridge. "Eli knows me too well. He was afraid I would get into trouble on this non-contact 100 planet."

Eli shrugged. "Theiv is not around to help me talk down whoever you rile up, Ziva. It's better I tag along. Someone has to play peacemaker."

Ziva grinned unrepentantly, and Thorne raised an eyebrow. "Keeping secrets, Creator?"

Eliana narrowed her eyes. "It's called timing, Guardian Feral. And my timing is always impeccable." She gave them all a look. "I have faith in you. Now, I'm off on my own Earth mission." Eliana disappeared.

Thorne shook his head. "Welcome to the Relentless. It's good to see you again Draakon." He clasped Eli's arm in the way of warriors.

"Deathstalker. I didn't expect you when Eliana told us of this mission."

"Creators." Thorne shook his head. "You know, there are some society's that report never having interacted with a being known as a Creator."

Eli and Ziva looked at each other, then burst into laughter. Thorne grinned. "Alright, let's get this mission done."

Chapter Forty-Three

EARTH DATE: JUNE 29 11:00 PM
Gardenside Alberta Canada, Brooke's home.

THORNE, ELI, AND ZIVA stood outside the alien dwelling, and contemplated what they presumed to be the entryway. None of them were certain how it worked. There was no communication pad to announce their presence, and they did not know Terran customs. A voice spoke out of the darkness. "Do not move. I'm holding a weapon on you, and I have enough back-up to take you all down. Who are you? What are you doing here?"

Thorne set his hand on the butt of his phase pistol and exchanged a look with Eli. "We're here to speak with Theiv Draakon." He was aware of Eli stiffening and the glance he shared with his wife. He shrugged. It had been Eliana's secret to reveal.

A light turned on without warning and they blinked against the sudden brightness. "Asshole." Thorne muttered, glad for the automatic updates to the translators as they entered the Sol Star System. Terrans had some colorful language. He could appreciate that. Three men stepped into the light, all of them holding weapons that he did not recognize. Thorne watched them warily, ready to go for his own weapon if necessary.

A dark-haired man watched them silently, his gaze hard, showing no surprise to be speaking to aliens. "Theiv mentioned he was expecting backup, but I assumed soldiers would be sent, and a lot more of them."

"This is what happens when a Creator interferes with a mission." Thorne muttered, clenching his jaw. "If you will bring Theiv out here, he can confirm that he knows me, and that Eli and Ziva are his parents."

Clay looked at the two men with him, then stepped closer and studied Eli and Ziva. "He looks like you both, but with all your advanced technology, that shouldn't be hard to achieve." He pulled his smartphone from his pocket and hit the number for Theiv. "Theiv, we have three aliens on the front porch. Two of them are claiming to be your parents."

The door opened instantly, and Theiv, his phase pistol drawn, stepped out onto the front porch. He stared at the three aliens who Clay was pointing his weapon at and shook his head then laughed. "The infamous Deathstalker, captured by a technologically less advanced alien. This is going to be interesting to explain to your warriors."

"Fuck you, Theiv." Thorne growled.

Theiv smirked and looked at his parents. "You guys checking up on me?"

Ziva shook her head and stepped into Theiv's embrace. "Stop poking at your father. Are you alright?" She stepped back, and looked at her oldest son, her hand lifting to brush back the hair that had fallen over his forehead.

"I'm a Dragon Warrior, mother."

"And yet, the Creator, Eliana, decided to pay us a visit and send us on a mission to retrieve you," Eli said, his arms folded over his chest.

Theiv raised his eyebrow. "The Creator? Are you serious?" He looked over at Thorne to see if the man shared his sudden concern for his parent's mental health.

"Don't look at me, Draakon. Rune fucking Aezorwyn, himself, appeared on my ship, demanding I rush to your rescue. You seem to have brought yourself to the attention of both Creators."

An exotic woman of undetermined origin stepped out onto the porch. "What's going on, Theiv?" Brooke's voice trailed off as she saw the massive man with long blue hair and pointed ears watching her. Her eyes widened, and she moved closer to Theiv before noticing the two people standing with him. Theiv put his arm around her, "Father, Mother, this is Brooke St. Claire. We are Jhaerithe, chosen." He hesitated. "But the situation is complex. Come inside and we will talk."

Chapter Forty-Four

EARTH DATE: JUNE 29
Gardenside Alberta Canada, Brooke's home.

WHEN WAS THE WEIRDNESS going to end? Brooke thought, as she led the way into her kitchen. Seated at the table were Clay, Jaxson, Dani, Nissa, Riak and T'lain. They slowly stood as she walked in with Theiv and the three new aliens. She could almost hear the shocked thoughts behind her family's wide-eyed stares. She'd long passed surreal, so she just introduced everyone. After inviting the new people to sit down, she joined Nissa in getting more cinnamon buns out and pouring more coffee. Just another of her new normal moments.

"I have a message for Havyn, where is she?" the big man named Thorne asked. Brooke looked at Theiv and bit her lip.

"Drace Aphelion managed to circumvent our security this morning. There was a fight, he was injured but managed to escape. Unfortunately, he had brought a Karisean prisoner with him. The Karisean was..." Theiv hesitated. "I have never seen a Karisean that enraged. He took Havyn when he escaped. He would have taken Brooke, too, if I hadn't arrived when I did."

"A Karisean?" Thorne stared at him.

Theiv nodded and shrugged. "I was stunned to be honest with you. Hell, it's fucking rare to see one of them off world."

Eli looked at Ziva, then turned to Theiv. "You can't stay here. If Drace got through your security then you are sitting mashulas when he returns, and he will return. It's not safe, Theiv."

Thorne nodded. "Your father is correct. Drace will not give up, and if the Karisean was going to take Brooke as well, then there is every possibility he, too, will return. Karisean's are not known for accepting defeat."

Brooke straightened, staring at the blue haired man. Her mouth opened, closed, then opened again before she found her words. "Leave? Where would we go? This is my home. This has been home to the St. Claire's for generations. We can't just leave."

Jaxson looked at his mom, then looked at Theiv and this new alien, and he knew they were right. Fuck. He exchanged a look with Clay, then turned to his mother. "Mom, the most important thing is that you are safe. This is just a house, and it sure as hell isn't worth losing you over. Believe me." He looked at Dani and Nissa exchanging an aching look with them, then back to his mom. "We know how empty this place is without you. Those days you were missing were the worst days of our lives. We are not going to risk your life, Mom. Not for a house."

"Besides," Dani spoke up, her voice husky. "I've always wanted to travel to an alien world. I'm in."

Brooke was shaking her head. "No. No. That is too risky. You have lives here. I can't ask you to just give everything up, and journey to some unknown place."

"We're going, Brooke." Nissa said quietly. "Adventure is good for the soul, and none of us ever want to be that far from you again. Also, you don't get to have all these good-looking men for yourself. I like what I've seen so far."

Everyone burst out laughing, and finally, Clay spoke, "Brooke, Mom, we are a family. We stand together. You taught us that. This is our decision to make. We're going with you."

"There is one more thing," Thorne said, his voice a low rumble of sound. "In Sarisia, my world, there are a few people who might be able to help you. They are called bondage breakers, and they have the ability to break the Zemyneah protocol bond."

Brooke looked at Theiv, her eyes filling with hope. "They could help me?"

Riak started to speak up, and Jaxson interrupted. "That decides it. If there is any chance that you could be healed, we have to take it."

Chapter Forty-Five

EARTH DATE: JUNE 30 1:00 PM
Gardenside Alberta Canada, Brooke's home.

BROOKE KNELT ON THE ground, pulling weeds from around the graves in the small family cemetery that held seven generations of her ancestors. From the top of this hill, you could look out over the whole valley. She'd come early and watched the sun come up, sitting by her parents' graves, and remembering the love they'd shared. Heart aching, she looked over at her grandparents' graves. They'd been a loving supportive presence in her life. How she missed them all.

Yesterday morning, she'd gone to the gardening centre. Instead of the usual bright annuals she normally planted around the headstones, she bought hardy rose bushes, lovely-scented lilacs, and a bunch of perennials that she knew would gradually go wild.

Today she'd set aside to clean up the small cemetery and plant the long-lived flowers. Caring for the ancestral resting place of her family was something she did yearly, though often Jaxson, Danielle, and Clay helped her, just as she'd helped her parents and grandparents.

After the conversation with Theiv and his friend Thorne, she knew that this might be the last time she set foot among her ancestors. This tiny place on the top of the hill, that the sun fed life to in the early morning hours and shaded gently in the heat of the afternoon. How she would miss it. She always found peace and a sense of belonging in the resting place of her family. She wiped away a tear with the back of her gardening gloved hand and sat back on her heels, wishing that her mama was still here. Wishing she could talk to her about this whole mess.

She remembered the last time she helped her mama with this task, her mother's words suddenly far more important than they'd ever been. *"Brooke, I know you love this land. I think it's in the blood of every St. Claire who has ever been born here."* Her mama handed her a battered tin mug with iced tea in it. *"And I have to say that I understand, I married into the St. Claire family, but this land grabbed my heart too. I find my peace here among the generations that came before me, that lived in our home and worked this land."*

They drank their iced tea and ate sandwiches before her mom continued. *"I think it's time for me to give you the message that your grandmother gave to me, the same one passed down to her from her father. It's been handed down through the generations from the beginning."* She reached into her bag and pulled out a very old worn leather-bound journal and handed it to Brooke. *"This is the journal of the first St. Claire to come to this land, Axton St. Claire. I hope you read the whole journal one day, but what I want you to see is this part."* She opened the journal to a place marked by an old ribbon and began to read.

"Last night, I made camp on the top of the tallest hill, in a small clearing on my new property. I could see for miles. This land is good, the water fresh, clear, and plentiful. I have a small campfire, and I can hear the wolves howling. Fact of the matter is, that I have never been frightened by the animals that live in nature. I have found that man is a much more dangerous creature. The wolf howl is a song to me, a song of freedom and uncontained wildness. And it is a feeling I know well since I made my escape from England and the life my father would have chained me to. I believe I have learned far more about the measure of who I am on this journey than I learned in all the years of sitting under the best tutors in the land.

"Tonight, I thought about my old astrology tutor, Mason Butterbee. All his lessons about the stars and the planets are spread out before me, as the majesty of the night sky fills me with wonder. Do you think that man will ever walk among the stars? I wonder if there are worlds we know nothing about, and people we haven't imagined.

"I hope that a hundred years from now, two hundred years from now, five hundred years from now, that my descendants will be filled with the same song of freedom, and uncontained wildness that drove me to seek out an unknown future. To those that come after me, if you read my words, be brave,

be courageous, and spread our seed far into the uni-
verse. And know that all who have gone before you,
journey with you, in your heart, and in your blood."

Brooke reached out and touched the rough hand-hewn headstone, with the name Axton St. Claire carved into it. Another tear slid down her cheek. "I don't know that I have the courage to do what is before me. To leave this land, this legacy that you gave us all. I don't know if I have that same song of freedom in me or any of your uncontained wildness. I'm so broken, and I'm afraid."

Hearing a slight noise, she swiped at her cheek and turned. Ziva Draakon was standing at the gate, Clay and Jaxson beside her. Her sons opened the gate and let Ziva through, then lifted their hands in greeting before disappearing into the forest that surrounded this quiet place of rest. She knew they would not be far. "Ziva." She smiled and started to rise, very aware that she probably had dirt smudges on her face, and her jeans were dirty from kneeling and planting. This wasn't how she wanted Theiv's mother to see her.

"Don't get up, Brooke. May I help you?" Ziva moved over to kneel by the old grave. "I have a garden at our home on Sarisa. The plants are quite different though."

Brooke nodded, and tried to ignore the fact that Ziva could not help but see she'd been crying. "I'm planting flowers that are hardy and should be able to survive even if no one is here to care for them." Her voice broke, and she blinked away the sting of tears.

Ziva reached out and gently squeezed Brooke's arm. "This is where your people rest?"

Brooke nodded. "My family. This is the first." She reached out and touched Axton St. Claire's headstone. "Axton and his wife, Sparkling Brook. She was First Nations and her people's ancestral lands border this property. When Axton found out that the land had been illegally seized, he made an unending agreement with her people, that they would always have entry to hunt and access water. Someday, when no St. Claires remain, the land will revert to them. Which will be sooner than any of us ever thought." Her voice broke, and she looked down.

"It is a place of peace and beauty, Brooke. Are you named for Axton's wife?"

Brooke nodded.

Ziva picked up a small trowel and dug a hole then gently placed a plant into the ground and covered its roots with dirt. "If you will allow us, Brooke, I think that, in this place of peace and beauty, surrounded by the protection and love of your ancestors, we could speak woman to woman."

Brooke took a deep breath, and her fingers trembled as she gently planted a hosta. Finally, she nodded, and braced herself for the rejection that she knew any Althanean wife would have over the thought of her son mating a Zemyneah slave.

Ziva's voice was gentle. "Brooke, evil has touched you and I see the wounds you bear." She reached over and gently lifted Brooke's chin. "I too was touched by the vile corruption that poisons my world. As any mother would, I attempted to protect my daughter from such depravity. The sentence for that crime was the Zemyneah protocol. And then I was sold to my husband's enemy."

Brooke froze as she stared into the light blue face of this beautiful woman, tears overflowing as she tried to find her words. "How can they justify what they do?"

"They are blinded by their ignorance, their fear, and their lust," Ziva said as she began to dig another hole. "It is as simple as that and far, far more complicated." The day passed as they talked about Ziva's story and planted a garden of strength and resilience in the small cemetery. A few times over the course of the day, one of the men would appear, Jaxson, Clay, Theiv, or Eli, and give them a wave before disappearing back into the forest, and Brooke knew they were being cared for.

Sitting back, Ziva wiped some sweat from her face and looked at Brooke. "I thought my life was over that day at the Zemyneah auction. I planned to end my existence." Brooke could tell she was serious, and understood, to the depths of her soul, why Ziva would make that choice. After all, she had contemplated the same thing.

"But my life was far from over. Eli. . ." Ziva smiled, the love for her husband apparent in her eyes. "Eli came for me."

"He threw away everything, risked everything; for me. His life as a Dragon Warrior was over. He was never a man who would tolerate injustice."

Brooke carefully planted another flower, considering Ziva's words. "Theiv is like Eli."

Ziva nodded. "My son is very much like his father." She watched Brooke for a moment before she went back to her story. "I tried to send Eli away, believing that I didn't deserve that kind of love, now that I was one of the Zemyneah." She shook her head and took off her gardening glove to push her long purple hair back. "It was a two-week space flight from Althanea to Sarisia. My sex drive was out of control. I was so ashamed that I tried to hide from Eli by locking myself in a cabin. Even though he risked so much to save me, I still thought I wasn't worth saving."

Brooke set down her trowel unable to meet Ziva's gaze, terribly aware of her own feelings of shame and guilt.

"Eli didn't agree with me. He tore the door off its hinges, and he spent the next two weeks demonstrating that a raging sex drive could be a very good thing between mates.

When we arrived on Sarisia, the bondage breakers met with us, and they were able to break the Zemyneah protocol, but even if they hadn't been able to do that, I learned a powerful lesson. Eli loves me, as I am. However, I am. There is no shame between mates.

Our son, Night, was conceived soon after that. I think it's fair to say that our love is deeper, richer than it ever was." She smiled at Brooke and reached over to touch her hand. "Brooke, you have so much to live for. Things will not always be this hard. Trust Theiv. He is a good man."

Ziva hesitated. "Brooke, I don't know if you have had this experience, but I found that some good meaning people told me that I should be thankful for going through this terrible experience because it made me who I am." She shook her head. "I won't say that to you, Brooke. What happened was a violation. It was brutally traumatizing. It's a crime that Drace should have to face the full consequences of the law for. There are no excuses that will ever make what he did right." Ziva looked Brooke in the eyes. "Every step you take past this trauma is what makes you the warrior you are. It is the surviving, the healing, the steps you make to take your life back that make you who you are. You are not defined by this crime. You are defined by the choices you make to overcome this. You are defined by your refusal to let that bastard win."

Brooke nodded slowly as the power of those words washed over her, and she wasn't sure what to think, what to say, but Ziva's words rang true. Her mind went to the young women she had counselled over the years, the women she had watched survive and thrive. She knew that it was indeed their survival that made them the courageous humans that they were, not the crimes that had been committed against them. Never the crimes.

Brooke reached out and brushed some dirt from the leaves of the rosebush she'd just finished planting, her mind swirling with a million different thoughts. It would take some time, but she was willing to allow the healing words to do their work. She did, however, have one concern that she had never voiced. "Ziva, I'm as old as you are. Theiv is a young man, I—." She swallowed, waiting for the condemnation she was sure would come.

Ziva shrugged eloquently. "Age is not as relevant to us once a person has reached the age of majority. The health protocols have reduced the effects of aging in most populations. We live long lives. Don't let such a small factor trouble your mind."

Brooke studied the woman in front of her. "You are gracious."

Ziva laughed. "Not really. I am simply a woman who understands, to a small degree, what you are facing. Brooke? I know this is a lot to consider right now, when you are still hurting, but perhaps you are the catalyst. Perhaps you will find a way out for the women who have also been forced into slavery. Our world desperately needs someone who will show us the way."

Chapter Forty-Six

EARTH DATE: JULY 2, 1:00 PM
Gardenside Alberta Canada, Brooke's home.

THE LAST FORTY-EIGHT hours had been a whirlwind of packing and making arrangements for all the details, small and large. It would have been nice to simply disappear in the night, but the risk of an investigation was something they couldn't ignore. Especially since the police would be after blood if one of their own disappeared. At Brooke's insistence, they spoke with Chief Wolf and his counsel, who agreed to become caretakers of her property and home. If she or a descendant did not return in fifty years, the land would return to them as Axton originally promised.

Jon Strongblood, Jaxson's right-hand man, became manager of Jaxson's construction business. After all debt and bills were paid, the profits from the company would be divided, with a portion going to Jon, and a portion going into an account in Jaxson's name.

Nissa sold her restaurant to Chief Wolf and spoke with Theiv about accessing her wealth through the Accord.

Danielle resigned from her job and Clay resigned from his. Storm and Sev were both at the end of their service with the military and they were released but agreed to be representatives for Earth on this journey. And that was it. They were all free in a way that scared Brooke to death.

As they boarded Thorne's ship, Brooke wondered if they would ever see Earth again.

Chapter Forty-Seven

EARTH DATE: JULY 5ᵗʰ
Somewhere between Earth and Sarisia

"BROOKE THERE IS SOMETHING we need to talk about," Theiv said as he walked into the suite he shared with her.

Brooke looked up from the computerized slot in the wall, where she had been trying to puzzle out how to work it and what on earth it was for. "What is this? How does it work?"

Theiv walked over to her. "This is a dispenser."

"You mean for medicines?"

Theiv paused and shook his head. "No. It's for all sorts of things. You simply touch this icon then tell it what you want." He touched a glowing blue symbol on the black screen. "Earth water with ice." A glass of cold water with triangular ice cubes floating in it materialized on the shelf beside the screen. "You can ask for a variety of food and drinks, and other necessities— Soaps, lotions, cosmetics, minor first aid supplies, book tablets, drawing tablets, holovids. Its purpose is to make our stay comfortable. If you touch here," Theiv touched a glowing green symbol. "A menu appears, and you can scroll to find what you want. I believe that this particular model has thousands of selections." He looked at her expectantly, then frowned. "Do you need medicine? I can take you to the medical facilities if you are ill."

Brooke shook her head. "I was just trying to figure out what it was." She turned with a small shrug. "This room is very... technologically advanced. I had to figure out how to use the bathroom. I'm way too old for that."

Theiv smirked and she narrowed her eyes. "Don't even go there." His laughter brought a curious kind of warmth to her heart, and she shook her head at him. "What did you want to talk to me about?"

Theiv rubbed his neck, then moved over to the wall and leaned against it. "You know in all of this madness we have not spoken about the Emperor and our meeting with him."

Brooke frowned. "What is there to say? We already fixed the problem of my being irresistible to him and driving him into a killing frenzy caused by unrequited lust. Honestly." She rolled her eyes and turned to eye the dispenser. "Does that thing have chocolate in it?"

"Brooke."

Something in the way he said her name made her turn slowly to look at him. What she saw in his eyes, made a chill seep through her body. "We have not solved the problem of the Emperor?"

"Why do you think we have solved this problem?"

"The Amberisian mating mark changed things, right? Havyn said the Zeptos have gone into stealth mode because of it. I..., I just assumed that meant the programming changed." Brooke wrapped her arms around herself.

Theiv shook his head. "I wish it were that simple. You're a very complex being, and nothing about the experiment has gone according to plan. We need to be prepared, because the only thing we know for sure, is that anomalies keep popping up. But those anomalies don't mean that you are safe.

Brooke swallowed and shook her head.

"Here are the facts as we know them: You were programmed to have a bond with two different men. One of those men was the Emperor, the other a handler. Technically, if things had gone according to the science, I'd be the handler, someone Drace could easily dispose of and take my place." He saw the tension in Brooke's body, the fine trembling that started in her hands. If circumstances were different, he would have taken her across the universe to somewhere safe, but this was about so much more than just them. His fist clenched. "The unexpected in all of this is my relationship with the Emperor. It's the unknown factor that messed with the science."

"You have a relationship with the Emperor? What does that mean?" Brooke's eyes were huge, a splash of deep green in her pale face. "I think you have forgotten one thing. I'm human. I'm not genetically predisposed to have two men bonded to me on a physical level. My humanity has to play into this somewhere!"

"You were human. Now, you're more. You are an entirely new species that the universe has never known. No one knows what will or will not happen when you meet the Emperor. Our hope is that, with our bonding, the pheromone levels have dropped enough, that he will not be affected by them."

Brooke shook her head. "It's simple then. I just won't meet him. Problem solved."

"There is no way you can avoid meeting the Emperor, Brooke." Theiv crossed his arms. "We have to tell him what is going on. He's the best protection your planet has."

"You can meet with him."

"He's going to want to meet you."

"So, tell him no. Tell him I'm sick, or I ran away."

Theiv shoved a hand through his hair. "Brooke, you can't simply tell the Emperor no. He won't take no for an answer."

"He's going to have to this time."

"He won't Brooke."

"How do you know that? He could be a very reasonable man."

"The Emperor is a reasonable man. He's also a determined man. He will insist on speaking with you."

"You don't—"

"I do know!" Theiv interrupted, almost growling in frustration. "I know better than anyone else. He's my brother."

Brooke froze, then took a step back. "Your brother?" Her voice was a faint whisper in the silence of the room. "My gosh, Theiv. Do you... I can't. I can't do this. Tell Thorne to take me back. I can't do this. I can't risk this. We... I was fall—" She turned blindly away, swallowing hard. Oh god, what was she going to do? Did he really expect her to risk everything, and to put him at risk too? Her wild thoughts stuttered into silence as she realized that they'd never actually spoken of love. Maybe he'd be relieved if she ended up with the Emperor.

"We are not turning around and going back to Earth, and we would certainly not leave you there. We have to put a stop to this madness!"

"No matter the cost?" Brooke whispered, her throat aching.

"No matter the cost." Theiv's voice was unyielding.

Whirling around Brooke stared at Theiv, her hands clenched at her sides. "So that's it? I'm just suppose to fuck your brother?" Brooke shouted, the words leaving a bitter taste in her mouth.

Theiv moved so fast she almost didn't see it. One moment he'd been leaning against the wall, the next he was in her space, his hands closing around her arms.

"You will never fuck my brother!" His cheeks were flushed, his eyes a deep stormy purple, a muscle ticked in his jaw. "Never! Do you understand me?"

"It's not like I'll have a choice." She struggled against his hold, then stomped on his foot when he didn't let her go. "I'm not your Zemyneah to give away! I refuse this! I won't do it! Do you understand? I. Will. Not!"

Theiv growled and shook her a tiny bit. "Stop it! I would kill my brother before I would allow him to touch you! You're mine."

Brooke froze staring up at him. "I'm yours?" Her eyes searched his. "What does that mean?"

"It means I will not share you. Not even with the Emperor. Especially not with him. You. Are. Mine." His mouth came down on hers in a hard possessive kiss, his tongue pushing aggressively into her mouth.

Some part of her wanted to slap him, but lust rose at the speed of light, a wildfire, burning away everything but this man. She reached up and clenched her hands in his hair, her tongue dueling with his.

He backed her into the bedroom, never ending the kiss. Lifting his head, his breathing harsh, his eyes glinting with emotion, he ripped her top right down the middle. She gasped. Her bra was next, and he picked her up, tossing her on the bed. Her breasts bounced, and he was on her before she could move. Her leggings and underwear were stripped off, and he was kissing her again, his hands moving over her body in a rough caress. She squirmed under him, and he growled, his hands grabbing hers to pin them above her head. "Be still."

Brooke pushed up, her teeth coming down on his lower lip, her eyes flashing with a jumble of emotion. He growled and pulled back, his hand raising to touch his lip, and she shivered at the look in his eyes. "There is a secret the Dragon Warriors hold close." His voice held a dangerous edge. "And I have decided there will be no more secrets between us."

His hand moved down her body and settled over her mound before his fingers slipped between her folds. "You are so wet, Dragoness. So ready for me." His fingers glided up and circled her clit, brushed over it.

She bucked, and a low moan escaped her lips. Her eyes stayed locked to his, her heart beating fast, because there was something utterly alien about the look in his eyes. Something she'd never seen before. Then his cock nudged at her opening, and she inhaled sharply. He eased forward, and as he did, scales rippled along his heavily muscled arms and over his chest.

Her eyes widened.

Blood red and overlapping, the diamond shaped scales, with their striated ridges and furrows had a matte appearance. She gasped at the sensation of her nipples rubbing against their coarse roughness, pleasure zinging through her.

His head dipped down, and his lips moved over hers again, the kiss slower but no less intense. She felt every millimeter of his cock as he filled her, her nipples rasping against the coarseness of the scales and flashes of exquisite pleasure forced her body to shift beneath his. When he drew back from the kiss, flames danced in the deep purple of his eyes. She swallowed, the slightest edge of fear shivering through her even as her arousal spiraled higher.

"The bite of a dragon is excruciating." His voice was a rough whisper that seemed to drift through the air around them, his, but also something utterly foreign that she'd never heard before. She trembled, even as she wrapped her legs around his hips, even as her blood heated, and a deep sensual awakening sparked like fireworks in her blood.

"It changes us." His eyes looked deep into hers, watching her intently as the scales traveled down over his abdominal muscles, his groin, and then unbelievably over his cock. She cried out at the exotic sensation of rough bumps and ridges gliding along sensitized nerve endings. "You are mine, Brooke, claimed by all that I am."

Fire seemed to lick over her body, and then there was no more talking. His fingers entwined with hers, low female moans and hoarse male groans filled the air, pleasure unlike anything she'd ever felt before drove her higher and higher as their bodies moved together in a frantic sensual dance. *What's happening? What's happening?* The extreme pleasure forced a cry from her throat as her body stiffened, then the heated splash of semen deep inside of her, and she fell over the edge, her world shattering into a million different colors. And on her neck, the image of a ruby red dragon slowly appeared.

Chapter Forty-Eight

EARTH DATE: JULY 21 10:00 AM
Sarisia, Galadin Star System

THEIV WALKED BACK INTO their rooms, more than a bit disgusted that he'd forgotten an important data strip. It had taken him two weeks, since their arrival in Sarisia, to arrange this meeting with the Emperor. He needed to drop this information off with his contact, and head over to see Night. His brother might be the Emperor, but he still managed to make time for Theiv, not that it had been easy to arrange.

It was the season of Yarl, and every dignitary or person of importance was trying to see him right now. Yarl was the time of granting favor, and everyone wanted the Emperor's favor. The festivities would get more and more exuberant, as the month slowly ticked by, in a blatant effort to impress the Emperor.

Today was the 9th of Yarl, only 21 more days to go. Theiv wondered what he would see today on his way to the Emperor's private office. There were some pretty outlandish displays during this time every year. If he weren't running late, he would have enjoyed the sights. He made a mental note to take Brooke to a couple of the festivals. She would probably find it fascinating.

It had been too long since he'd seen his brother, but that was the life of a Dragon Warrior. Especially when they lived on different planets and their planets were not exactly friendly with each other.

The room flashed bright and Theiv dived behind a table, but it was too late. A phase pistol fired, then another. Theiv was struck in the arm but managed to palm his own weapon with the other hand. He ducked behind a chair and returned fire. His aim was true, and the man crashed into the table as he went down. The other man fired, and the phase stream burned across the top of Theiv's shoulder. He swore and fired back, then ducked behind another chair.

"Drace sent us to collect you, Draakon. He doesn't want you interrupting his dinner plans."

"Tell Drace I have my own plans tonight, and he is going to have to be satisfied with fucking with one of you instead."

The huge Althanean with long messy hair laughed, an ugly sound that grated on Theiv's nerves. "Our orders are to bring you to him. We've been promised a night with that sweet little Zemyneah he keeps with him. I'm not missing out on that, Draakon, so you might as well make this easy for all of us and surrender." Theiv replied with another burst from his weapon. The room flashed bright again, and several more of Drace's men appeared.

Theiv began laying down a heavy volley of weapons fire. He had to get to the door. He had to finish his mission. Brooke. He tried to send her a warning over their bond, as he stood up and continued to fire, trying desperately to take out as many of Drace's men as possible. A blast caught him full in the chest, and he fell, his last thought on the woman that everyone wanted.

Chapter Forty-Nine

EARTH DATE: JULY 21 1:00 PM
Sarisia, Galadin Star System

BROOKE PACED IN THE beautiful alien gardens as she waited for Theiv to come back. He'd gone to a private meeting with his brother, The Emperor. His plan was to reveal everything to his brother and come up with a plan, while she waited with Eli, Ziva and her family and the men who protected her. But he should have been here by now.

Eli decided that the palace's royal garden would be the best place for them to wait. There were festivities taking place all over the city, and no one would think it odd that they were resting in the gardens of the Emperor. The garden was public, and that would make an attack unlikely. No one would dare to touch a marked Dragon Warrior's woman, especially in such a public space.

She was worried, and she could see that Eli was also concerned. "Perhaps I should go back to our suite, in case he's there?"

Eli shook his head. "You're safer here with us, but one of the others could go."

Jaxson and Clay volunteered, and she went to sit with Ziva and Nissa.

CLAY AND JAXSON SURVEYED the mess. Tables and chairs overturned, drawers dumped out, and blood drying on the wall. A note was stuck to the dispenser.

"Somehow it never occurred to me that an alien asshole would leave a note," Clay muttered as he stepped over to the dispenser, careful not to disturb the crime scene. *Zemyneah, I have the Dragon Warrior. If you want him to live, come to me. My craft is at docking spaceport 793 on the east side. Do not delay or it will go badly for him. Come alone.* Clay shook his head. "Fucking criminals are all alike." He pulled out his new communicator and hit the code for Eli. "Eli, there's a problem. It looks like Drace was here. The room is in shambles. There's a note instructing Brooke to go to a docking spaceport. Alone."

Eli swore. "Come back here Clay. If this were Althanea, I would simply gather up my warriors and we'd deal with the bastard. Permanently. However, I suspect that the Sarisians will not be pleased if some Althaneans have a shootout in their city."

By the time Clay and Jaxson returned, Eli had formulated a plan that scared Brooke, but also met with her approval. And that was how an hour later she found herself just outside the private suite of the Empress of the known universe. Eli squeezed her arm and touched the symbol that activated the communication system. Moments later they were being escorted into a private room to wait for the Empress.

"Eli." An exotic woman entered the room. Stunningly beautiful, she was tiny with rich brown skin, short spiky blue hair and pointed ears. Her eyes were silver, not grey, but a deep glimmering silver. She wore a soft silky turquoise tunic and black leggings, with black leather flat-soled boots on her feet. On her arm was the same unusual dragon bracelet that Ziva wore. She looked nothing like what Brooke was expecting. Especially, with the dagger belted at her waist, and the tiny ruby red dragon mark on her neck. "I did not expect to see you before the royal dinner. Is everything alright?" She glanced over at Brooke.

"Kahea." Eli walked over and hugged the tiny woman. "No, everything is not alright. Is Night here?"

Kahea shook her head. "No, I'm sorry, but there was some kind of disturbance about his recent health protocol injection, and he went to speak to the doctor about it."

Eli traded a glance with Brooke, then turned back to his daughter by law. "Empress Kahea, this is Brooke St. Claire, she is Theiv's mate, and she is in need of your help. I must go and speak to Night about this situation. It is urgent. Please lock your doors and do not let anyone, including Night into your rooms."

"Including Night? You don't want me to allow my shield, my mate, into our chambers?" Kahea's voice was hard, and a dangerous glitter entered her eyes.

"Brooke will explain." He turned to Brooke, and gave her a reassuring look, then squeezed Kahea's arm gently. "Trust me." After another look at both women he hurried out of the room.

Well, this was awkward. Brooke looked at the Empress, and the Empress looked at her. What on earth did you say to an Empress? "Hello, Empress Kahea, I'm uh—"

"Theiv's mate?"

"Yes. Sort of."

"Sort of? You wear the mark of his dragon. There is no sort of when you've been marked." The Empress gave her an amused look. "Come let us have something to drink, and you can explain this urgent situation that my brother by law has got himself into."

"We need to hurry, he's in danger, and we need to save him."

"In danger? Save a Dragon Warrior?" Kahea laughed. "Oh, Brooke, I like you already. What has the mighty Dragon Warrior done that requires us to save him?" She rang a bell, and waved Brooke to a seat, then strode over to open a cabinet and took out an assortment of weapons. A young woman entered, and Kahea asked her to bring them some cold winterberry nectar. "It's been far too long since I've had an adventure." The young woman returned with their drinks, and Kahea thanked her then waited for her to leave before sitting down with Brooke. "Tell me everything."

Brooke told Kahea everything. If they were to save Theiv, and the Emperor, then there could be no secrets between them. The Empress rose to her feet, a dangerous angry smile curving her lips. The glint in her eyes warned Brooke that this woman was not one to dismiss easily.

"These Althanean's, and their obsession," Kahea practically spat the words, "with keeping their women under control! We are talking about illegal genetic experimentation, and murder, multiple murders! I won't turn a blind eye to this. What they have done is tantamount to a declaration of war with several planets in the Accord. Are they fools? They have no idea what they have stirred up."

Kahea belted on several weapons as she spoke. "Brooke, you and I are going to save your Dragon Warrior, but before we leave, I need the doctor to come and take a sample of your blood. He would need it to figure out if they succeeded in their bid to alter my husband's health protocol."

After the doctor took his sample, Kahea led Brooke into a private room, and flung open a closet door. "I believe sister by law, that since Drace is expecting a Zemyneah, we should give him one."

Brooke gasped, clenching her hands into tight fists. "If that bastard sets one foot near me, I'll kill him."

Kehea turned that dangerous smile on her. "A few years ago, I would have approved your plan, hellfire, I would have joined in, but Drace must stand trial for what he's done. That means we must take him alive. You are going to be the distraction." The Empress set about pulling some of the most shockingly bare gowns that Brooke had ever seen out of the closet.

"Why do you have a Zemyneah outfit in your closet?" Brooke asked faintly, aghast at the almost transparent bits of cloth that floated around her, revealing far more than they concealed.

"It was given to me by the Althanean delegation, a few years ago. I'd just become Night's Empress. It was intended as an insult of course," Kahea said with a harsh laugh, and she grew serious. "I don't take the Zemyneah slave trade lightly.

It is evil, and we are working with the rebels to save as many women as we can. I was tempted to throw that entire delegation into prison, let them discover what it means to insult an Empress who is also a warrior, and deadly with a blade." She sighed, "But Night said that would only start a war." She paced, her memories awash in that day. "I was ready to go to war. I wanted war. I wanted to slaughter every man that thought it okay to enslave women. Night insisted I find another way to deal with their arrogance."

Kahea walked over and adjusted a few of the transparent scarves that Brooke was struggling with. "So instead of prison and torture, I gave orders for the entire delegation's wives to wear Zemyneah clothes for the duration of the conference, and I also wore the outfit, a public declaration that we wore these ridiculous outfits as a sign of solidarity for all Zemyneah slaves." She shrugged. "Of course, the delegation was terribly insulted, and they left immediately. I did receive a note from one of the wives who thanked me for my brave stand against the Zemyneah slave trade.

"That was a very courageous thing to do, Kahea." Brooke stared at her reflection in the mirror, it always seemed as if she was looking at a complete stranger, when she saw herself. An alien stranger. Her eyes met Kahea's. She was starting to recognize that look in people's eyes. It meant that she needed Theiv. The pheromones she released were potent, and gender did not seem to matter. Kahea put her hand on Brooke's shoulder. "You're safe Brooke. And you're the courageous one. Let's go save that mate of yours."

She did not feel courageous as she hurried along by Kahea's side out of the castle, and into a ship that would take them to the docking spaceport. But, Theiv had saved her more than once, and now it was her turn to save him. She refused to allow Drace's crimes to go unchallenged. Evil could only prevail if good people did nothing.

Chapter Fifty

BROOKE STOOD OUTSIDE the small personal cruiser docked at the spaceport and waited for a reply to her hail. A door slid open, and a ramp descended. She looked up, and there, standing in the doorway of the ship, was Drace Nakieya. "Zemyneah, you've chosen wisely." His smile was unpleasant at best.

Brooke swallowed, and glanced away from Drace hoping to catch a glimpse of Kahea, but the woman had hidden herself too well. "You will release Theiv now. I won't come one step closer until he is released."

Drace laughed, "Look at you, all fire and command. That is your old life, Zemyneah."

"Brooke. My name is Brooke." She clenched her hands into tight fists and glared at the alien who had created such pain and chaos in her life.

Drace smiled at her, but his eyes were hard and cold. He started down the ramp. "You no longer have a name. You are my creation. My Zemyneah slave. Your sole purpose in life is to bring me pleasure, until such time as I see fit to pass you on to the Emperor. Your purpose will then be to please the Emperor and gain the information I need."

"You arrogant ass!" Brooke hissed, and glanced around before meeting his eyes. "We are standing on Sarisian soil. You have no power over me. There is no slavery on this planet."

Drace wrapped his hand around her arm in a hard grip. "And what do you think the Dragon Warrior is? My power is very real. You're the one who is arrogant, Zemyneah, but I will cure you of that failing. You are here, of your own free will, choosing the life of pleasure that I created you for."

Brooke drew back, a shudder running through her at his touch. "I am here to free Theiv. I'm not setting one foot on that ship until he is free."

"That's not how this is going to work." Drace leaned down, his breath caressing the skin of her neck, and inhaled deeply. "These pheromones were an inspired idea. With this alone, I'll be able to control the Emperor and set this universe to rights."

Shuddering, Brooke's hand clenched in the fragile fabric of the scarf skirt, and she forced herself to remain still, as Drace's other hand settled on her hip. Her eyes met Kahea's as the woman slipped from behind some containers, gave her a nod, and raced silently up the ramp.

Slowly, Drace straightened away from her. "Come, you will demonstrate your willingness to submit."

"N––No! First release Theiv. I won't—"

"You will." Drace gripped her chin in a punishing hold and lifted, staring coldly into her eyes. "You will demonstrate thoroughly your acceptance of my control, or I will kill the Dragon Warrior. Do I make myself clear?"

Brooke was shaking. The first part of their plan had gone exactly as they thought it would, but she was not sure she could go through with the next part. The idea of using her body's seductive powers to keep Drace distracted made her skin crawl. There was a prickling feeling in the tips of her fingers, and she realized that the claws that helped her escape the military compound on Earth were reacting to the threat she now felt. A feeling of relief swept through her. She was not defenseless. If worse came to worst she could tear his face off. She almost laughed at the shocking thought. Instead, she swallowed. "What guarantee do I have that you will release Theiv."

"Come, we are drawing attention, Zemyneah." His arm went around her back as he ushered her up the ramp. "The Dragon Warrior is useless to me, more of a problem than I need at this time. As soon as you have demonstrated your compliance, I will have him released."

Lying Bastard! She thought, a terrible feeling of dread rising inside her, as she walked beside the monster up the ramp, and into his ship. Reaching out through the telepathic bond she shared with Theiv, she sought any sign that he was alive. What if he'd already killed Theiv? Her breath caught, and a hard lump rose in her throat. No. She forced herself to take a deep breath. Theiv was alive. He had to be alive. She reached out again, picturing the satisfied look on Theiv's face this morning after they'd made love, holding it close to her heart. "*Help is coming. Be ready.*"

Drace yanked off one of the flimsy scarves that were her only covering, and she flinched. He backed her up against a wall and she knew the pheromones, that he felt were his secret weapon, were getting to him. His lips touched her neck and she stiffened, but carefully pulled out the tiny injector hidden in the scarves. His tongue licked across her neck, and revolted, she jerked almost dropping the syringe. Her heart pounded in her chest and she fought the nausea building in her throat. Staring past him at the wall in front of her, she shifted her head to the side to give him better access, fighting visions of being raped right here in the hall. She couldn't prevent the whimper that escaped her, as she struggled with her urge to knee him in the balls. His hand lifted to her breast, and she lifted the injector, jamming it hard against his throat. A tiny hiss, and Drace collapsed against her.

Kahea stepped out of a darkened doorway, her face furious, and helped her to drag Drace into the nearest room. "I was just about to kill him when you pulled out that injector. Sick Bastard!" They quickly bound him with some of the scarves from her outfit, the fragility of the fabric a deception. As Kahea explained to her, the scarves of the Zemyneah outfit were often used to bind a Zemyneah for her master's pleasure. Drace would not escape his bonds easily. "Are we just going to leave him here?"

Kahea shook her head. "We'll come back for him. I plan to lock him up in the fortress dungeon and interrogate him, as slowly and painfully as possible."

They worked their way through the ship, using a scanning device, and the directional computers located at regular intervals in the corridors. It still took them precious minutes to find the section where Theiv was being held. When the scanner showed Theiv's bio signs, Kahea pushed her around the corner and quickly handed her a weapon. "Point and fire. It's that simple. Look at me, Brooke." The urgency of the Empress's voice caught Brooke's attention. "We're going into a dangerous situation. If there is fighting, it will hurt. You must expect that and be determined to carry on. Focus on our goal. We'll succeed, no matter the cost. We will get Theiv out. Do you understand?" And then the wild woman winked. "I've been in situations much worse than this one. Remind me to tell you about the time that Thorne and I faced off a pack of deathstalkers."

Deathstalkers? What the hell was a Deathstalker? Brooke took a deep breath and nodded. It was clear to her that Kahea was a fierce warrior, and it was becoming glaringly apparent that she, herself, needed training in self defense and some fighting skills. If they survived— No. After they got Theiv out, she was going to insist on it.

A rough looking man exited through a sliding door and they waited till he was out of sight before ducking inside. Theiv was sitting propped up against the wall, his face swollen and bruised. Multiple abrasions, cuts and contusions covered his bare chest and hands. Brooke gasped and rushed over to him. "Theiv!"

Kahea swore.

He opened his swollen eyes and then tipped his head. "Brooke?"

"It's me Theiv. And Kahea. We are going to get you out of here."

"Kahea?"

"Right here, Brother by law." She ran a scanner over Theiv before helping Brooke to get him standing. "Night is never going to let you live this down."

"Night is going to spank your ass, Kahea."

"Goddess, I hope so. What's an adventure that doesn't end in great sex?"

Brooke stared at them both and shook her head. "Come on, let's get out of here before we're discovered."

They began to work their way back through the ship, ducking behind the metal framework of the passageways, and stepping into empty rooms to avoid the crew. They were almost to the room they'd left Drace in when a couple tough looking men, supporting an unconscious Drace stepped out. There was a frozen heartbeat of time, and then Kahea shot her weapon. One of the men staggered, then the corridor lit up with neon flashes as they returned fire. A glowing particle beam of intense plasma energy seared Brooke's arm as she fired her blaster. She stumbled back against the wall before lifting her weapon with shaking hands, ignoring the terrible burning, and fired again. Kahea was down on one knee firing repeatedly, a burn mark on the leg of her pants and Theiv was propped behind a steel frame, swearing. "Give me that blaster!" Brooke wanted to say no, but her hands were shaking so badly that her shots were going wild.

"Dammit!" She slapped the blaster into Theiv's outstretched hand. She was going to get training on these damned alien weapons! A growl left her throat, and she froze then looked at Theiv. He shot her the beginnings of a brief crooked grin, then began to systematically lay down fire. Alarms were blaring, and it would only be a matter of time before reinforcements arrived. "We gotta go!" Kahea shouted, and surged to her feet, firing repeatedly at the men who stood between them and freedom.

She was going to have to help Theiv if they were going to get out alive, Brooke realized. She pushed her way out from behind him and wrapped her arm around his waist.

"Leave me, Brooke. Get the hell out of here!"

Stubborn male. She ignored his cursing and shoved her shoulder under his arm. "I'm not leaving without you."

Theiv cursed and drew deep on the strength of the dragon he was bound to. Ignoring the pain that every move cost him, he fired again and again. A man dropped, hit dead center in the chest by Kahea's shot, then the other man went down. Shouts sounded down the corridor and they began to run. Stagger was more like it, but they staggered as fast as they could. Suddenly, the airlock in front of them blew, and through the smoke and debris Eli burst through.

"You're late." He growled as the ship's engines roared to life. "The emergency bulkheads are closing! Come on!" He grabbed Kahea, and tossed her out the hatch, then wrapped his arms around Brooke and Theiv and jumped, just as the ship shot up into the air. They landed hard on the ground and rolled. When Brooke opened her eyes, they were surrounded by Sarisian warriors. A tall muscular blue man, his face chiseled and hard, was staring down at her. He had a long, jagged scar running down one cheek, giving him a dangerous air, and a fierce intelligence glowing in his eyes, and he looked remarkably like Theiv. She swallowed.

Chapter Fifty-One

EARTH DATE: JULY 22 10:00 AM
Sarisia, Galadin Star System

"STOP STARING AT HER, Night." Kahea frowned at her husband. "You're making her nervous."

"She should be nervous, she almost cost me my Empress, my brother, and my father." Night's voice was hard, his face expressionless.

Kahea rolled her eyes and looked at Brooke, who was sitting beside the bed that Theiv rested in. "I'd tell you that Night is more growl than bite, but that would not be true. However, he's not a tyrant. He's a fair ruler of the known universe. Just tell him what you told me."

"I've already been briefed by my father." Night turned his stormy purple eyes on his wife. "You're also in trouble, beloved."

Kahea grinned and winked at Brooke. "Does it involve spankings and being tied up?"

Night crossed his arms and glowered.

Brooke was terrified for a lot of reasons by this hardened warrior king, not the least of which was the fact that she could smell the pheromones that her body was releasing. She wanted to disappear, to run, to hide, but the small medical suite they were in did not allow for any of that.

"Drace's formula was a success," Night said, his voice a deep growl of displeasure. Kahea's eyebrow rose, and Brooke shrank back in her chair, glancing towards the door.

"You would never make it." Night said, his voice a whip of fury. "I'm glad that my father, at least, had the common sense to come and talk to me." He looked at Theiv who pushed himself half up in the bed as if he would attempt to protect the woman who sat beside him. "We believe this might be an antidote." He set a small vial of shimmering gold liquid down on the bedside table. "It's untested, and there is a high chance that it will fail, and it comes with the risk of unknown side effects." He set an injector down on the bed-side table. "This is a potent, instantaneous sedative. At the first sign of a loss of control I would have injected myself, and my medical staff would have given me the experimental antidote."

Kahea shoved back her chair and stalked over to her husband. "And yet you came into this room knowing the risks."

"The blood samples from Brooke, when combined with my blood, prove the experiment was a success, but there were anomaly's. Things the doctors could not explain. It was decided that we must know for certain if the formula Drace devised would work the way it was supposed to. The instant I came in this room, I could scent the pheromones that Brooke is releasing. And, yes, they have a powerful effect on me, but with a twist. All I can think about is fucking Kahea."

Kahea grinned and winked at Brooke. Brooke blushed, and Theiv let himself drop back on the bed with a laugh that turned into a pain filled groan.

Night continued to look fierce. "Don't think it is that simple. Drace's formula is a success. There is still danger. We don't understand the anomalies in Brooke's blood. My medical staff is running tests to see if they can figure this out. It is imperative that we speak with Havyn. Where is she?"

"The Karisean we told you about escaped with Havyn as his captive." Theiv said. "There is something you need to know, Night. The Karisean was Raine, King of the Windborne."

Night swore. He exchanged a look with his wife, and then he stalked over to the communication system built into the medical suite's wall and punched in the code to his Prime Commander, Jorel Wildhaven. "Jorel, we have a situation, please set up talks with the Karisean's at once. And listen to this discussion, I'll need your input later." He looked back at Theiv and Brooke. "This has the potential to turn into a bloody war. Did Raine see Brooke?"

Theiv nodded, "He spoke with her, scented the Karisean in her and discovered that she's developed a wing base. He would have taken her with them when he escaped, if I hadn't burst in at that moment."

Night Draakon, Emperor of the known universe, shook his head. "He'll send someone to collect her. Rain is going to want her under Karisean protection. You know the Karisean's are fanatical about remaining isolated from the rest of the universe and preserving their genetic uniqueness." He paced across the room and back. "This is an incredibly volatile circumstance. Your woman contains the DNA of four of the most dangerous species in the known universe. By the Creators, every one of those races is so protective of their females, that to even consider harming one is to court death. Drace is insane. He may have started an intergalactic war!" Night shoved his hand through his hair and turned, furiously pacing the room again. After a moment he came back, and Kahea put her arms around his waist, leaning against his chest.

Brooke sat in her chair, a growing horror seeping through her veins, stunned by what she was learning.

"They're all going to want her, Theiv. Every damn one of those species is going to claim her!" Night was furious. He turned to his Commander. "I want emergency meetings with the Liege Commanders of each of these species. I want an emergency session of the Accord set up. And I want an overhaul of our security protocols! I won't tolerate this threat! And get my medical staff in here. Theiv needs to be given the antidote."

An icy coldness slid through Brooke. It was right. She knew it was right. Theiv needed to be free of her, but even though she understood, she had to fight the panic. Wrapping her arms around herself she nodded, her voice faint. "Yes, please, give him the antidote at once."

She swallowed to relieve the dryness in her throat, then jumped when Theiv's hand grasped her arm and he hauled her onto the bed with him. "No." His voice was flat, hard, and Brooke stared at him sensing a terrible fury.

"Brooke is mine. You have seen the mark of the dragon on her. She is mine. I will not take the antidote."

Night turned and looked at his brother. "Theiv, you don't have to—"

"No." Theiv slashed his hand through the air. "I choose to be with Brooke. I am her Protector."

"Think, Theiv. There is no choice in an addiction. There is no choice when you are forced by this formula to mate with her."

Brooke felt that hissed truth like a slap. She bowed her head and fought the tears. She couldn't hold Theiv to her like this. She wouldn't force this man of honor to live with the repercussions of Drace's evil. And she would not risk his life with the dangers that would follow her.

"Night!" That was Kahea's shocked voice, but Brooke did not look up.

"Theiv." She spoke softly. "You should take the antidote." Silence, dark and dangerous, met her words. She looked at Theiv, and the fury in his gaze made her tremble. She looked away.

A low masculine sigh, then the Emperor spoke again. "I will send a diplomatic mission to your world, Brooke, to establish first contact and invite Earth to join the Accord. We won't allow your world to be destroyed by the evil intentions of this man and the powers that back him.

Night looked at Kahea, his eyes showing regret for his angry words. "I will send ambassadors to meet with your leaders. There are many things to discuss. And if your leaders are open to it, we will provide a squad of warriors to patrol your star system until a Terran squad can be established."

Chapter Fifty-Two

FOR THE FIRST TIME since they rescued Theiv from Drace, Brooke went back to their personal suite. She couldn't permit Theiv to make this sacrifice for her. Somewhere in this universe, his true mate must reside. And yet, she knew, that as long as her life was in danger, there was little chance Theiv would take the antidote. Tears rose at the thought, but she pushed them away. She had to find a solution. She had to find a way to free Theiv so that he could have the life he was meant to have.

She walked over and looked out the window, the alien landscape spread out before her in glorious beauty. The sky was blue here, but the grass was teal, and the leaves on the trees were varying shades of purple and red. The flowers were a profusion of color just as on Earth, but their shape and form were different in many ways. She'd been told that the winters were harsh, and the wilderness around the city was dangerous. She had no intention of experiencing either.

She paused, a frown crossing her face. Thorne. What had he said about someone called a bondage breaker? Someone who freed Zemyneah slaves. Still frowning she walked over to the communication system and put in a call to Thorne.

A mere hour later, she sat beside the big warrior on a personal flyer, skimming over the wilderness of Sarisia. "How long till we are there?"

"Not long, Brooke. Why are you doing this?"

Brooke shrugged pretending a nonchalance she was far from feeling. "I do not wish to be a Zemyneah slave. It's abhorrent to my people."

Thorne laughed, a rough growl of amusement. "It's abhorrent to all intelligent people. You and Theiv seemed well suited though. I thought it was more. He did not treat you as if you were merely a slave for his pleasure."

Brooke glanced at Thorne, her eyes troubled. "Theiv had no more choice than I did in this situation. It's not right that he risks his life for me. Drace is never going to give up. I am going to be running from him forever. If this 'bondage breaker' can break the bond with Theiv, then he will be free and safe."

Thorne tapped a few commands into the panel before him, then turned and regarded Brooke. "How does Theiv feel about this?"

Brooke shook her head, "He doesn't know. We tried to get him to take the experimental antidote, but he refused."

Thorne watched her silently for a long moment. "He will be angry I think."

"But he will be free, and he will be alive." Brooke turned away from Thorne. "That is all that matters."

"No, I do not think so Brooke. Theiv is a man of honor, a man who feels deeply. He wouldn't stay with you if he weren't committed to you."

Brooke sighed wistfully. "It's not something that we will know for sure unless this bond is broken, and he is no longer addicted to the Zemyneah—to me."

Thorne expertly guided the little craft down in the courtyard of a stone keep, deep in the wilderness.

"Welcome to the Scarlet Light Fortress." A woman dressed in a red leather uniform, greeted them as they disembarked from the flyer. "Hello, my name is Ava. I'm the Guardian of this fortress. Thorne sent me a message regarding the nature of your Zemyneah technology. Walk with me, Brooke, and we will discuss what can be done. Thorne, please avail yourself of our comforts.

Thorne gave a short nod and headed into the fortress. Ava held out her hand to indicate the direction they would walk. "We will go to the gardens. They are peaceful and we will not be disturbed."

They'd been seated only a few moments when they heard the arrival of another flyer. Ava assured her that her second would take care of the new visitor and urged her to continue her story. When she was done Ava looked deeply concerned. She lifted her hand, a scarlet glow appearing. "I would like to examine you if you don't object. There will be no pain, or harm, I assure you."

Brooke nodded her consent, and Ava reached out a hand, careful to not touch her. "You're Zemyneah, but..." she walked around Brooke, her hand still held out, the red glow growing. "I've never encountered the Zeptos that inhabit your blood, and your heritage is confusing. You're not a species I've encountered before, and yet you also contain DNA from several other species. How is this possible?"

"Stop!" A hard male voice, that she knew all too well, interrupted. Brook turned slowly. Standing just a few feet away was Theiv. His legs planted widely, arms crossed, he glared at her, his eyes cold and flinty. "I've warned you about running away from me. Why are you doing this, Brooke?"

"I told you, Theiv. It's not right that you give up your life for me. That you risk your life. That you risk never finding a true mate."

His expression tightened. "I never do anything I don't want to do."

"It's still not right, Theiv. It's too much to ask of anyone."

Theiv growled, and Brooke looked at him, alarmed. "Go ahead, Brooke. Have the bond broken. You're still not leaving here without me, and I guarantee you that I will fuck you until that bond comes back stronger than ever. You're mine, and I will never let you go."

"You want a Zemyneah slave that badly?" Brooke flinched and looked away.

Theiv strode forward and grabbed her by her arms, giving her a tiny shake. "You are not my Zemyneah. You're my dragon marked mate. A Zemyneah slave doesn't bear the mark of a mighty dragon. It's impossible. Zemyneah slaves don't bear an Amberisian mating mark. It's not possible. And yet you bear both marks. Put there by my hands, by my seed spilled deep inside you, by my lips and tongue as I tasted every inch of you. You're not my slave, Brooke. You never have been. You're my heart, you're my soul, you're my beloved, the woman I will protect for all eternity.

A tear slipped down Brooke's cheek, and she lifted a trembling hand to Theiv's face. "You love me?"

"Without limits, Brooke. I love you with all my heart and with all that I am. It is my honor to protect you." His hand lifted and he cupped her neck, the warmth of his palm covering the small red dragon that marked her as his. "I've told the Emperor that we will be mated tonight."

Brooke laughed and wiped a tear away. "Don't you think you need to ask first?"

Theiv regarded her seriously for a long moment. "I'm asking, Brooke. From the beginnings of time the dragon warriors have joined with their women in a sacred binding that can never be broken. You are the keeper of my heart. I am your defender, your protector, your shield. With great reverence I ask for the gift of your trust. I ask for the right to call you mine. I ask for a place for my soul to call home."

Brooke's hand covered her mouth, tears filled her eyes as she understood the depth of his feelings for her. "Yes," she whispered, then louder. "Yes!"

Theiv solemnly indicated a box carved with exquisitely detailed dragons, that Brooke hadn't noticed in the heat of their words. He opened the lid and withdrew something, turning to Brooke. "As a symbol of my protection, I ask you to wear the emblems of the Dragon Warriors. He held out a slender band of gold, which sort of looked as if it could be a bracelet. Brooke looked at it, puzzled, but nodded her consent. Theiv took her right hand and slid the band onto her wrist. The metal began to warm, and in a sudden blaze of ruby red light, transformed into a dragon that curled itself from elbow to wrist around her arm. The head of the dragon came to rest on the back of her hand, the tail winding around her arm to settle by her elbow. Its eyes were ruby red jewels, it's scales intricately etched and edged in a deep ruby red, every detail from its eyes to its wings were so finely wrought that it appeared to be a living creature. Brooke gasped and looked at Theiv, her eyes wide. He smiled. "It's an automation. Your Zeptos are even now coding it to you. It will protect you if it ever senses danger."

Brooke moved her wrist experimentally, the weightless automation moved with her in a smooth undulation, never hindering her movement in any way. She looked up with wide eyes. Theiv turned her slightly and then he fit a delicate semi-circle of gold over her left ear, again the burst of ruby red light and the warmth as a delicate dragon transformed and clung to the side and point of her ear. She reached up, touched it, and turned questioning eyes to him. "If you are in danger, it will fly directly to me. It has the capacity to travel great distances, even through space if needed."

He took her left hand, pressed a kiss to the palm, and slid a band of gold over her ring finger. Once more, the band transformed into a dragon. A tiny glittering red dragon. "It sends a signal that is coded to my Zepto's, Brooke, so that I will always be able to find you. It also creates an impenetrable force field around the wearer to prevent it's removal and to protect the wearer from harm."

Theiv slid his hand along her cheek, and into the short strands of her hair, as he leaned down and rested his forehead against hers. "I love you, Brooke," he whispered as he took her mouth in a gentle kiss.

"I love you, too, Theiv," she said between kisses, knowing that, finally, she had found a safe place for her heart.

~The End~

Next Book

The Codes of Creation Multiverse: Realm of The Forsaken
Series:

Forsaken

Coming Soon

You can find me at:

https://www.arliesheelin.com[1]
https://www.facebook.com/pursuingdreams.ca
https://www.instagram.com/arlie_sheelin/
https://twitter.com/ArlieSheelin
https://www.patreon.com/arliesheelin

---

1. https://www.arliesheelin.com/

Glossary

CREATORS: Beings who exist out of time and space. The last two surviving Creators, created the Multiverse

Godsdamned: A common swear word throughout the multiverse. There are two Creators, so this expression is plural.

Heliosphere/Heliosheath: Our sun generates a bubble that surrounds our solar system, called the Heliosphere. This bubble is made up of solar winds from the sun.

The heliosheath is the point where those solar winds begin to slow down and interact/merge with interstellar matter.

Hyper warp drive: Hyper warp drive combines the ideas of hyperdrive and warp drive

1. **Hyperdrive** (Star Wars) is a fictional propulsion system that enables a starship to travel at lightspeed and cross the empty space between star

systems using an alternate dimension of hyperspace

2. **Warp drive** (Star Trek) is a fictional technology that enables space travel at faster-than-light speeds. The idea behind Warp drive is to create warp fields that form a subspace bubble surrounding a spaceship. The subspace bubble distorts the section of the spacetime continuum around the spaceship (rather like folding space), and results in the ship being able to travel at velocities that would exceed the speed of light. (Warp Drive is thought to be theoretically possible in the real world.)

3. **Hyper warp drive** is the idea that a spaceship could enter hyperspace and while in that dimensional highway they could generate a subspace bubble. The results being an even faster way to travel between star systems, and galaxies.

Laser Pistol/Phase Pistol/Blaster: Space age weaponry similar in appearance to a gun or rifle that uses a particle beam of intense plasma energy instead of bullets.

In-between: The in-between is the place where the creators existed. It is a place out of time and space, existing between nothingness and the Multiverse.

Millennia: The plural form of millennium. A period of a thousand years.

Multiverse: A multidimensional universe.

Non-contact 100 world: A world that is to have no Alien contact for 100 years to allow them to advance at their normal rate.

Planck Epoch: In Big Bang theory, the Planck epoch or Planck era is the earliest stage of the Big Bang that created the universe.

Sol Star System: The Star System that the Earth is part of.

Terran: A person from Earth (Earth is also known as Terra).

Translator: A highly advanced device that translates foreign languages into the language of the person using it.

SoSwI' SoH'a'? Are you my mother?
(This is Klingon as translated by The Klingon Language Institute. Thank you qurgh. Check it out!)
https://www.kli.org/

- **tlqwIj puqloD SoH:** You are the son of my heart
  (This is Klingon as translated by The Klingon Language Institute. Thank you qurgh. Check it out!)
  https://www.kli.org/

Yottasecond: A unit of time equal to 10^{24} (1000000000000000000000000) seconds. The unit is equal to 31.7 quadrillion years.

Yoctosecond: One yoctosecond is one trillionth of a trillionth of a second ($10-24$ s) and is comparable to the time it takes light to cross an atomic nucleus.

Zeptosecond: A zeptosecond is a trillionth of a billionth of a second. That's a decimal point followed by 20 zeros and a 1, and it looks like this: 0.000 000 000 000 000 000 001. The only unit of time shorter than a zeptosecond is a yoctosecond, and Planck time. A yoctosecond is a septillionth of a second.

Zepto Technology: Zepto technology is a real thing in our world. Basically, it is nanotechnology (10^{-9}) but on a much smaller scale. Zepto technology (10^{-21})

Acknowledgements

THE CREATION OF THIS book would not have been possible without these people. They have contributed a lot on this crazy journey. Thank you for your steadfastness, and your belief in me.

To my beta readers and my cover review team: Brandy, Andrea, Cara, Ann, and Michaele and Johannes. Thank you for your patience and eagle eyes. My books are made better by your skills and the conversations we have had about this story.

To my editor Dennis Doty, who told me I spin a great yarn. Thank you for so clearly hearing my voice and seeing my vision for this book and respecting it. Thank you for encouraging me to walk my own path.

Don't miss out!

Visit the website below and you can sign up to receive emails whenever Arlie Sheelin publishes a new book. There's no charge and no obligation.

https://books2read.com/r/B-A-SLWO-ZFLPB

BOOKS 2 READ

Connecting independent readers to independent writers.

About the Author

Writer, introvert, and a bit of a geek. **Favorite Authors:** Nalini Singh, Angela Knight, Sandra Hill, and Louis L'amour. I've raised my kids on a steady diet of **Star Trek** *and* **Star Wars,** which resulted in *them taking me* to sci-fi/cosplay conventions. Bonus points! I'm also an Indie RP writer - which means I write short story fiction online as some of my favorite characters. My drink of choice is tea, Earl Grey, or Chai. But on cold days, I go for Hot Chocolate with the odd venture into Peppermint Mocha. Caffeine is the magic elixir that helps fuel the imagination. I have a New Media Production and Design Diploma. - Which is a fancy way of saying I have creative skills with computers, mainly graphics.

Read more at https://www.arliesheelin.com/.

About the Publisher

Creating a publishing company for my books is all about pursuing dreams, creating the life I want to live, and believing in myself. I invite you to join me on this incredible adventure, as I create worlds filled with daring adventure, brave heroes, and strong heroines. Do you need a new adventure that washes the dust of life from your soul? Dive in. You want to just forget life for a little while? Open the pages of my stories and step into my worlds ? Just watch out for the dragons. ~ Arlie

CPSIA information can be obtained
at www.ICGtesting.com
Printed in the USA
BVHW081832010721
610987BV00008B/314

9 781777 756413